THE

WRITING

ON MY

FOREHEAD

THE
WRITING
ON MY
FOREHEAD

⸙

NAFISA HAJI

wm

WILLIAM MORROW
An Imprint of HarperCollins*Publishers*

This book is a work of fiction. References to real people, events, establish-
ments, organizations, or locales are intended only to provide a sense of
authenticity, and are used fictitiously. All other characters, and all incidents
and dialogue, are drawn from the author's imagination and are not to be con-
strued as real.

FIRST EDITION

Designed by Cassandra J. Pappas

Library of Congress Cataloging-in-Publication Data has been applied for.

ISBN 978-0-06-149385-0

09 10 11 12 13   OV/RRD   10 9 8 7 6 5 4 3 2 1

ISBN 978-0-06-177118-7 (international edition)

For Mummy and Daddy, Majee and Bapajee,
Nanima and Nana, Khalajan, Mariyah Khala,
Auntie Mamma, Ma, Big Nanima, Mamma,
Banoo Khala, Habiba Khala, Phupijan, and Bibi—
whose stories helped me to understand what was

For Ali,
my hero in the story of what is

And for Khalil,
my window into the story of what will be

The Moving Finger writes; and, having writ,
Moves on: nor all your Piety nor Wit
Shall lure it back to cancel half a Line,
Nor all your Tears wash out a Word of it.

—RUBAIYAT OF OMAR KHAYYAM,
translated by Edward Fitzgerald

THE

WRITING

ON MY

FOREHEAD

ONE

I CLOSE MY EYES and imagine the touch of my mother's hand on my forehead, smoothing away the residue of childhood nightmares. Her finger moves across my forehead, tracing letters and words of prayer that I never understood, never wanted to understand, her mouth whispering in nearly silent accompaniment. Now, waking from the nightmare that has become routine—bathed in sweat, breathing hard, resigned to the sleeplessness that will follow—I remember her soothing touch and appreciate it with an intensity that I never felt when she was alive.

I shake my head to dispel the longing. The world has changed around us, and, because of all that has happened, I know it is my time to give comfort and not to receive it—not that I have yet proven equal to the task. Shoving myself out of bed, I make the quiet nightly journey across the hall. I pause in the doorway of my sister's childhood room. Her daughter, Sakina, is asleep—a little lump, rising and falling slightly with each even breath, curled up in the corner of Ameena's old bed, apparently at ease with the night and its quiet in a way I have not been for a very long time.

Every night, I have the same nightmare.

I search through a crowd of people on an endless expanse of green lawn, pushing past bow-tied waiters in white uniforms who carry trays piled high with biscuits, sandwiches, and tea. There are tables draped in white linen, chairs occupied by aunties and uncles. Beyond the garden, there is a pavilion trimmed in teak, furnished with cane-backed chairs where the pale, white ghosts of British officers and their wives, the founders of this place, whose names are still etched on plaques at the front entrance, congregate to laugh at the antics of the natives, swirling their gin and scotch, clinking their glasses.

My search is urgent, every moment that passes means loss. And death. I know I am dreaming. But the knowledge doesn't alleviate the urgency. If I find Ameena in time, then everything will be all right. As I approach the edge of the crowd, I see what I did not see before— that the endlessness is merely an illusion. There are high walls surrounding the lawn. From beyond them, I hear a roar of sound, which drowns out the clinking of glasses, the laughter and chatter of the people around me. Over the walls, which seem to be shrinking, getting lower so that what is outside is starting to become visible, I see crowds of angry people, clouds of dust and debris that hover over a city of ruins. In the distance, I see twin plumes of smoke rising up out of the chaos.

I turn away from the fearsome sight and see her. She stands alone, at the other edge of the crowd. A path clears. I run. Before I can reach her, I am distracted by voices behind me, calling my name. I stop and turn to see whose they are. There is an old woman urging me to hurry. Another old woman, my grandmother, who shakes her head sadly. An old man dressed like Gandhi, battered and bruised, throws his shoulders back and shouts something I cannot hear, raising his fist in protest. There is another white woman, different from those officers' wives in the pavilion, dancing by herself to a tune I cannot hear, her arms encircling an imaginary partner. These are all familiar characters from stories I know, stories I have lived my life by.

I turn my back on all of them because Ameena is still there, alone, at the edge of the crowd. She is wearing red, the color she wore at her wedding, her head draped by the long dupatta of her outfit. I begin to run when I see her, shouting a warning she does not hear. From somewhere behind me, a gun is shot. Ameena falls to the ground, the red of her blood darkening the red of her clothing. I scream, but I make no sound.

There is someone beside me. A child. She was with me all the time, running through the crowd, trying to save her mother. I turn to face her and see her arms outstretched. I lift my own to meet hers and find I am holding something in my hand. She sees it, too, and recoils. I look down and understand why. I was wrong. The shot did not come from behind me. It came from the gun in my hand.

There are no secrets here—I know exactly what the dream means. It is what I should do that I cannot resolve. I approach the bed and stare down at Sakina for a moment. Her face is hidden, turned away from mine. Her arms are wrapped tightly around a little doll that used to be Ameena's. I wrap mine around myself and marvel at how easily she has staked her claim. On Ameena's room. On Ameena's toys. I remember battles fought with my sister in trying to do the same. Battles and skirmishes, which always ended with a story from our mother. But that was long ago—in the days when I was young enough to want whatever Ameena had. In the days before I began to roll my eyes at our mother's stories. As I turn to leave the room, my eyes fall on a jewelry box on the dresser. And the memory of one of those battles is so clear that I can feel Ameena's arms around me, now, as her daughter sleeps in the room where the skirmish took place.

Ameena's grip around me was so tight that I had to struggle to free one hand. But I did, reaching up immediately to grab a clump of hair and pull for all I was worth. She shrieked, but not as loudly as the howling I had commenced upon losing hold of Ameena's jewelry box, which she had found me playing with in her room. Her hair was her Achilles' heel, long and straight, easy to grab and hold on to. Also a target, perhaps, because I was jealous of it. My own, my mother kept boyishly short—because I was a wild creature, she said, and it was too much trouble for her to try and keep it tame.

"Let go, Saira! Ow!" Ameena tried to regain control of my wayward hand, but it was no use. In any case, we both heard the angry stomp of our referee in the hallway, coming to break up the fight.

"*Bas! Junglee* girls—I will not have this wild-beast behavior in my house!" Mummy had pulled us apart already. "What has gotten into you, Ameena? To fight like a shameless creature?" Mummy didn't ask me the same question. Because she had long ago decided that I was just that—a *besharam* creature, brazen by nature. Unlike Ameena, who could be chided in this way because she was not.

"Saira was in my room without my permission! She took my jewelry box—" Ameena retrieved the item from the floor where it had fallen during our dispute.

"I was just playing with it!"

"You have your own, Saira."

"But—it's—"

"She broke it!"

"Not on purpose!"

"She broke it and now she wants to break mine!"

"The ballerina came off of mine." I was crying. The ballerina had been important. "There's no dancing now."

"*Oof-ho! Junglee* girl. Always breaking things, jumping here and there like a monkey."

"I wanted her to dance faster. I didn't mean to break it."

"That's what being *junglee* is. Doing things without thinking, without meaning to, breaking things because you're not careful."

I didn't think that was fair. Though it was true that nothing of mine seemed to last as long as Ameena's. But it wasn't fair that Ameena would get away with her half of the fight. "Ameena hit me. She grabbed the box out of my hand and hit me. And then she pushed me and grabbed me and hurt my arms."

"Ameena!" The shock in my mother's voice was enough to make Ameena lower her head in shame. Mummy nodded, satisfied with Ameena's show of remorse. Genuine remorse. Not the kind I trotted out on occasion. Then Mummy turned back to me. "And you, Saira, you didn't pull her hair? I saw when I came in the room, both of you rolling around on the floor, pushing and hitting. Haven't I told you what happened to my cousin Laila? When she and her brother were fighting, pushing and pulling each other, over a pencil? Her brother poked her in the eye with that cursed pencil. Not because he *meant* to, Saira. *Junglee* boy, he always was. Poor Laila!" Mummy shuddered. "She lost her eye. No one would marry her when she grew up. And her brother had to take care of his poor, unfortunate, unmarried sister for the rest of his life. Even now, she lives with him, instead of having a husband and a home and children of her own. You see? You see what happens when children fight like animals?"

Ameena lowered her head, again, in shame. I felt my own eyes widen in gruesome fascination. "So—she had no eye, Mummy? Was there a hole? Did she have to wear a patch? Like a pirate? What about a glass eye? Why didn't she get a glass eye? Sammy Davis Jr. has a glass eye! And Colombo. Daddy told me. That's why they look like this—" I scrunched and squinted one eye in an attempt to show her. "This wouldn't be so bad. See? See, Mummy?"

My mother shook her head in disgust. She looked at Ameena, who shook her head, too. They laughed.

"Shameless creature! What will I do with you? Is there nothing you are afraid of?"

I didn't laugh with them. Not then.

Now, I smile as I take a seat on the floor across from the bed where Sakina is sleeping, the first genuine smile I have managed in weeks, though the muscles required to achieve the expression have been well exercised by the failed attempts at strained, cheerful assurance that I offer her by day. I get the joke now. The one my mother and sister had laughed at. That I had missed the point, the moral of the story: that fighting with your sibling can lead to serious injury, including the loss of important body parts, and, worse, marital eligibility—the last a primary theme in most of Mummy's stories.

Sakina sighs and mumbles something indistinct. I wait for a few moments of silence to settle. Carefully, I rise up from the floor, finding Sakina's discarded clothes there, which she has kicked off and across the room. I pick them up, holding up the T-shirt, the shorts. When I was nine, three years older than Sakina is now, I was no longer allowed to wear shorts.

6

At nine, Mummy believed, shorts and dresses and skirts that ended above the knee were no longer appropriate forms of attire for girls—her girls, anyway. The day before I turned nine, as Mummy sorted through my closet and dresser, tossing shorts into a pile that she would later give to Goodwill, she told me about a childhood friend of hers who had nearly died of snakebite back in India, because she was wandering heedlessly through the garden in a dress that was way too short when a cobra, which had escaped from a snake charmer's basket, struck her on the thigh. I was not too young then to question the logic of that moral: beware of snakes when scantily clad. I remember asking Mummy why boys weren't subject to the same rules, whether she considered them to be immune to snakebite or somehow less attractive to snakes.

I fold away Sakina's clothes and notice how small they are in size. She is six years old. Too young to bear the burden of what she has witnessed. I exit the room that is now hers, as quietly as I entered. Wandering through the house, I think of India—so very far away from the Los Angeles suburb where Ameena and I grew up. Mother India, where both Mummy and Daddy were born, was the source of all of Mummy's improbable fables. Stories that always ended with a twist—of fateful, karmic proportions.

Mummy's was an extremely comforting worldview—to believe that bad things happened to bad people. Or, at least, to not-so-good people who made bad choices. It gave the world an ordered sort of logic, where roles were clearly defined and duty and obligation comprised the script. It was a logic wholly convincing to my sister.

Yet, from the beginning, I resisted. I focused instead on

tangents—on pirates and glass eyes. Later, I was much too pre-occupied by the whats, wheres, whos, and whys of the plots, stopping Mummy often to interrupt, focusing always on what she considered to be the unimportant details.

But it was the details that mattered most to me—those devilish details that caused Mummy's stories to spill over and out of the boxes that she had constructed for them. In eighth grade, I asked permission to go to the prom.

"No dancing! We don't dance, men and women together, Saira. It's wrong. It leads to other things that are wrong."

"But, Mummy—"

"No! No buts. I know what can happen, believe me." Mummy paused—a long, calculating pause. "I knew a man once, who loved to dance, who shamed himself and his family because of it." Mummy gave the pot on the stove a final stir, banging the spoon on the edge of it before lowering the heat, putting the lid on, and sitting down at the kitchen table, indicating with her hand that I should do the same. "It was a monumental scandal! And it all happened because of that man's love of ballroom dancing."

"What was the man's name?"

"He—his name is not important, Saira. Who cares what his name was?" Mummy stopped to frown at me for a moment. "You would not know him anyway." She paused again, still frowning. Then she resumed her story. "He was well-to-do, head of his family's trading business in Bombay, a respectable leader in the community. His family had come a long way from its very modest beginnings, when luxuries were unheard of and it had taken careful budgeting to maintain the appearance of respectability that made the keeping of at least one servant necessary. And all of the credit for this advancement belonged to him. Though, to hear him talk, one might never know this. He was the eldest brother in a family of four sons, and, because his father had died young, when this man was only seventeen, he had shouldered responsibility for the younger ones. None of them could complain about the job their brother had done. All that was his, all that he had gained, was theirs as well."

"What did his father die of?"

"Blood cancer."

"Blood cancer? What's that?"

Another frown. "Leukemia, which we used to call blood cancer. But that has nothing to do with the story! Really, Saira, I cannot tell you anything when you constantly interrupt in this way."

"Sorry." But I wasn't really. Just curious.

"Yes. Well. His reputation in the community was unparalleled. Everyone knew him as a gentleman. And they were right. A more thoughtful, generous, and upstanding man would be hard to find among the business leaders of Bombay. Everyone knew that he was the man to see during hard times, and many, many people came to him when they were down on their luck. He never said no. All anyone had to do was ask. He often said that this was the secret to his success—a firm belief that all of his wealth was just an *amanat,* a trust, given to him and his family by Allah but which belonged, really, to his fellow man. That it was his duty to share it with those less favored by God."

"Did he?"

"Did he what?"

"Did he share his wealth?"

Mummy wrinkled her nose. "Yes. He did. Some of it. A lot of it." Mummy sounded defensive.

"But he was still rich?"

"Yes! Yes. I told you. He was very well-to-do. But he was kind to those less fortunate. And generous. His only weakness was his love for things from the West. After Independence, his business boomed. And what he didn't spend on the poor, he spent on the merchandise that Westerners of high status seemed to treasure. He wore elegant Italian tailored suits and shoes and expensive Swiss watches. Nothing but the finest. He drove a big American car with fins and tails.

"When he and his beautiful wife were first married, in the days before his fortunes were made, he took her to a beauty salon and asked the stylist to cut her hair according to the latest trends to be found in European beauty magazines. They cut off her yard-length, dark, silken hair. She cried for days, not consoled by her husband's praise and assertions that now, at least, she looked 'modern' and 'Western.' He made her wear her saris with sleeve-less blouses, the kind that were in fashion among the Bombay film crowd. Her mother-in-law pursed her lips disapprovingly when she first saw her in one of these. Her grandmother-in-law said, 'Your arms will burn in hell from here to here.'" My mother's hand swept down from her shoulder blade to her wrist.

"Did she tell her husband?"

"Yes, of course. When his wife told him, in tears, what his grandmother had said, he said, 'Next time tell her that her arms will burn from here to here.'" This time, my mother swept her hand down from mid-upper arm to wrist, which the traditional sari blouse left exposed. "'Don't worry,' he said, 'it's only a few inches' difference. It won't hurt much more than hers.' He took her to all of the latest clubs and nightspots. She was from a conservative family, like his own, and she was pitied and admired for gallantly suffering the whims of her husband. He even took her ballroom dancing, actually hiring a tutor to teach her the steps!

"The word we use to describe men like that is *shaukeen*. It means 'keen'—he was keenly interested in trying out new things, keenly enthusiastic about the way things looked and tasted, keenly excited about life in general." Mummy sighed. She got up to pour a cup of tea. "It's always wonderful to meet someone who is *shaukeen*. You find people sort of riding along in their wake. They bring a kind of energy with them when they enter a room." Tea in hand, Mummy turned back to face me, walked back to the table, and stared at me for a moment before getting on with the story.

"This man's wife learned, very quickly, how to ride quietly in that wake. It wasn't easy for her. She had been a young bride, a child. The transition from her parents' home to her husband's had been a challenge. But she was lucky for two reasons. One was that she had been brought up well enough to understand the difference in what was expected of her—before, she had been a pampered, youngest child. Everyone in her house, her parents, her brothers, her sister—had spoilt her and cherished her. But now, she was a daughter-in-law. And she had to learn to obey not only her husband, but also his mother and grandmother. They were constantly complaining and criticizing. But she managed to learn the steps of this dance, too. To maintain her composure, to nod her head respectfully in front of her in-laws. The other reason that she was lucky was that her husband really was a charming gentleman. He was kind with her, and patient and loving.

"During the time of Partition, when India was divided into India and Pakistan, *her* family, her parents, decided to leave Bombay for Pakistan, where they settled in Karachi. Like so many,

many others. Though she was sad to have to say good-bye to her family, she knew that her place was with her husband. That her home was where he was. That her happiness depended on his.

"She built her life around him. They had three children. When her grandmother-in-law and mother-in-law died, she finally gained control of her household. She supervised the servants—there were many of them now that her husband had become a rich man. And took care of her husband's brothers and their wives, whose marriages she had helped to arrange. They all lived together, still, as a joint family in a big, new house he had bought. She took pride in maintaining an ordered and disciplined home. She was not a materialistic person, but she took pleasure in her husband's success, because it gave him pleasure. She had always been a pious woman, but she became more religious as the years passed—spending more and more time on her prayer rug and focusing more of her thoughts on the remembrance of God. Her husband was pleased. He used to say that his wife's piety was another reason that God smiled upon them with such favor."

"Was he religious, too?"

"Religious? Yes. He prayed. He didn't drink. He tried to always do what was right."

"Except for the dancing?"

Mummy seemed to have forgotten the point of her story. "Hmm? Yes. Of course. Except for that. A good man—a satisfied husband. Still kind enough to often express his appreciation for the efforts and virtues of his wife, publicly, as their children grew up around them. He was well loved by his children, respected by his brothers, honored by the community. He had everything a man could want." Mummy took a long sip of her tea before saying, "His wife was happy, too. Her children were all well settled." Mummy looked up at me, her forehead creased. Then her face relaxed as she set her cup back down onto the saucer and reached out to touch my cheek with her fingers, tucking a lock of my short hair behind my ear as she said, "She was happy the way that I will be when you and Ameena are grown and married." My mother sighed—lightly, happily—at the thought and didn't speak for a few moments.

"When their eldest daughter, who was married and settled in London, was due to deliver their first grandchild, husband and wife decided to await its arrival in person. They leased a flat there—close to their daughter's—and settled down to wait well in advance of the baby's arrival."

"Why didn't they stay with their daughter?"

"Hmm? Well, it wasn't done. In the old days, it was not considered right. For a man to stay in the house of his daughter. That is, his son-in-law's house. It is like trespassing."

"Even for a visit?"

"Even for a visit. So, every day, in the final days before their grandchild was due, they would walk together, after breakfast, to their daughter's flat and take tea with her. Then, he would go for a walk. To Hyde Park. That's where the scandal began. Somewhere, somehow, the man met a woman there—a girl, really. Young enough to be his daughter. Who knows how it happened? How that girl, an Englishwoman, seduced him? How it began, how long it went on? Within a few weeks of the birth of their grandchild, the man came home and told his wife that he was in love. That he was leaving her for some woman he had met at the park. A hippie girl." Mummy stopped talking then. She took some more sips of tea, quick now where the last one had lingered.

"What did his wife do?"

"What could she do? Nothing. There was nothing she could do to stop him. He walked away from her. From his life in India. From his business, his social connections, making a fool of himself in the eyes of the whole community, humiliating his wife, shaming his children. He left his whole family behind without a second thought."

I was shocked, I remember, at the idea of an Indian man—a Muslim man—behaving in this way. "What happened then?"

Mummy's eyes met mine for a long moment. Then she looked away and said, "He died soon after that. Alone and cut off from his family."

I didn't have anything to say to that. For a little while. Then I remembered why my mother had begun this story in the first place. "But, Mummy—what has any of this got to do with the prom?"

Mummy clicked her tongue impatiently. "Don't you see, Saira? Dancing—that's what led to that man's downfall. He—he didn't follow the rules of his own culture and community. He liked to dance in the Western way. In our culture, men and women only touch each other when they are married. And in private. When you forget the rules of your culture, you lose it. You forget about what is right and wrong. You forget that the reason we are here is not just to enjoy ourselves selfishly. What we do affects other people who love and care for us. It's not right to overlook other people's love and loyalty, to be selfish instead of being mindful of what you owe them. We all have duties and obligations in life. And those duties come first, before our own selfish pleasures and whims."

Duty and obligation. Did I roll my eyes at this conclusion? I must have. I must have pouted, stomped out of the kitchen, and sulked for hours at the prospect of having to forgo the prom. I never considered going to my father. The feminine triangle of our family dynamic left my father, geometrically speaking, on a plane far off in the distance, a single point whose relation to us could not be traced in precise mathematical terms. I suppose that was natural—he was male. But I was uneasy about that rather simple explanation for his exclusion, feeling responsible in some way for not having been born a son.

Simple explanations always made me uneasy. I suppose that's why I became a journalist. For years, I have traveled the world, uncovering the details overlooked by others, avoiding the details of my own past.

Those details are unavoidable now. Still, I try, seeking refuge on the couch, my hand reaching for the clicker. Images of war pour into the room. James Earl Jones announces that "This is CNN." And I realize that I am not ready to be mesmerized by twenty-four-hour news, Darth Vader's voice notwithstanding. The voice of Authority. The voice of the Empire. Telling neat and tidy stories, with neat and tidy morals. Like my mother's. Stories with all the messy details removed, because they don't serve the message. In different circumstances, I would be there, halfway around the world, working hard to uncover those details, those babies killed by bombs, those wedding parties showered with shrapnel, those soldiers scarred and wounded, killed and killing—all of the collateral damage that Darth Vader's voice dismisses as insignificant. Details. I click off the TV.

I wonder how this has come to be—how it is that I am back

in my parents' home, alone, my sister's daughter asleep and in my care. I breathe in the silence and darkness of the night—and think about the details. How to separate them out of the past, which I thought I understood, and reclaim them in the present, which I cannot.

TWO

❧

No. No! I will not come to the wedding. Not if *she* is invited . . . that *kuthi* with her brood of *haramzadas.*" I remember walking into the room, hearing my mother's words as she turned down the invitation to my cousin Zehra's wedding. I had stopped short at the entrance to the kitchen. *A bitch? With a brood of bastards?* I was fourteen and I couldn't recall ever hearing my mother use an obscenity before. In any language. I remember how quickly she changed her tone when she saw me staring at her, mouth hanging open in surprise. Maybe it was my shock that prompted what followed.

"*Acha, baba, acha.* All right. I'll send the girls, *teek hay?* They'll enjoy the wedding and it's a long time since they visited you all in Pakistan. Yes, yes of course they'll stay with you." She was speaking to my Lubna Khala, her younger sister. (It was amazingly easy to figure this out. Among the three sisters—Jamila, the eldest; Shabana, my mother; and Lubna—sentences began in Urdu and ended in English with liberal lingual hybridization sandwiched in between, which none of them had any trouble following. They were loud, too, something that perhaps became a habit from having spent all of their adult lives apart—Jamila Khala in London, Mummy in Los Angeles, and Lubna Khala in Karachi—connected by long-distance phone calls.)

My thrill at the thought that Ameena and I would be traveling to Pakistan, unaccompanied by our parents, almost outweighed my curiosity about the nature of my mother's refusal to attend the wedding. Almost. But here, Ameena proved to be typically less cooperative than I could have wished.

"I don't want to go to Karachi for Zehra's wedding," was her response to my triumphant announcement of Mummy's decision.

"What?! Why not?"

"I just don't, that's all," said Ameena, with the familiar stubborn twist to her lips with which she met most of my suggestions. But those suggestions usually involved breaking rules or defying Mummy. Now, I was baffled. We already had permission for this particular adventure. Baffled and frustrated.

"But Ameena, why not? It'll be so much fun. We get to go on the plane alone and it'll be so cool. Please, please don't say no." There was no hiding my own selfish motives. "And Mummy won't let me go if you don't come. Please, Ameena, please!" I could feel my voice getting shrill in my desperation.

Too late, I realized my mistake. There is a particularly nasty quality among older siblings. Something to do with the sheer pleasure of power, the ability to withhold an object of desire from a younger brother or sister . . . whether through the use of brute strength, the physiological advantages of height, or the mere flaunting of privileges yet to be permitted the younger child . . . the older sibling, I am convinced, develops a sadistic streak that younger siblings everywhere will recognize. Ameena never failed to take advantage of the weakness she sensed when the pitch of my voice began to move up.

"I don't care. I don't want to go."

Always, in situations like these, I strived to maintain my composure. To hide the fact that I was desperate for what she withheld. But it never worked. Ultimately, I always succumbed to the only recourse left to a younger child. I went to Mummy.

Who, finally, was able to get to the bottom of the matter. I was—at Ameena's request—sent out of the room. But that had never stopped me from keeping myself abreast of the news. I stood, in my usual position for such situations, just outside the door, listening anxiously for the no doubt ridiculous reasons my sister had for refusing to go to Pakistan.

"But why not, *beti*? I thought you would be happy to go. You've always enjoyed yourself there."

"That was different, Mummy." Ameena's voice lacked the power and authority that she had wielded over me just moments ago. "That was before. It will be different now."

My brow furrowed in puzzlement. I honestly did not understand what she was talking about and had to stop myself from asking what she meant. My mother, when I chanced a peek, was nodding her head. She seemed to know what Ameena was thinking.

"I know, *beti*, I know. It will be hard to go there now that Nanima has gone."

Of course! I slapped my head, silently, in realization. And then lowered it in a gesture that might have resembled shame. I had forgotten. Worse, even now it didn't bother me. Our grandmother's death, the year before, had meant little to me then. It was so far away. And we hadn't been to Pakistan since, not Ameena or myself. But for my sister, of course, it would be different. She had been the favorite grandchild. Then, Ameena asked the question that formed in my own mind.

"Is that why you're not going?"

"Well, *beti*, you know that I went to Pakistan when Nanima died."

I remembered that vividly. The day and a half that Mummy had spent crying and mourning before we saw her off at the airport, racing to Pakistan to be able to attend her mother's funeral. Her mother's funeral. That night, when Mummy was gone, I had tried and tried to imagine life without Mummy. The thought had driven me out of my bed to seek out Ameena. She had welcomed me, had held me close, and we had cried together—Ameena for the death of our grandmother and I at the prospect of ever losing Mummy.

"So, I've already faced that. And it was difficult. But, no, that's not the reason I'm not going. I—" I leaned closer to the door in anticipation of hearing more about the *kuthi* and her *haramzadas*, the bitch and her bastards. "I want to go in the winter. The weather will be too hot now. I can't bear the thought of it."

It was a lie. But I don't think Ameena realized it. She was starting to cry now.

"I still miss her. Do you think she can see us?"

"I think she is always with us. I dreamt of her last week, did I tell you?" I peeked into the room again to see that Mummy had put her arm around Ameena, pulling her head close into her armpit.

Nanima was the only grandparent that I had ever known. My

father's parents had passed away when Ameena was a baby. On his side of the family there was only an uncle, my father's brother, whose family we were not very close to. My mother's father had died, as far as I knew, before Ameena and I were born.

Widowed, Nanima had left India and moved to Pakistan to live with her maiden sister, whom we called Big Nanima and who was *my* favorite relative. My first memory of Nanima was when I was about four years old and Ameena was eight, on one of our then annual trips to Pakistan. When Nanima greeted us at the airport, she kneeled down in front of me, put her hands on my shoulders, and stared into my face as if searching for something.

After a moment of scrutiny, she patted my shoulders, as if in sympathy, and declared in Urdu, because she didn't speak English, "This one has totally gone after her father." The way she said it left no doubt about the disappointment that this entailed.

Immediately after, she put her arm around Ameena, rubbing her back as she said, "Now, this one! This one is totally ours." It was a scene that was repeated at each subsequent visit with Nanima.

It wasn't that she was wrong, empirically speaking. It was merely the confirmation of what I had already observed. But it was the first time that I remember making a judgment about my own appearance with respect to that observation. The most important feature she looked for to determine a likeness, I suppose, was color and complexion. Ameena had our mother's smooth, milky-white skin tone—the kind that reminded me of Dove soap commercials. My own skin was dark. Like my father's. But that wasn't the only proof of Nanima's accuracy. Ameena was sharp-featured. Her nose was long and thin, her cheekbones high and well defined. She was slender. Long-legged and high-waisted—sleekly built. I was shorter, of course, because I was younger. But my proportions were also stubby, compared to hers, in a way that had nothing to do with the developmental differences between us. I had shorter limbs, stumpier fingers. I was round and plump, too. Nanima was the first person to bring these differences to my attention and she reinforced them in a less than positive light every time we met.

My memories of Big Nanima, who was still alive, an English professor at a women's college in Karachi, were far more vivid and warmth-filled than those of my grandmother. She was very unlike her younger sister. Nanima was thin, while Big Nanima's clothes were daily challenged by the effort to contain her rather large and generous proportions. Truly, the amount of flesh that spilled out of the sleeves of her sari blouse defies description. It rolled and waved as she spoke, gesturing, it seemed, with the whole of her massive self to emphasize her words. As a child, I believed that the "Big" in Big Nanima referred to her size rather than to her being my grandmother's older sister.

Nanima disapproved of dining out in general and of Karachi street cuisine in particular. She insisted, with good reason, that the food made on the streets of Karachi was dirty and not fit for consumption. Big Nanima scoffed at such caution. Food, as her figure could attest, was her friend, and the cheap and spicy fare sold in the stalls at every corner in Karachi was what she thrived on. *Bun kabab*s, a hybrid hamburger made mostly of potatoes smothered with sweet and sour tamarind chutney and chili paste, were among her favorites. And *pani puris,* deep-fried, crispy, and puffed up little flatbreads dripping with a spice-flavored water that had never known the process of boiling, which was mandatory among people respectable enough to afford the luxury of having a kitchen. She introduced me to these delicacies, among others.

One of my favorites was *paan*, a betel leaf stuffed with ground betel nuts. These were prepared to the specific taste of each customer by *paan-walla*s all over the city. I liked them sweet, oozing with multicolored coconut shreds. Nanima especially condemned this particular treat, trying to scare us off of them with dire predictions of premature tooth loss and ominous warnings about the possibility that they may contain illicit drugs. The one time that Ameena went along with Big Nanima and me and succumbed to the temptation of the colorful pastes and powders that went into the complicated process of *paan*-making, she spit it out after only a few chews, convinced that she was feeling dizzy from the drugs Nanima had persuaded her they contained.

There wasn't any secret to the fact that Ameena was our grandmother's favorite, or that I was her sister's. One incident in particular, memorable because of its sheer absurdity, illustrated this beyond a shadow of a doubt. Ameena and I were both suffering from our regular bout of dysentery, which usually kicked in within a week of our arrival in Pakistan. Ameena, careful to abstain from all street-hawked food and unboiled water, was especially susceptible to this disorder and usually became pretty queasy for the rest of our visit. I, on the other hand, merely suffered for a day or two at most before recovering fully enough to continue to partake of all that the filthy streets of Karachi had to offer—a fact that Big Nanima never failed to crow about to Nanima.

Both of us, on this occasion, were running low-grade fevers. It was the middle of summer and the heat was unbearable. Even more so in the small home that was too modest a household to have air-conditioning. Ceiling fans were the only remedy. And, of course, there was only one in each room. And here lay the foundation for the controversy that was about to erupt.

Whenever we visited Karachi, Nanima would move into Big Nanima's room, leaving her own accommodations for my mother and father. Two small cots were set up in the middle of the grand-mothers' room for Ameena and me. It was the placement of these cots, now, that was to be hotly contested.

Nanima had just finished readjusting the location of our cots when Big Nanima walked into the room with a bowl of ice water and a couple of hand towels to put on Ameena's forehead and mine. Ameena and I had been playing *Ludo,* a primitive form of Trouble, which always seemed to be more fun than its American counterpart, despite the lack of a pop-o-matic dice. We were sit-ting on Big Nanima's bed, because Nanima had strict rules about the hours of operation for hers. It was a bed, not a chair. Not de-signed for sitting on, but for sleeping in. I don't think I took these rules very seriously, and I am not sure what consequences break-ing them would have entailed, but playing with Ameena always meant playing by the rules.

Big Nanima stopped short in the doorway to the room, took one look, and saw what Ameena and I had not.

"What are you doing?" She had set the bowl and towels down and the fact that her hands were on her hips was a good indica-tion that she had already drawn some conclusions.

"I'm shifting the cots over a little," Nanima said, as she shifted her own slight weight a bit from one foot to the other. "Ameena needs the fan. She's burning up with fever."

"Oh? And what about Saira? She's sick, too."

"Yes. And she'll be fine. She's a sturdy, hearty child. Ameena is too thin and weak. You know she can't take the heat. I've just moved her bed over a little to make sure she gets the air directly from the fan. Poor child." There was a brief pause before Big

Nanima's sudden motion caused Nanima to ask, "What are you doing?"

Big Nanima let her actions answer for her as she, not very gently, shoved Ameena's bed over with her leg and pushed my own into the favored position directly under the fan. Ameena and I forgot our game as we stood up together, near the foot of Big Nanima's bed. Our heads began to move from side to side, like tennis spectators', as the drama unfolded and the cots began to be volleyed back and forth in a battle of wills that, looking back, I am sure had nothing to do with us. The contested space was a difference of about eight inches and neither position was going to make the difference between life and death for either of us.

"What are you doing? I have decided, haven't I? Ameena has the greater need. She will be under the fan!" Nanima said this in an imperious voice as she, once again, arranged the cots to her liking. Her volume was going up, and the fact that she had to stop to tuck in a lock of steely hair that had strayed from her tightly wound bun was a grave indication of the loss of her composure.

"No! Saira is very sick. She has a higher fever than Ameena. She needs the fan more!" Big Nanima's long, wild, and curly locks of gray and black hair swung forward onto her face as she shoved the beds back again.

"Yes and she wouldn't be sick, would she, if she hadn't eaten all of that trash with you? *Her* illness could have been avoided. Poor Ameena has been good. She has eaten only what I make for her at home." Nanima tried to push the cots back, but Big Nanima had planted herself in her way.

"And it's no wonder she's sick!" shouted Big Nanima.

Nanima stood up, lengthening her spine to its usual straightness. Her thin, frail figure was no match for Big Nanima's bulk, and Nanima, realizing this, turned and walked out of the room with a "Hmmph" that left us no illusions about the depth of her anger.

Remembering Nanima, I felt guilty that I seemed to suffer so little grief over her death. I supposed it was my own fault that she preferred Ameena to me. For more than one reason. Though I understood the language, I didn't speak Urdu as well as Ameena did, and Nanima never hid her displeasure at that fact. I also remembered running away from her on several occasions when she'd stopped me to request that I massage her aching and arthritic legs. Ameena took pride in the task. She believed, as we were taught in Sunday school, that service to our elders was a sure-fire way of earning the points needed for gaining eventual entry into heaven.

For me, the potential long-term gratification was not worth the short-term pain. Any moment alone with Nanima meant the onset of a lecture—which was odd, considering that her sister, Big Nanima, was the one who actually lectured for a living. It was easy to see where Mummy had gotten her moralizing tendencies from. But Nanima recited essays rather than stories. Her themes of virtue and vice were always illustrated through the abstract. There was a lot of talk about heaven and hell. Good and evil. And little representation of what that might look like in actual fact, making these little sermons, devoid as they were of people and plot, rather too dry and humorless for my taste.

Big Nanima, too, told stories. In beautiful English, which made my communication with her less lopsided than the kind I ran away from with her sister. Her stories, however, had no apparent moral messages. They were rude, crude stories, peppered with plenty of practical lessons on the process of human digestion with all of its funny sounds, sights, and smells. They were told solely for the purpose of eliciting laughter . . . totally devoid of any ulterior motive that I could ever find. And they were usually accompanied by demonstrations. The sounds of belching and farting, coming from Big Nanima, never failed to bring on a giggling fit. Even Ameena, when she could tear herself away from Nanima long enough to hear one of Big Nanima's stories, couldn't help but laugh.

As I spied on Mummy consoling Ameena, I remembered another conversation I had listened in on one afternoon in Karachi, on our last visit there, when Nanima was still alive. I was restless, pacing the hallway, waiting for Big Nanima to finish her prayers. It was even hotter than usual and she had promised me a *gola ganda*, a snow cone, one of the deadliest sins and a sure harbinger of deathly illness in Nanima's eyes because of the unknown quality and origin of the water used to form the ice that was its primary ingredient. Ameena and Nanima were in the dining room, both seated at the table. Ameena was shuffling her fingers through a tray of uncooked rice, sifting through it for stones and pests. Nanima was slicing onions as she talked, her quiet, firmly uttered words punctuated by the rhythmic thud of the knife falling effortlessly, it seemed, and repeatedly, on the cutting board. It was the only time that I remember being drawn into their company—the topic was personal and there was a wistful, smiling tone to Nanima's voice that, because her back was to me, I am not absolutely sure I would have found confirmation of on her face.

"You never met him? Never even talked to him before the wedding?" asked Ameena, who was so engrossed in Nanima's words that she didn't notice me standing in the doorway to the room.

"Oh, no. It wasn't done. No, no. Not until the wedding day. And even then—I was veiled, my face was covered. So was his. He wore a veil of roses, a *sehera*. When I peeked up, once—when I thought no one was looking—all I could see were strings and strings of bright red roses." Nanima laughed, "Your poor grandfather! He must have been so hot! Oh, yes. It was a very hot day. Maybe as hot as it is today."

"But how could you have—I mean—" Ameena's relatively fluent Urdu seemed to fail her.

"Well, that was the way it was done. It was very, very different then. And it worked. Your grandfather and I—" Nanima faltered inexplicably for a moment, using the end of her scarf to wipe her face, her eyes. For one brief second, I thought she was crying. Then I remembered the onions. And she continued, her voice strong again, "Your *nana* and I were very happy. For many, many years."

They were both quiet for a few moments, had both seemed to settle back into the tasks at hand and into the cheerless, boring kind of companionship that they enjoyed in each other, when Ameena's fingers stopped shuffling. She pushed the tray away from her, put her elbows on the table, and propped her face into the cup of her hands.

"Nanima, that's the way I want to get married. Like you."

Nanima laughed and shook her head. "No, Ameena. Times are different. I was only sixteen when I got married! Just a child! You will meet your husband before you marry. Like your mother met your father, at your uncle's wedding. He will be someone they find for you, yes. Someone they approve of. Your mother and father will have a tough time of it, I know." Nanima's head tilted as she looked into Ameena's face. "You are a beautiful child,

Mashallah. Like I was. The boys will line up at your father's door, like they did at mine. But you will get engaged only after you have seen the man your parents find worthy of you. And met him. Then, he will take you out. For ice cream, maybe. And you will get to know each other. You will not marry a stranger."

A hand touched my shoulder. I gasped, but not loudly enough to disturb Nanima and Ameena. It was Big Nanima. I don't know how long she had been there, how much she had heard. She had a thoughtful look on her face when she beckoned silently for me to come. She took my hand as we left the house, unusually quiet. But then, so was I.

When I had finished my *gola ganda,* I asked, wiping the sticky red syrup on my clothes before taking Big Nanima's hand again, "Is that true?"

"Is what true?" Big Nanima squeezed my hand, unconcerned about the residual stickiness that I could feel clinging, still, to my fingers.

"Is that the way it used to be? The way that Nanima got married? She and Nana didn't even know each other?"

Big Nanima frowned and paused before answering, "Used to be? It still is! Too, too often. Girls married off before they become women, like cows at an auction. Before they are old enough to understand what the world is about and what it has to offer. That there is more to life than breeding and birthing." The frown faded into a smile. "But not for you, that same old story. Not for my Saira. From you, I expect big things." She tweaked my nose and challenged me to a race home. I remember feeling glad and proud of myself, too. As if in advance for all that she hoped I would accomplish.

THREE

IN THE FACE of my rather traumatic, tantrum-filled railing against Ameena's refusal to accompany me, Mummy arranged for a way to let me go to Pakistan alone. Almost. As far as London, at least. From there, I went on to Karachi in the company of Razia Nani, a distant relative of my mother's—I tuned out when my mother tried to clarify the exact nature of the connection and have no idea of whether the tie was by blood or marriage—whom I vaguely recalled as a somewhat elderly lady. It was a compromise that I could live with, if reluctantly. The same was planned, in reverse, for my return three weeks later, when I would stay with my father's brother and his family for a three-day visit before coming home. I was nervous about this, because it had been several years since I'd seen my paternal cousins, Mohsin and Mehnaz—eighteen-year-old twins whom Ameena and I had always tried to avoid, finding them more than a little frightening and exceedingly weird.

Razia Nani would, my mother said, take good care of me. "Besides," she'd added, probably to try and avert the objection I was about to offer regarding the need for anyone to take care of me, "she needs you, too. She's a lonely old woman. It will be good for her to have your company on the plane, poor dear."

As it turned out, I found Razia Nani's company to be highly educational. She was a bona fide gossip, talking nonstop for the duration of the ten-hour-long journey from London to Karachi —with no regard for the tenderness of my young age; with no notice of how close or far my relationship was to the people that she tore through with a generous impartiality that included people she considered to be friends as well as foes; and with no care for the possibility that I may repeat the sensitive and potentially dangerous information that she shared with me.

But for one detail, it would have been a perfect trip. The volume of Razia Nani's voice—quite unconsciously, it would appear—seemed to increase in direct proportion to the delicacy and sensitivity that her subject should have commanded. While I was thrilled to get the lowdown on so many family secrets, I have to admit that I was quite mortified at the sinking certainty that everyone on the plane seated even remotely within our vicinity would be privy to the same information. I remember spending much of the early part of the flight slumped down in my seat, desperately balancing the need to keep these secrets in the family by urging Razia Nani to "shhhh" against the knowledge that such a "shhhh" would, in my mother's estimation—and, more important, in Razia Nani's—not be acceptable behavior toward an elder. Whenever the impulse to hush her became overwhelming, I entertained nightmarish visions of Razia Nani cozying down to tea with my other relatives and making loud declarations about how rudely I had behaved with her on the trip to Karachi, saying, "how ill-mannered and disrespectful that Saira girl is," and "how badly Shabana has brought up her *besharam* daughter."

My fear of being overheard was compounded by my childish belief in the degrees of separation between people who could trace their heritage to the Indian subcontinent. That there were, essentially, very few of them. It was an irrational belief, I know, but one that I have never really outgrown. Perhaps, originally, it was born from the curious perspective that growing up as part of a very small minority population afforded me. When we were children, my mother always seemed to make friends with anyone and everyone who could claim any connection to the geography in question—so that strangers, encountered in grocery stores, malls, movie theaters, or restaurants, became part of an intimate circle of friends that always felt like family.

This feeling was underlined by the culturally appropriate titles of "auntie" and "uncle" by which Ameena and I referred to these friends of our parents. Totally different from the less intimate Mr.'s and Mrs.'s that we used to refer to neighbors and acquaintances outside of that circle: people who were white, black, or anything other than *desi*—a slang word for compatriot that was more about geography than religion, ethnicity, race, or even nationality.

It was always rather confusing, on visits to Pakistan, to be confronted with a whole population of aunties and uncles. To look into the faces of racially familiar people who looked back at me with the blank strangers' stares that I unconsciously associated with people of another hue. And part of my discomfort, on that journey with Razia Nani, was due directly to the fear that all of the brown people on the plane must know who we were . . . must bear some relation to my family within a number of degrees that made their passive participation in Razia Nani's discourse less than disinterested.

Her revelations began just after we boarded. I was breathless, having barely managed to lug both of our carry-on bags on board and into the overhead bin, where Razia Nani had decided they must rest.

"*Hanh, Beta. Shabaash.* Very good. You see, I must have the room for my poor old legs. Ahh! They are already hurting. They swell up so badly on an airplane. And carrying all that luggage only makes it worse. And my bag is soooo heavy! All those chocolates to carry! I hope they know, in Karachi, all the trouble I go to, bringing them soooo much chocolate. I know how they like it. But still, I don't think they realize how difficult it is. I'm an old lady, now, and my legs can't take it. Of course, I love to give people happiness. And if suffering a little, carrying all those expensive chocolates—they're so expensive nowadays, I don't think they realize how much I'm giving them—if suffering a little is what it takes to make others happy—well, then, I'm glad for my suffering. Yes, I am glad to do it."

Since the only one who had suffered so far was me—I had bruises on my legs, I could feel them, from where the heavy bag kept banging against them—I was rather skeptical about the depth of her sacrifice. Her bag was heavy, that was true, and I worried about the weight restrictions that had been written and displayed clearly at the check-in counter. I had pointed them out to Razia Nani, thinking she may have been unaware of them. But she had waved her hand furiously, worried that the attendant might hear my concern and actually check the weight of the bag, which she told me to carry casually, in a manner that would disguise how heavy it was. I briefly imagined the plane crashing, all because of the weight of Razia Nani's chocolates, and hoped that her self-described willingness to suffer for the happiness of others would not have to be stretched to lethal limits.

We buckled our seat belts and Razia Nani made herself comfortable. She took both the armrests and spilled a little into my seat, making me shrink toward the window a bit in an unsuccessful attempt to avoid getting pinned in.

She issued forth a long, deep sigh, suggestive of much greater burdens than a bagful of English chocolates. "*Aré, Beta!* How I wish your mother were here! It has been *such* a long time since I've seen Shabana. My heart longs to set eyes on her. But of course, one can understand. I don't blame her for not coming. I don't know what your Jamila Khala is thinking." She shook her head, placed her hand hard on her voluminous chest with an audible whack, approximately where I suppose she thought her heart was, and continued, "It breaks my heart! Breaks my heart, I tell you!"

I tried my best to give a coolly sympathetic nod, trying to let her know that *of course* I knew what she was talking about. And hoped desperately that she would elaborate.

I needn't have worried. She was only just getting started.

"Poor, poor Zahida! So disrespectful to her memory, your *nanima*, you understand. Of course Shabana couldn't come to the wedding. She's a loyal daughter, your mother is. Not that Jamila, your *khala*, had any choice, mind you. Who would have thought that such a thing could happen? That your cousin Zehra would actually become friends with one of *those* creatures? That she would insist on inviting them to her wedding! Unthinkable! Who would have thought? Not that Jamila's not responsible, of course. I mean, keeping up with *them*—with that family—for

appearances' sake is one thing. But to actually allow a friendship to develop between the girls! *Tawba!* Lord forgive us! Have
mercy on us! That such a thing could happen! What would dear
Zahida have said, your poor *nanima*, I mean? Yes, Jamila should
have put her foot down. But there is this also, I suppose—that if
there was coming and going between the two houses, then what
could be done? Order the children not to speak to them? No!
That would not be right also."

It was a bad beginning and I regretted the decision to pretend
to have any knowledge. I was lost in pronouns, innuendoes, and
obscure references that only enhanced my appetite for solving
the mystery of whom and what my mother had referred to on the
phone weeks before. It was like walking into a story already in
progress—a juicy story, I could tell—but how could I get Razia
Nani to start at the beginning? At the "once upon a time" part?

"No, you're right, Razia Nani. Jamila Khala had no choice, I
suppose. I guess it's all really Zehra's fault?" I don't think I managed to keep the question mark off of my statement, but Razia
Nani didn't seem to notice.

"Zehra's fault?! Of course not! How could it be your cousin
Zehra's fault? No, no, of course there is only one person to blame
after all, isn't there? Or maybe there are two? Well, I'm sure it's
not Zehra's fault, at least. If anyone, it has to be your grandfather's fault. Your *nana*."

"*Nana?*" My voice croaked a little, but she didn't notice. "But
he's dead."

"Yes, yes. And you're quite right. One shouldn't speak ill of
the dead, I know, but what that man did to your grandmother!"
Another whack to the chest. "It broke my heart to see Zahida
so humiliated. And now your mother won't even attend the

wedding of her dear sister's daughter. All because your grandfather had to go off with that Englishwoman—that witch, that
flower huppie! Gone off and had children, too, would you believe?
And Zehra—befriending one of those girls, her own *khala,* isn't
she? *Chee, chee, chee* . . . such a shameful thing. *Bap re bap,* it happened so many years ago, so many . . . and it's still so shocking!
The whole of Bombay could talk of nothing else for months and
months, you know. Mind you, not that *I* was surprised . . . Kasim
Bhai was always like that, you know. Causing scandals here and
there and everywhere! From the very beginning I could see how
it would turn out. And poor, poor Zahida! Such a good wife your
grandmother was to him, so very beautiful! And the way she put
up with his mad whims for all of those years . . . wearing whatever shameless clothes he bought for her, cutting off all of her
beautiful hair just to suit *his* tastes! Going ballroom dancing also!
She suffered so much for him . . . everyone blamed her for it, you
know, when all she did was try her best to please him!"

"Ballroom dancing?" I knew then, with the kind of knowledge that comes upon you suddenly, followed by a disbelief so
strong that acceptance takes a while to achieve. That the old
man from Bombay of my mother's story was her father. I'm not
sure what, if anything, I might have said next. Thankfully, the
conversation halted for a few minutes when the flight attendant
reached our row of seats to ask our beverage preferences.

"I'll have a tea, please," said Razia Nani to the flight attendant, in a thick, *desi* accent that I had failed to notice before.
"With sugar and milk, too. And can I have two teabags also?"
She waited for the flight attendant to serve her the tea and me my
soda before turning to me in explanation. "These white people
don't know how to make tea. *Chee!* It tastes like muddy water,

the way they make it. Sooo weak! *Akh-thoo!* But what choice do I have only, *nah?*"

I sipped my soda slowly, eating a few of the bite-sized cubes of ice as I chewed over what I had learned and tried to fit my unfamiliar grandfather into the familiar story of dance and downfall that my mother had told me when she refused to let me go to the eighth-grade prom. I was fascinated, I remember, struck by the scandalous glamour of what my grandfather had actually dared to do. That he had survived the consequences of his actions, at least long enough to have fathered more than one child—I was shocked at the realization as the meaning of what I had learned started to sink in—seemed to lend him a victorious light. As if he had fought a battle with fate, broken the rules of culture and convention—and won. It certainly cast a whole new light on the story my mother had told. Where were his just deserts? What else was there that I didn't know?

My mouth was cold, now, from the ice my tongue had flirted with, and my mind, too, had settled a bit when I decided to try and steer Razia Nani back to the course she had begun before we were interrupted, jointly, by my shock and the flight attendant's service.

"Her *khala?* Zehra is friends with her aunt, Razia Nani? I'm so bad with understanding these things. How exactly are they related?"

"Well, it's simple, *nah?* The English witch's children—that is, her children with your *nana,* your grandfather, are the brothers and sisters of your mother. And of Zehra's mother. Of course, they are not full brothers and sisters. Only *sautella.*"

I wasn't as ignorant, when I was paying attention, as I had claimed. And I knew that in Urdu, *sautella* was a word used for relatives and siblings who were not full or real—that there is no distinction, in the translation of that word, between step- and half-. But if my grandfather was the father of these children, then they were the half-siblings, not step-, of my mother. Which made them, as Razia Nani had pointed out, my aunts? uncles? How many were there?

Razia Nani started fumbling in her giant purse, in search of something. *"Aré!"* She was clicking her tongue between her teeth in dismay, her hands getting more desperate in their quest. "Oh, no! I've left my *paandan* in my hand luggage. *Beta*, please get my bag down for me. I must have it."

I stood up, squeezing myself past Razia Nani and into the aisle, and brought her bulky bag down for her. I waited, standing awkwardly exposed in the aisle, while she searched her bag for the round stainless steel box in which she kept all of the ingredients and paraphernalia she needed for the creation of the homemade *paan*s, laced with tobacco, which she ate at regular intervals. When she had found and removed it, I put the bag back into the overhead bin before making the return trip to my seat in eager anticipation of hearing more.

I had to wait for a few minutes while Razia Nani used little spoons and spatulas to sprinkle and brush mysterious and strangely aromatic powders and pastes onto the shiny green *paan* leaf that she prepared. She hummed to herself a little as she scooped a pinch of finely cut betel nut onto the leaf and folded it up expertly into a triangular kind of pocket. I watched her stuff the triangle into her mouth, tongue it over to one side, and park it, before finally prodding her back to the beginning of the story, which I had heard already from my mother. And then on, through it, to the end, which I had not.

"So, after Kasim Bhai left Zahida—your grandmother—she moved to Pakistan. To live with her older sister, Adeeba."

"With Big Nanima."

Razia Nani nodded. "Exactly. It was good for Adeeba. She had no children who would have visited, bringing little ones. So she was able to share Zahida's. And your grandfather? Well, he lived out the rest of his life with his Englishwoman—Belle— and the children she bore him in London." Razia Nani's voice, after having run a monologue of marathon proportions, came to a sudden halt.

I was silent for a moment. Then, all of the questions that I had been stifling, in a way that I would have been incapable of during the course of one of Mummy's stories, came pouring out. "But Nanima's home was in India. Didn't she ever go back?"

"Never."

"Why not?"

"At first, it was because she couldn't face them, poor thing— the rest of the family in Bombay, Kasim Bhai's younger brothers and their wives. Before, it was *her* house that they all lived in together. I remember visiting her in Bombay. Before it happened. With what grandeur she used to live . . . so many, many servants she had. And your grandfather kept her like a queen! She was the *begum sahiba* of the house. Now, with no husband, she had nothing and no place in that home. Oh, they made a lot of noise on her behalf in the beginning, the family in Bombay, swearing up and down that they would never forgive their older brother for what he had done to Zahida. But Kasim Bhai was the head of the family. And the business. So, when he brought Belle to India a few months after he took up with her, they had no choice but to accept her. It was a humiliation for Zahida. What a fall she took. From where she started and where she ended up! She never went back to India. And neither did your mother, who was furious with her father's family for accepting what her father had done."

It had never occurred to me to wonder why we visited Pakistan and never India, where my mother and father were actually from. Now, I knew. That Mummy had forsaken her country because of her anger at her father. That in breaking ties with him, she had also broken off with the rest of his family.

"Did Nana ever go back to India with Belle? After that first time?"

"Every year. With their children."

"Are they all coming to the wedding, Razia Nani? All of the children? Have you ever met them?"

"Well, of course! Many, many times. They are beautiful children, of course. Fair and beautiful. But then, they would be, wouldn't they? Being half-white as they are, *chee*! Let's see . . . Tara is the oldest." Razia Nani held up her finger, bending it backward with her other hand at a painful-looking angle as she spoke. My eyes focused on the finger, associating her words with it as if it truly represented, as she meant it to, the person she was describing.

"She has light eyes . . . not blue, but light-colored. She is your cousin Zehra's friend. I think she is a year, maybe two, younger than Zehra. Though, who knows what the truth is?" Razia Nani's brows lifted suggestively.

Her second finger went up, alongside of the first, and she subjected it to the same awkward contortions that the Tara finger had gone through. "And the middle one is a boy. I think he's about sixteen years old." Razia Nani nodded. "I remember the shame of it, your grandfather having children at the same pace that his grandchildren were being born! His name is Adam. Only they say it in the English way, *chee, chee*. He's a very quiet boy. Tall. His hair is golden."

It was the third finger's turn to be punished. "And the last one is Ruksana. But they say it the English way. Roxanna." Razia Nani's lips were pursed in disapproval and her pronunciation was an unconscious parody of the English one. "She's very sweet. The most like your grandfather. Round and plump. And darker than the others, though, of course, she's still very fair. I think she's twelve? Eleven? No, twelve, I think."

"She's younger than me?" For some reason, this was the most shocking news of all.

Razia Nani seemed surprised. "Well, yes, I suppose so." She was quiet for a long moment and I regretted my outburst, fearing that she might be reflecting on my age with regard to the appropriateness of the subject. She gave a little shrug, finally, and said, "Well, you will meet them all yourself soon enough. They will be at the wedding, after all. With their mother."

"The reason Mummy's not coming to the wedding." I managed to say it with confidence, leaving off the question mark.

"And who can blame her, after all? Shabana—your mummy— is a very strong woman, you know. She decides what is right and what is wrong. And she sticks with it. Very strong. Like her mother. Your Jamila Khala is different. She likes to make people happy. Likes there to be peace. Your mummy said she would never forgive her father. That he was dead to her. And she kept her word. Never spoke to him again. I suppose it was more difficult for your Jamila Khala. They lived in London, after all. And he was her father. She didn't want to tell your *nanima*—when she started to keep up with *them*. With your *nana* and Belle. She didn't want to hurt her, after all."

Over the course of her story, Razia Nani's betel nut had softened and marinated to a consistency that she found quite enjoyable. I could tell by the way she swished it around in her mouth, lingeringly, and by the maroonish-red hue of the spit that she collected and cradled in a pool between her lower lip and gums, which spilled over, from time to time, and stained the crevices at the corners of her mouth. I remember, quite vividly, thinking how ghoulishly like blood the stains on her mouth appeared to be. The darkened lights of the airplane cabin and the shadows they cast on Razia Nani's face did nothing to detract from the vampiric impression. Her mouth was full, which caused her words to be muffled, and though I had found it more and more difficult to follow her story as the plot and the *paan* progressed and developed, I worried less about eavesdroppers because of it.

I watched her manipulate her mouth with her tongue for a few seconds more and then prompted Razia Nani again, "You were saying about Jamila Khala not wanting to hurt Nanima?"

"Of course she was hurt, your *nanima*, very badly, when she found out that her own daughter had betrayed her."

"How did she find out?"

"Who knows how? People talk. God knows I am not one to speak about other people's business or to break a confidence. But there are some in this world who like to talk—to gossip— regardless of who they're hurting and without thought to the damage their words can do." She said this, endearingly enough, with a wholly convincing kind of sincerity that left no room for any level of self-consciousness.

"Did Lubna Khala"—I was referring to my mother's younger sister—"keep in touch with Nana?"

"No. But then, she was so far away, settled in Pakistan. Far away, like your mother. Who was furious with Jamila, when she heard that they were in touch. But Zahida interfered. She told your mother that it was wrong to fight with her sister."

"And what about Nana? When did he *really* die?" I remembered that my ignorance was something I had tried to cover before, and quickly added, "I mean, when exactly? I forget."

Razia Nani was too busy riding the wave of her own knowledge to notice my slip. "Oh? Let's see, was it May? June? Yes, June. Of last year. A massive heart attack. Your *nanima* had a stroke and died one week later. Poor Zahida. As if she was still waiting for him. As if, when he died, there was nothing left to wait for. So now Adeeba is alone again."

"I never met him. Nana." This was not a question.

Razia Nani glanced at me for a second, probably looking for material for her next news hour. I kept my face blank. Disappointed, she said, "No, well—your mother never forgave him, ever. She said she wouldn't and she didn't."

I leaned back in my seat and yawned, falling asleep to the sound of Razia Nani's voice, which had moved on to lament other scandals and tragedies involving people I was less interested in.

When my eyes opened, I heard the captain's voice, more muffled than Razia Nani's had been, announcing the beginning of our descent. Razia Nani, hand on chest, exclaimed at how time had flown—I don't think any pun had been intended—and directed me back to the overhead bin to retrieve her hand luggage. She extracted an old blue-and-white-striped grocery bag—from Tesco, I think—stuffed full and as wrinkled and creased as the face she began to pat and primp with the creams and cosmetics that came out of it.

Before long, we were on the ground. And welcomed, embraced, and folded into the sweaty armpits of loving relatives. For a few seconds, I felt lost among them, looking for Nanima before remembering that she was gone.

Jamila Khala and Lubna Khala, my mother's older and younger sisters, were there to receive me. Along with Zehra, the bride, whom I was surprised to see. She was beautiful, radiating happiness and health and hope. Her eyes were lined thickly with kohl, emphasizing the shine of their whites, her hair long— much longer than when I last saw her—straight and smooth, like Ameena's.

I hugged her, laughing a little as I asked, "What are you doing here? Isn't the bride supposed to be locked up indoors for weeks before the wedding?"

She laughed back, making a face as she nodded toward her mother, and said, "If Mum had her way I would be."

"Nonsense, Zehra." Jamila Khala frowned up at her daughter with the same expression my mother so frequently frowned with at me, its effect greatly diminished by her being a half a head shorter than Zehra, four-inch heels notwithstanding. "Of course she had to come to the airport to receive you, Saira. You've flown all this way to attend your cousin's wedding. We are only sorry that Ameena didn't come with you. And your mother also, of course." Jamila Khala pursed her lips, slightly, on these last words, running a hand through her short, perm-frizzed hair.

"Where's Big Nanima?" Hers was the other face I had looked for and missed.

"She's at my house," Lubna Khala said, "waiting to see you. You have all your bags? Good. Say good-bye to Razia Nani and we'll go." She turned to her driver, an old, bearded man with red, hennaed hair, and pushed my luggage cart toward him, gestur-

44

ing with an imperious wave of her hand, setting off clinks with her gold bangles, every red-tipped finger ablaze with the sparkle of diamonds and emeralds and rubies. "Driver, take these bags to the car! *Chalo, chalo!* Let's get out of here as quickly as we can."

I turned to Razia Nani, who put her hand on my head, "*Khudahafiz*, Saira. We'll meet soon. When the wedding functions begin, eh?" As she turned to walk away with her son and daughter-in-law, who had come to receive her at the airport, I heard her say, "Such a good girl she is. So respectful and well-mannered. Shabana has done well with her."

As Lubna Khala promised, Big Nanima was waiting for me at the house. Opening her arms wide, she folded me into flesh that felt less substantial to my arms, which were longer and stronger than the last time I had embraced her, two years before. She asked after my mother and father and Ameena. And then cried a little as she remembered her sister, my grandmother. I shed a few tears myself, sharing in the grief of my grandmother's sister as I had not been able to with my own.

"So," Big Nanima said finally, wiping the corners of her eyes with the end of her sari. "Your mother didn't come."

"No." I was not sure what else I should say, self-conscious about the revelations I had received from Razia Nani on the plane.

Big Nanima put her hand under my chin, telling me again how much I'd grown. "You are starting to bloom, eh, Saira? All of my sister's grandchildren have blossomed into such beautiful young men and women."

"*Your* grandchildren, too, Adeeba Khala," Jamila Khala chided Big Nanima. "Are we not your children also?"

"That you are." Big Nanima, whose eyes were still on me,

asked, "Has your Jamila Khala told you about the foreign guests that are to be present at Zehra's wedding? Did your mother tell you why she refused to attend?"

I shook my head. "No." My chin lifted a little, in defiance or resentment, I'm not sure which. "But Razia Nani told me."

Big Nanima clicked her tongue. "So you found out the truth from a stranger. Your mother should have told you before, warned you."

Jamila Khala spoke then, clicking her tongue between her teeth, too, her expression one of exasperation, "*Oof!* Shabana didn't tell Saira because she is stubborn. For twenty years she has carried her anger upon her head, refusing to even discuss our father. Stubborn, she's always been stubborn, since she was a lit—"

Lubna Khala interrupted with another clink of her bangles, "None of us are happy that you've invited *that* woman and her children here. To Pakistan. Don't blame Shabana! If I didn't live here myself then I probably wouldn't have come also!"

"But why? What is the matter with all of you? You think it didn't affect me? She was my mother, he was my father, too. And I was there when it happened! You think I have forgotten? *Oof*—tell me, what does it matter now? It's all in the past. He's dead, she's dead. Both of them gone, what difference does it make now? Tara is Zehra's best friend. They went to the same school, same college. How would it look? To invite her and not invite her sister and brother? And if I invited them, I had to invite their mother, too. Who knew she would have the cheek to actually come? And her children, don't forget, are our sisters and brother, after all."

Lubna Khala had nothing to say to this. Neither did anyone

else. Zehra, who looked as if she had been witness to this argument many times before, sighed, "I'm sorry I've caused so many problems for everyone." She turned to me, "And I'm sorry that Shabana Khala isn't going to be here. But Tara is my best friend and I don't want to talk about this anymore." She glanced at her watch. "I'm late for an appointment. I have a fitting for the wedding outfit. Saira, you're going shopping with me and Mum tomorrow, so rest up, okay?" She came over to hug me and left, shouting, "Borrowing your car and driver again, Lubna Khala. 'Bye!" over her shoulder as she scurried down the hall, *chappal*s flapping, past the servant who was carrying in my bags.

Jamila Khala looked at her watch now, and exclaimed, "*Oof!* Look at the time! I have an appointment, also, with the jewelers. I'll see you all later. Don't forget about the shopping tomorrow, eh, Saira? We have to get you measured up for your clothes, too." She hurried out the door, too, heels clicking comically fast, oofing and tsk-ing her way out of the house about how little time there was left to get everything done that needed doing.

After Jamila Khala left, Lubna Khala left the room to supervise the servant's delivery of my bags to the guest room.

Big Nanima took a seat on the sofa in the lounge and beckoned me to her. "Come, come, *beti*. Tell me, what shall we call for to eat? *Paan*s, *bhel puri*, *bun kabab?* Let's call for a little bit of everything, eh? We'll tell Lubna not to bother preparing anything for lunch and spread all of the food out on the table so you can choose."

I smiled. But my heart wasn't in it, she could see.

"What's wrong, *beti?*"

"I wish I could stay with you, Big Nanima."

"With me? What would you want to stay with an old lady

47

for? When there's a wedding in the house and all of the *hungama* that goes with it? Your place is here, with your aunts and your cousins, where you can practice all of the songs and dances you will perform for Zehra and her bridegroom. I will come every day myself, to watch you and clap and cheer."

Lubna Khala reentered the room and said, "Adeeba Khala, please! I've told you a hundred times—you must stay here for the wedding. You tell her, Saira. Tell Big Nanima. She'll listen to you. Everyone knows you are her favorite."

"Stay here? I have my own place to look after, Lubna."

"Yes, yes. We know, Adeeba Khala, you have your own place. But there's nothing to keep you from staying with us for a few days. You don't have your students to use as an excuse, now, during the summer holidays."

"No. No students now. But Lubna, *beti*, I have my own routine and rhythm, which you know I am very particular about. And I am used to my own lumpy bed. Your house is too big, your mattresses too soft for me." Big Nanima glanced up at me and laughed. "This one is swaying from side to side from exhaustion. Go, Saira. Go and wash up and rest a little. I'll wake you up for lunch. Then we'll eat and we'll talk. Go now, *beti*, go."

I got up a little unsteadily and obeyed.

BIG NANIMA KEPT her word and came every day. But, with one exception, I never got to spend any time with her alone. In this way and others, Karachi was a totally different place for me that summer than it had been on any of my previous visits. Staying at Lubna Khala's house, which had become Wedding Central, had never been an option in the past. Now, finally, Lubna Khala had become the ruler of her own domain, in charge of her own domestic affairs, where before the title had belonged to her mother-in-law, who had also recently passed away. Lubna Khala's house was a vast structure, laid with marble, trimmed in teak, each room humming with the boxed air-conditioning that so few in Karachi could afford. Very different from Big Nanima's modest home.

Even though I saw Big Nanima every day, I missed the dynamic that she and Nanima had combined to create. Instead of the gentle rhythm of their elderly company, I found myself to be part of a crowd of extended family—and lonely nonetheless. I missed my mother. I missed my father. And most of all, I missed Ameena. I missed being her younger sister. Letting her do the talking for me. The bossy, self-important advice she offered uninvited and that I normally resented—orders, really, that I flouted more often than not. I wished desperately that she, at least, had come with me. She was part of how I defined myself and I felt off-course without her.

This was my first visit to Karachi as a "young adult." By which I mean I had a regular period and breasts—a fact that affected my experience there far more than I would have expected. As soon as Razia Nani and I had gotten off the plane, I had noticed. How male the world around me was. I felt the eyes, men's eyes, drilling holes into my clothes in an attempt to see what lay underneath them. I was wearing jeans that day—a mistake I realized and rectified from the moment I arrived at Lubna Khala's house, thinking that the sight of a young woman in trousers was what was causing all of the fuss. But wearing *shalwar kameez* and a *dupatta* didn't make much difference. At one point, on a shopping expedition with Jamila Khala and Zehra—we were looking for bangles to match the yellow outfit Zehra would wear at her *mehndi* ceremony—I started trying to outstare the men who lounged around the doorways of the stalls in the bazaar.

"What are you doing, Saira?! Look down, for God's sake!" Jamila Khala yelped when she noticed what I was doing. "You have to look down. It's the only way to handle them. Look down, ignore them, pretend you don't notice. Staring back only gives them a cheap thrill—as if you were inviting them to look more."

"But it's so disgusting! Why do they stare? They make me feel so—so dirty!"

"They stare because they're men," my diminutive aunt snorted with impatience, directed with equal force at me and the men around us. "If you don't like it, use your *dupatta* to cover your head."

"What?" But I did as she suggested. "What's that going to do?"

"It gives them a message. That you're a good girl, a modest girl. It won't stop them from staring. But you'll feel more comfortable, more protected."

But I didn't. I felt fragile and painfully aware of my own femininity. Vulnerable. And resentful for being made to feel so.

FOUR

I WAS ABLE TO spend only one afternoon at Big Nanima's house on that trip alone to Karachi. Everything was the same and I spent the first hour exploring it all, discovering things I must have seen before but, some at least, I had never noticed. All of the bookshelves, floor to ceiling, in the living room and bedrooms, stuffed with books. There were *Jane Eyre* and *Pride and Prejudice*—these I was familiar with from our last visit, when Big Nanima had given them to me to read for the month we had spent there—and hundreds of other books with which I was not yet acquainted. There was a globe on a stand in the corner of the living room. On a desk, next to it, there were stacks of paper, handwritten pages, in English and Urdu.

"What's this?"

"Ah—you naughty child. You have discovered my secret."

"You—you're writing something?"

"Translating. Which is very different from writing."

"Translating what?"

"Well—those pages, there"—she pointed to one of the stacks—"that is no secret. Only some Urdu poetry that I am translating into English. I have worked on two books already which have been published."

"Really?"

"Yes. And that pile of papers—that is something new I have begun in my spare time. A television screenplay."

"TV?"

"Yes. It's a script for an Urdu drama. A serial adaptation of Jane Austen's *Sense and Sensibility*. They have begun filming it already. Very exciting."

"You're in show business!" I laughed.

"Shhh! After all the negative things I have said about television, I am afraid I will be rightly accused of all kinds of hypocrisy when my role in the production is found out."

I went back to wandering around the room, taking a stand in front of some photographs, fading, on a table in the corner opposite the globe. Some needed no explanation. A series of them: Big Nanima, getting bigger in each successive photograph, standing beside groups of young women dressed in crisp white *shalwar kameezes,* pressed and starched to perfection—college students, hers. Others of a young woman with curly short hair, sari-clad, umbrella and pocketbook at hand, posing in front of Imperial fountains and statues and monuments.

Of course I knew who these pictures were of. But I had no idea when they had been taken. I took one of these off one of the shelves and turned to the subject herself to ask, "Big Nanima, when are these from?"

"London, *beta*. From when I went there to study."

"I didn't know that you went to London to study."

"Hmm. Well, I did."

Something struck me as odd. I remembered Nanima's conversation with Ameena. About how she had been married to a man she had never met, at the age of sixteen. I couldn't reconcile that with the photographs of Big Nanima on the wall in front of me.

"But Nanima was, like, a child bride, wasn't she? I mean, why did *she* have to get married so young? While you were allowed to go to London to study?"

Big Nanima knew me well enough to hear no accusation in my question. She smiled. "That's a very good question. Something I would have asked myself, at your age. Something I ask myself, still, today." Big Nanima sighed, took the picture frame from my hand, and sat down on the sofa, patting the cushion next to hers, inviting me to sit down with her.

When I did, she continued, "It's a good story, Saira—the answer to your question. In the beginning, you see, I thought *I* was the unlucky one. But time has a way of proving all of us wrong in the end. Every single one of us. Sit. Listen, and I'll tell you." Big Nanima set the photograph down on the coffee table and reached for the food she had spread there earlier. She unwrapped one of the *kabab* rolls she had called for from down the street, scooping extra chutney on the side of my plate before handing it to me.

Then, picking up the photograph, she ran the end of her *dupatta* over it, as if removing dust I could not see. "See how short my hair was in this picture? How I always hated it—so curly and unkempt! Since our days in Bombay, before Partition, I had longed to chop it off. But only when I was in London, far away from my mother, did I have the courage to finally do it. I was never very interested in such things—in my appearance and in what others thought of it. Though, truthfully, that is because I knew that the impression I made on others wasn't a very favorable one. Only once do I remember spending any length of time in front of the mirror, which was little Zahida's favorite place in the house!" Big Nanima laughed. "That day—I remember it so well! Important for me—because of what did not happen. And for Zahida—because of what did.

"It was—when was it? Oh—1941, if I'm not mistaken. We were still living in Bombay. Yes, I remember standing at the mirror in the room I shared with your grandmother, smoothing my hands down over my *kameez*, hating myself for the sweaty palms that made the action necessary. I put my hands together, squeezing them, trying to suppress the nervousness that filled me up, 'til here." Big Nanima pointed to her throat. "I looked in the mirror and saw myself the way his mother would see me, and his grandmother. A plain face. With skin that was—well, rather dark." Big Nanima smiled gently at me, shaking her head ruefully. "And hair that is easier to laugh at now than it was then. I tried everything. Pigtails, a ponytail, braids, a bun. But nothing could tame that unruly mass.

"It is one of the few times I remember resenting my father—for being so brutally honest regarding the situation about to unfold. I thought that perhaps Gray, the poet, was right, and ignorance, in this instance, would have been preferable to the folly of knowledge. That is, preferable to the painful awareness that my father's words had caused. That everything hinged on the outcome of this meeting. That one of my flaws, for once, might actually become an asset.

"The boy's mother and grandmother were due to arrive at any moment. To meet and assess my worth as a potential wife for the boy they represented. A boy who had expressed the specific and very unusual desire to be wed to a 'read and written' girl. An English-speaking girl. *'Beti,'* my father had said bluntly, 'this might be your only chance. And finally, I hope, we will prove your mother wrong. That I was right to allow you to study.'

"You see, I was already a little too old to be single. My parents were worried for me. There had been few enough inquiries made about me. And of those, I had suffered, in the way of comparison. Because my younger sister, Zahida—your Nanima—was startlingly beautiful. She had light brown hair, green eyes, and sharply symmetrical features. Zahida's skin was translucent and luminous, and she was pale. With oh-so-beautiful, silky, straight hair that fell to her waist. She was also—well, not academically inclined." Big Nanima looked up at me, a smile in her eyes. "Why lie? Your grandmother was only sixteen. And she was a stupid girl. *I* should know, as her occasional tutor, unkind as it is to say, to even think such a thing about one's own sister. But, in the situation which I was about to face—when a suitable boy's family came to call to size up the available girl in question— intelligence, or the lack of it, did not seem to count for much. Our parents had been fending off proposals for Zahida before she had even reached puberty.

"I was not surprised by my father's straight talk. He had never been very diplomatic in his characterizations of his children. The boys—there were four of them, all older than me and Zahida— were, respectively: sharp, lazy, too handsome for his own good, and hardworking (at least). I was considered to be the brain. And Zahida, the beauty.

"Though I must put aside any claim to modesty to say so, I was the most educated girl in the community. And I suffered for it. Gladly. My mother never ceased to complain, saying that I would be left unfit for marriage. Even my father, who was my greatest champion in my quest to study, was less than sensitive in his advocacy." Big Nanima winked at me, letting me know that her tongue was in her cheek. "He said, 'Let the poor girl study! What's the harm? God knows He didn't gift her with the beauty He granted her younger sister. Let her make the most of what He did grant her.'

"Our mother had better luck—trying to protect her daughters from educational corruption—with Zahida. When she was five, Zahida was sent off for her first day of school, the same convent school which I attended. She came home crying—so pitifully that our father affectionately gave in to our mother's objections to having sent her in the first place. 'All right, all right! *Acha, baba, acha!*' he said. 'Stop crying, Zahida. You can stay at home with your mother. No schooling for little Zahida, all right?' I remember our father's words as he turned to my mother and said, 'She's a pretty thing, and doesn't need to worry her little head over studying and learning English. Everyone can't be a scholar, just as everyone can't be a beauty. Her sister can teach her the basics—reading, writing, a little English—at home.' But Zahida was very naughty. She ran away from the lessons I tried to give her. Despite my best efforts, she never did learn English.

"I was ashamed to admit that I was grateful for that fact. On that day, standing in front of that mirror. For once, I needn't worry about being upstaged by my beautiful little sister. And— just to be safe—our mother had taken the precaution of giving Zahida strict instructions to stay out of sight. In the meantime, while I waited for our guests to arrive, I did the best I could, tried to do something with my hair, wishing, not for the first time, that my mother would have allowed me to cut it down to size, like so many of the Englishwomen I had gotten to know through school. They were visitors from England, educational experts who had been invited to observe and help to improve the British-run convent school that I used to attend. The school where I now taught English. Though no one but my father knew *that*."

"What do you mean? You—your job was a secret?" My mouth was full of *kabab* roll, my eyes watery from the spicy chutney that I dipped into before each bite.

"Yes. From everyone except my father. My mother was suspicious, I think, when my father told her that I would continue to go to school every day, for 'special studies' that the teachers had deemed me worthy of. 'Why? What is the point of all this study?' she had asked him. 'It is time for her to be married. It was time for her to be married a long time ago!'

"'Yes, yes! We know all that,' my father had replied, 'but it's not that she has a choice, is it? Let her study . . . what difference does it make? It keeps her busy. She's a very good student. And those silly old British women think she's a very clever girl.' My father had winked at me then, and I could see the amusement that twinkled in his eyes as his plan to trick the family fell into place.

"'Just go along with whatever I say,' he had told me. 'Don't contradict me. And make sure you hide whatever your earnings are. Don't go showing off to your brothers and sister, mind you! Or there'll be hell to pay!'

"That instruction had been more difficult to follow than expected. Since the marriages of my two eldest brothers, things in the household had become complicated. My new sisters-in-law had proven their value and fertility very quickly by producing one son each, within one year of matrimony. Household expenses had increased dramatically. And my father's small business, never a very profitable enterprise, had taken a downturn that made it difficult for him to pay the bills. My hand had itched with the desire to ease the burden that now fell on my father's head. Ultimately, his need had outweighed his pride.

"He had come to me within the first two months of my employment. His embarrassment, even now, makes me cringe in sympathy for how his dignity must have suffered. His head had hung low and his eyes were cast downward. 'Adeeba, uh, well— things have been very—uh—difficult lately. All of the strikes and boycotts. They have affected the business. And with all of the talk of Independence, so many of the British are leaving. And you know that some of them have been our best customers. Adeeba, *beti*, I am ashamed to ask, but I have to do it—'

"I interrupted him then, 'No, *Aba*, please don't ask. You don't have to ask. I have been saving my salary. I wanted to give it to you from the beginning. I don't need it. I have everything I need. Please, please take it.' I went into my wardrobe, rummaged through it to find the old talcum powder tin, which I had wrapped in an old shawl, and took out my meager savings.

"My father stared down at my hand, full of money and extended toward him. I can never be sure, but I thought I saw moisture collect at the corners of his eyes as he put his hand over mine, held it firmly, caressed it, and withdrew it, having accepted the transfer of funds within his hand. That day, in front of the mirror, as I waited for the guests to arrive, I worried about what might happen if things turned out the way my father and mother hoped they would. I knew, with all humility, that my secret contribution to the household finances was what kept up the appearance of even a minimal level of prosperity. And yet I was practical enough to realize that marriage was a requirement for my own future security.

"I was not a stranger to ideas of romance. Part of the reason I so loved English literature was because of the importance it gave to romantic love. It was an abstract ideal, however, and one which I was perfectly happy to wait to discover within the context of social acceptability and economic necessity. One of my favorite authors—you know, Saira—was Jane Austen, who well understood the need for reason and pragmatism with regard to matters of the heart. The success of a marriage depended no less on economics than on an intellectual understanding between its participants. And here, finally, there was hope for that. I had not given much thought to the boy in question, beyond marveling at the progressive nature of his desire to be wed to an educated girl—a girl who spoke English, no less! My father had met him before, had known his father.

"'He's a very good boy. Decent and kind. He's taken care of his family from a very young age. Since his father passed away. Not rich, mind you. But he has a lot of potential. Very clever chap. I'm sure he'll go places. I would be happy to have him as a son-in-law.' My father had made his approval clear. There seemed to be no escaping the favorable implications—that the hand of destiny might have something to do with the meeting about to take place.

"The only obstacle to happiness in this story, that I could foresee, had to do with the short-term needs of my own family . . . the financial considerations of the present. Because in the long run, I believed, my single status would only lead to unhappiness. My sisters-in-law were very good to me. I had no doubt of their sincere affection. For the moment, however, their position in the household was subservient to that of their mother-in-law, my mother. Change was an inevitable part of the future. And who could tell how future shifts in the balance of power might affect their view of me?

"Already, there was an underlying tension in their feelings toward Zahida. It was easy to understand. It was difficult to like Zahida. Her beauty was such that it inspired automatic envy and dislike among all young women, even those who were not in a position to have to compete with her directly. In this sense, I knew, I myself posed no similar threat. And Zahida, spoilt by the attention she had received since birth by loved ones and strangers alike, did nothing to aid in her own defense. She was demanding and selfish. She was used to getting things her own way, and wheedled and charmed her way around the house among our brothers, parents, and servants, who all served as her willing victims. Thankfully for all concerned, there was no fear of Zahida remaining in the household for very long. Her marriage prospects were assured.

"But my future was not so certain. And I knew that my sisters-in-law's present affection for me was no guarantee for my future position in the household. By the dictates of our culture, it was their responsibility, as the wives of my brothers, to care for any of my parents' surviving dependents, maiden daughters included. The limited independence that my work afforded me, however, had spoilt my taste for a lifetime of dependent toleration. So, marriage was my only long-term option."

Big Nanima sighed, long and hard. She looked at my plate, saw that I had finished my *kabab* roll, and reached for the jug of sugar cane juice that she had called for with the food, pouring me a glass, handing it to me, before continuing her narrative. "I sat there for a long time, in front of that mirror, thinking of all of these things. And then, from the window in my room, which opened out into the open-air courtyard, I heard unfamiliar voices, their tones raised in an exchange of polite greetings. I knew that my summons was imminent and gave myself one more doubtful look in the mirror and laughed at the nervous expression that I saw there.

"'That that is, is,' I quoted Shakespeare, softly, to myself. 'And that that will be, will be,' I added, laughing at myself, very pleased with my own improvised wisdom.

"A little while later, from where I sat, things seemed to be going well. I had made my entrance, tea tray in hand, quite some time before. The conversation, carried by my mother and the younger of the two ladies visiting, was flowing. Cordialities and compliments abounded. They had praised the room, its furnishings, the home, and the residents they had yet met. The tea was declared to be delicious. The *pakora*s perfectly spiced. And the bearer of both, myself, assessed surreptitiously between sips of tea, the ladies declared charming. My English skills had not been tested. But then, I had held little expectation that they would be, rightly assuming that the examiners present would themselves not bear the expertise required to make such an evaluation. The fact that I had them had been confirmed, and the verbal assurance had seemed to be sufficient.

"And then, events took a turn which was all the more regrettable because it had been foreseen. Zahida made an unplanned and specifically forbidden entrance. She seemed to stumble in accidentally—though the verb hardly applied to the gliding grace with which she arrived."

"She——?! Didn't you say that your mother told her not to be

around?! Did she do it on purpose?" I don't think I even tried to hide my outrage. But then, my loyalty had been firmly engaged some years before, in a fight over fan rights.

Big Nanima laughed at my tone, bringing her story back to human scale. Then she shook her head, still smiling. "I'll never know the truth of her motives. At the time, it was hard not to believe it was deliberate. And yet I could not let myself give in to the temptation of such a suspicion. I could not see any motive for what Zahida did . . . not one that would preclude a level of spite and malice that I believe my sister was incapable of.

"In any case, the change in the air was immediate and obvious. In mid-conversation, the attention of both visitors shifted from one of my mother's daughters to the other. And—I saw it happen before my very eyes—so did their interest. My mother tried to steer them back onto course, pointing out in the first few moments of Zahida's arrival that she was a rather simple girl, not inclined to study and therefore non-conversant in English. The two ladies exchanged a glance and I saw the grandmother give a little shrug before asking another question of Zahida. My own presence, I knew, was no longer required or even noticed. There was nothing for me to do but wait politely for my mother to dismiss me, along with Zahida.

"When she did, we left the sitting room together and ran into an awkward pause in the hallway outside. Zahida was wringing her hands together and biting her lip in obvious discomfort. I looked at her. The words, in reference to the scene that had just unfolded in the sitting room, remained unsaid. These were matters that we sisters had never before discussed, and I saw no reason to change that now. I turned and walked down the hallway toward our room. And Zahida, who was apparently less content with the silence, followed me.

"'Adeeba?' Zahida said. Resenting her urge to communicate, I didn't answer right away. 'Adeeba? Are you angry with me?' she tried again. Big teardrops gathered at the corners of her eyes. I watched them make a trail down my sister's beautiful face. And I saw—I couldn't help it—how the marks of sorrow seemed to enhance her loveliness. 'Please, Adeeba. I can't bear to have you angry with me.'

"I sighed. It was no use. It would be like the leaf resenting the flower. And we both belonged to the same plant. 'No, Zahida, I'm not angry with you.' I remember that I paused before asking, out of sheer curiosity, 'What reason would I have to be angry with you?'

"She said, 'I'm not sure. I shouldn't have gone in. But I couldn't help it, really I couldn't. I was so curious! I wanted to know what was happening.'

"I shook my head and said, 'I understand.' And then I turned away, wishing to let the matter drop.

"But it was picked up again later. I overheard my parents that evening, as my mother recounted the afternoon's events to my father. 'But didn't you tell her to stay away?' My father sounded angry.

"My mother, no less so. 'Yes! Yes, of course I did. I told Imran to take care of her for the afternoon. They were supposed to have gone out.'

"'So? What happened?' my father asked.

"'I don't know,' my mother answered, sounding as puzzled as I had felt.

"'Did you ask Imran?'

"'No. Not yet. I wasn't sure what I could even say . . .' My mother's voice had trailed off. And I had understood her dilemma. Had faced it myself in my brief exchange with Zahida. What, exactly, could one say? To be frank was to be less than delicate. And the situation called for nothing if not delicacy.

"My father was silent for a moment before he sighed and said, 'I don't know. There's nothing that can be done, I suppose. Or said. And how did the visit go?'

"'Before or after Zahida danced her way into the room?' I remember that I winced at the sharpness in my mother's voice as she asked the question, rhetorically, sighed, and then continued, 'It went well. They seemed to like Adeeba. And then, they seemed to like Zahida even more.'

"'Hmmm. Well, I suppose there's nothing that can be done. What will happen, will happen.' I remember smiling at my father's words. They echoed exactly what I had said to myself earlier in the day, in front of that cursed mirror. 'He's a good boy and we would be lucky to have him marry our daughter. Whichever daughter that may be.'"

Big Nanima had picked up the photograph again, having laid it aside when she poured me the juice. She looked at it for a long moment and then stood up to put it back on the shelf I had taken it down from. Then, instead of coming back to the sofa where I sat, she began to pace up and down the room. Her hands were clasped behind her back. She wasn't looking at me, but at the floor, at the wall, out the window. I had never seen her in a classroom. But I imagined that this is what she might look like there, in the middle of a lecture, engrossed in her own thoughts, formulating the sentences she would utter to express them. I didn't have much time to marvel at the contrast—between the introspective, intellectual person pacing in front of me and the fun-loving, food-loving, sound effect–prone storyteller I knew her to be.

Because, after a few lengths around the room, Big Nanima spoke again, as she had been speaking, in perfectly chosen words, which she delivered flawlessly, as if reading to me from one of the novels she had read aloud when I was younger. "In the way that partly held expectations can still come as surprises, my father received a visit, the following evening, from the uncle of the boy. The men were served refreshments in the sitting room, this time, less controversially, by the servant. The uncle waited until the servant had left the room before embarking on an explanation for his call.

"'Well, uh—Mahboob Sahib—uh—er—my sister was quite taken with your daughter yesterday. She has asked me to bring a proposal on behalf of her son. She has also asked me to remind you of your friendship with the boy's father. She hopes that this friendship would cause you to look favorably upon my nephew, Kasim. He—uh—he's a very intelligent and able young man. Not wealthy, you know. But a very good boy. With a bright future, I am sure. The blessing of such a marriage would, I have no doubt, seal the promise of that future.'

"My father cleared his throat delicately and said, 'I am flattered, Abbas Sahib, but I have to point out that I have two daughters.'

"The visitor said, 'Yes. Oh, yes. I am sorry. I am speaking of your younger daughter, Zahida.'

"My father was silent for a long moment. He put his hands together and leaned his chin forward onto them before saying, 'Zahida. Yes, Zahida. I had heard that Kasim—' He broke off and was silent for another moment and then seemed to change his mind as well as the direction of his words. 'Yes. Well, I am sure you will understand that I will have to defer an answer to you until I am able to consult with the members of my household.'

"The boy's uncle said, 'Of course, Mahboob Sahib, of course. Take your time, please. I will come back for an answer whenever you call me. I am at your disposal.'

"Kasim Bhai's uncle took his leave and my father saw him out before returning to the sitting room, sinking into the favored armchair that his guest had just vacated, and putting his head into his hands. I had been hovering near enough to have heard everything—the identity of our guest, the purpose of his visit, the fact of his departure as well as the dilemma he would have caused for my father. Now, I entered the room and sat down on the rug, at my father's feet.

"His eyes still closed, he moved one of his hands from his head to mine and said, 'I am sorry, *beti*. I wish that things could have been different.'

"I said, 'I don't, Aba. I'm glad they turned out this way,' and as I said the words, I realized that they were true. 'I like things just the way they are. I know that this may change. But whatever happens, happens for a reason. If I had to go away, to leave you, then I would worry.' I regretted saying the words as soon as they were out of my mouth.

"My father froze. And then he sighed, a long and heavy breath, saying, 'It's all right. I know what you mean. And the truth is, I don't know what I would do without the help you have been giving me. I should be ashamed to admit that. But it's true. I would miss you if you went away, that's true. As I will miss Zahida. But you, Adeeba, right now—I don't know if

I could spare you. Maybe Allah has decided to let me keep you for a little while longer. Only Allah knows . . .' He broke off on a ragged breath. And then continued, 'Adeeba, forgive me, but I will even need your help for the wedding expenses. If it had been your wedding I had to plan, then I would have had to go into debt. More debt, even, than I am in already. So, you see, maybe it's a blessing in disguise. A blessing for me. A blessing for Zahida, and for the family. I'm not sure it's such a blessing for you, though, *beti*.'" Big Nanima stopped pacing and talking at the same second.

I took advantage of the brief pause. "But—what did Nana say when he found out that Zahida—I mean Nanima—didn't speak English? Was he mad?"

"What could he say? It was too late by then. They were already married. And besides, she was so beautiful that I don't think he cared what language she spoke or didn't speak."

"But—did she ever say she was sorry? That she stole—"

"No, no, Saira. She didn't steal anything. Nothing that wasn't hers already."

"But—if she hadn't come into the room—"

"If? There's no if. There is only what is. What was. What will be. I am not giving you this history lesson in order to find blame. No story worth telling should ever be about blame or regret. What happened was what was meant to happen. *Kismat*. My life was not over. My *kismat* was different than my sister's. She had her journey to travel. And I had mine." Big Nanima paused to give me a piercing look, the look of a professor pausing to assess how well her student understood. Whatever she saw in my face made her shake her head and sigh. "You won't understand this now, Saira. Later, perhaps. When you are older. When you learn that life is not only about the choices *you* make. That some of them will be made for you."

"But—"

"No, Saira. There are no buts. No ifs." Big Nanima cocked her head to one side and smiled at me for a long moment. Then she resumed her pacing. "Some years later, in 1947, we moved to Karachi, leaving Zahida behind with her husband, with sorrow in our hearts."

"Why did you move to Pakistan? I mean, you didn't *have* to."

"No, no one *had* to move. Though some thought they must. Most came out of fear—there was anger everywhere and they thought it was better to be among our own than among angry neighbors of a different faith. Yet more Muslims remained in India than those who moved to Pakistan. My father moved because business was bad already. Being a Muslim among angry Hindus didn't bode well for the future. He thought a fresh start would be a good thing.

"But that fresh start came with a high cost. No one realized how much blood would be involved in the birth—the birth of twin nations. It seemed to happen overnight: the sudden fanfare and formalities of Independence had hardly been a matter for celebration in light of the need for hasty decisions over the question of national loyalty. The chaos of leaving and the tears of leave-taking blurred in our minds, like the scenery that whizzed by from the train on our journey. Each time we passed populated areas, my father made us draw the shades and keep carefully quiet, praying silently to be left in peace and undiscovered by the mobs of angry people that attacked from—and on—both sides. Each mile took us farther from home and paradoxically closer to it, too. It was impossible not to be collectively afraid.

And equally impossible not to be collectively exhilarated: to arrive at our destination and to consciously forget the horrors of our travels, to pretend that the new borders that were constructed were not newly imposed. As if their very artificiality could be ignored in the fury of a nationalism that was as fervent as it was new.

"I was twenty-six when the flag of Pakistan was raised for the first time and I was intoxicated by the promise of change and progress in a totally new context. Not surprising, really, when one considers the rather limited options left open for me in the life and city that we were leaving behind. Immediately, I began teaching in a girls' school near home, a school whose governing board was still comprised mostly of British do-gooders.

"In Pakistan, there was no longer any need to hide the fact that I was teaching. Our family's downward-spiraling fortunes were at their lowest ebb, and during these turbulent times no one dared to voice any objections to the fact that I was employed and earning. My economic contribution to the household, now, was something that everyone, and not just my father, acknowledged and appreciated. In any case, I was no longer young enough to merit the careful cultivation of the kind of reputation that young, single men would require in a bride. Since Zahida's marriage, inquiries about me had been few and far between. The last few had been from much older widowers—eager to foist their growing children on a new wife who could also serve as a substitute mother. One of them actually had children older than me!

"My mother, thankfully, had been as insulted as I was. 'She is not that old!' she said. 'Not yet! And we are not that desperate! We can wait. We can wait for whatever God wills for her.'

"Two years after settling in Pakistan and two years further

away from marital eligibility, I was offered a scholarship to study in England. And I hoped that my mother would view my good fortune in that light. Knowing, of course, that there was no way that my parents could agree. But for a moment, I allowed myself to hope." There was a light in Big Nanima's eyes, which sparkled as she clapped her hands together, reliving the moment in a way that made my presence superfluous. "It was an easy thing to do—a natural outcome, really, of living in a newborn country. Opportunities seemed to be abundantly swimming in an ocean of hope. All one had to do was catch them. The optimism was universal . . . the whole nation seemed to be on a family fishing trip, laughing and chatting companionably as we baited our hooks in the naïve assurance that there were plenty of them—opportunities—to go around. Plenty of potential for industry. Plenty of arable land. Plenty of work. And plenty of progress to roll up one's sleeves for.

"Progress." Big Nanima smacked her lips, savoring the taste of the word. "A wonderful word that implied movement forward, to a better state of being. Unbelievably, the chance to be a part of progress was within my reach and I could hardly imagine what that might mean—to go to England and be able to study English literature! To come back and share my knowledge, my expertise, with my countrywomen on a mission of educational progress! It was an opportunity I had never dared to dream of . . . a cruelly tempting glimpse at a life that was beyond imagining.

"But if it was meant to be, then—well, then, it simply was. That is how I approached it with my parents. After meeting the challenge of first finding a private moment alone with them both—away from my brothers, my sisters-in-law, and my nieces and nephews—I told them, 'It is a wonderful opportunity. I

70

feel it in my bones. That this is the right thing to do. That this is meant to be. All of the expenses would be paid.'

"'But England?' My father was shocked—my mother's silence an indication of being no less so. 'Adeeba, how can we let you go so far away? Alone? It is not right, *beti*, it is not right that a young woman—an unmarried young woman—should be so far away from her family.'

"I pleaded with him, 'But, Aba, it would only be for a few years. And I would stay with a sponsor family. I would not be alone. And it is so important! Not just for me—think of what it means for the country. If everyone thinks as you do, then we'll never get ahead. Never! Aba, you have always supported me in my education. Please. This is the opportunity of a lifetime. I cannot pass it up. I cannot!'

"Finally, my mother had spoken, in a daze, 'But why? Why would they do this? Offer you so much? For free? What do they get out of it?'

"I was happy to have the chance to explain, happy that my request had not been refused without a chance to do so. 'It's a charitable foundation, Ama. They want to help developing countries through education. They want to help train and educate teachers so that we can come back and share our learning with others here. They're helping to build a college here, too. And will work in partnership with the board. If I go, and if I complete the degree, then I will be guaranteed a position at the college. As a professor.'

"Something flickered in my mother's eyes. Suddenly, the person I had thought of as my biggest obstacle switched sides to become my biggest ally. The first sign of support came in the form of silence. That night, my mother offered no further argument against my going.

"That first evening, my father closed the discussion by saying he needed time to think it over. He had seemed to run out of things to say and had looked in my mother's direction several times in confusion—trying to gauge her uncharacteristic silence and failing to take its measure.

"The next day, I anxiously waited for my father to raise the subject again. But he did not. After dinner, when I dejectedly served him tea, convinced that his reticence was an indication of his continued opposition, it was my mother, finally, who broke her own silence in order to force my father to break his.

"She asked, 'How many years, Adeeba? How many years would you be away?'

"My father had looked up from his tea in unhappy surprise and I took a deep breath before answering, 'Three years. Only three years.'

"'And you realize, don't you, that this might make marriage out of the question?' My mother's face was never very expressive to begin with. Now, it looked like it was set in stone.

"I tried to hide my excitement, my hope, as I answered her look with one I hoped would be as expressionless, but which I knew was not. 'Yes. But that may be so even if I stay.'

"'No!' My father's voice had rung out in protest. 'No, it is out of the question! I will not permit it.'

"My mother shocked me with her next words, rearranging my whole view of life, as she said, 'I'm not sure if she is really interested in whether you permit it or not. She has done enough for you. Enough for all of us. The boys' business is doing well, now. We will survive without her. The only thing left to consider is her future. Her feelings. Not ours.'

"My father's eyes flashed in angry disbelief. But my mother

had more to say: 'It is her life. She has to decide. I cannot say I approve. But the whole world has changed. Everything is different. And she has been a good daughter—is still a good daughter. Because she has given us the option to refuse her. I don't want to test her obedience any further. I don't want to give her reason to defy us. And I'm afraid that if we say no, we will.'

"I could feel my own eyes widen in surprise. Defiance had never been an option. Until now. Until my mother had suggested that it was. She was right. This was a question of my life. My future. I would have liked to have my parents' blessing. But, for the first time, I realized—because of the argument that I would never have dared to offer myself, the one that my mother had just offered on my behalf—that the choice was mine to make.

"My father saw it, too—saw the power that my mother had just granted to me, his daughter. And his own power in the matter was suddenly lost in the face of it. No one said anything else that night. Nor for the next few nights.

"One week later, my father took one of the shipping trunks out of the storeroom. He was dusting it off, himself, with a rag, when my mother and I and the other women of the household walked in from the kitchen area where we had been washing and preparing unripe mangoes for pickling. I was too afraid to hope. I looked at my mother and saw the same combination of puzzlement and anxiety that I felt reflected on her face. My sisters-in-law were frowning, only puzzled, not having any knowledge of the dilemma that we three had faced, in isolation, over the past week.

"My older sister-in-law stepped forward as she spoke, 'Aba, please, let me clean it for you,' her hands outstretched in a gesture of solicitous service.

"My younger sister-in-law was not to be outdone. She stepped in a little closer, actually reaching out to take the rag from her father-in-law's hands in order to take over his task. Neither one of them thought to question the reason for their labor. My father, brow and upper lip beaded with moisture, took his handkerchief out of his pocket and wiped his face, avoiding the questions in the eyes of all of the women before him.

"His older daughter-in-law, finally, seemed unable to contain her curiosity and took a deep swallow for courage before asking, in a carefully respectful voice, 'Are you going on a trip, Aba?'

"He only said, 'No,' and didn't reward her courage with any further explanation. Until his eyes, finally, met mine. 'No. But Adeeba is. A very long journey. I am very happy for my daughter.' With these words, my father turned and left the room, oblivious to all of the mouths he left hanging open behind him.

"Immediately, the braver of my sisters-in-law jumped to the wrong conclusion. 'Is Adeeba getting married? But that's wonderful news! *Hai, Allah!* A long journey? Is she going back to India? Oh! We will miss her too much! Who is the boy? Ama, how could you have kept this from me? Am I not the older daughter-in-law? Surely I should have been consulted! When did this all happen? Why all the secrecy?'

"I could not fault my sister-in-law for her mistake. Until a few days before, the only journey I had ever again contemplated taking was the same kind that she envisioned. The kind that all girls are prepared, from a young age, to have to take. The physical journey from father's home to husband's home—the one that symbolizes the journey to becoming a woman and, most important, the transfer of power from one *mehram* to another. When the burden of responsibility that men bear—the mantle of protection—passes from a father to a husband.

"My mother said, 'Adeeba is not getting married.' I saw the looks of bewilderment on the faces of my sisters-in-law. Saw, too, the hesitation on my mother's. This was, for her, the point of no return. The point at which the whole question of my future ceased to be, strictly speaking, a family matter. Because though my sisters-in-law were part of our family, they were also still a part of their own and were therefore a link that connected me to countless others—to the whole community, in fact. Their reaction, my mother was well aware, would be the first indication of how the community at large might view me in the future.

"It was not a good sign, therefore, when the explanation that my mother offered to her daughters-in-law was met with absolute silence. It meant that their reaction was strong enough that they felt the need to hide it. Which meant that the disapproval they would share, later, with their own families would be the most dangerous kind—the kind that is expressed behind one's back, in the form of gossip, impossible to defend oneself against."

Unwittingly, I stepped into a cultural chasm with my next words. "But—did it really matter? What *they* thought? What *any*body else thought? If you and your parents were okay with it, I mean." The sugarcane juice was long finished. I was now working on a little bag of chili chips—spiced potato chips—that had somehow appeared on the table in front of us over the course of Big Nanima's story. I was eating them mindlessly, totally engrossed in the pictures Big Nanima was painting, my eyes glued to her face as if it were a television screen I could not tear myself away from.

She laughed at me, hooted really, so that her whole self shook, like it used to when she was a little more substantial than she was now. "Spoken like a true American! Here, *beti,* we have to care what people think. We live among people, around people, in the midst of people. Our decisions affect them. Theirs affect us. We cannot just jump on a horse and ride away into the sunset"—Big Nanima's tongue was in her cheek again—"as I believe they do in America."

I could see what she was saying. But I was struck by how unfair it all seemed. Though I was too interested in hearing more to stop and debate the point. "Go on. That's when you went to England."

"Yes." She walked again to the shelf, the home of the photograph that had prompted the story she had almost finished telling me. Again, she wiped off the imaginary dust with her *dupatta*. "That was a wonderful time. A gift. That would never have happened, you understand, if *I* had married your grandfather." Her eyes lifted and met mine to watch the point hit home.

I nodded, understanding—kind of—what she had meant when she had talked of *kismat* before.

"Three years in England! What an adventure that was! All the more so because of how unbelievable it all was!" The smile on Big Nanima's face, the light in the eyes, which were trained on that photograph, said all that she didn't. Because when she picked up her story again, she was already back. "In such a short, short time, in 1952, I was back home in Karachi. And you are right, in a way. I was more fortunate than most. Whatever people may have said about me did not matter. I was older. Wiser. I had a degree in hand. And though I was less eligible for marriage than I had ever been, now I had a well-paying job, too. That gave me a level of independence that made my marital status—or lack of one—palatable in a way that most spinsters, as I was now officially referred to, could only envy.

"Then, one of the many excellent fringe benefits that came

with my position became the subject of further contention in the family, and this time my sisters-in-law were part of and loudly active in the discussion from the beginning." Big Nanima put the photograph back on the shelf. "I came home from having signed the contract for my new position and told them the news I knew they would not consider to be good. That I had been offered housing on the new campus.

"My father was the first to react. 'Housing? What kind of housing?' He was looking up from the meal that my sisters-in-law, in less than harmonious concert, had prepared for the family. He had welcomed me back from England a few weeks before, and the expression of pride and happiness on his face, not yet faded, rivaled the one it bore upon the birth of each of his grandchildren, adding to my own happiness in a way that I cannot begin to describe.

"I explained, 'They're building homes on a housing compound adjacent to the campus. They showed me the plans when I went to sign the contract today. They look like they will be very nice homes. Not very large. There are two- and three-bedroom houses, which will be assigned according to need. There are servants' quarters as well. I would be eligible for a two-bedroom house next year, when they are completed.' I added the last with a quiet, casual tone. A tone that did not reflect how I felt as I looked first at my mother's face and then at my father's.

"My older sister-in-law had caught the looks. And followed them up with her own. She was apparently unsatisfied with the silence with which her parents-in-law had responded. She said, 'But surely you told them, Adeeba, that you would not be needing any housing? You have your family, after all. You are not some lonely orphan girl in need of some service quarters.'

"It was my turn, now, to be silent. I did not know what to say and was further intimidated when I looked up to find all of the eyes of the adult members of the family trained on me with remarkably similar expressions of expectation.

"Again, my sister-in-law was discontented by the silence. 'Adeeba? You did refuse the housing, didn't you?'

"I stammered out an answer, nervously, 'Uh—no, I haven't refused. Yet.' I added the last word hastily as everyone at the table began to speak at once. Only a few of the voices, however, penetrated the general cacophony to be heard.

"One was my father's. '*Beta?* There is no need for such a sacrifice. Perhaps you don't know how well your brothers' business is doing. We are prospering.'

"Another, my mother's. 'Adeeba! There is no question! Your *bhabi* is right, you must refuse this housing immediately!'

"My sister-in-law, the one who had, it appeared, developed an aversion to silence in my three-year absence, provided the best example of its opposite state with her words, 'Adeeba! Isn't it enough what you've gotten? That you went to study abroad and made us the talk of the town! For God's sake, I will not have it! What will people say now? That we didn't keep you? That we treated you badly? Do you even care? About the shame that we will all have to endure? It is just not done! For a sister to live by herself when she has brothers who can care for her! A father and a mother, too! You are our responsibility! And it is a burden that we carry gladly, Adeeba, gladly!' The silence that followed was deafening, and my sister-in-law, the one who spoke these last words, at last gave up trying to fight it.

"Finally, I spoke. '*Bhabi,* I am sorry, but I—' I cut my sentence off abruptly as I thought better of what I had been about to say.

"My mother then surprised me, as she had a few years before, picking up the words I had reluctantly set aside: 'Perhaps Adeeba doesn't want to be anyone's burden. No matter how gladly she is carried.' There was no indication, in the soft words that my mother spoke, of how she felt about my place of residence or her daughter-in-law's feelings about it. Her gaze was fixed on the curtain beyond the dinner table, fluttering lightly in the hot wind that blew outside. My sister-in-law, hearing the words she had uttered so excitedly reframed in the level tones that my mother employed, seemed to wilt and whither. In any case, the tide of this conversation had turned. And I took up residence in my own home in August of the following year." Big Nanima waved her hand around the room. "I've been here ever since."

I looked around, obligingly appreciative. "Was this the best part of it all? Of going away to study? Having your own place?"

"It was one of them, that is certain. *A Room of One's Own.* Virginia Woolf. But teaching itself was its own reward. How to explain it? The sheer joy of it! Have you ever heard that song—I think it was a Beatles' song? 'Getting Better'?"

Thrown off, I frowned, unsure of what she was talking about. "I—I'm not sure."

Big Nanima began to sing, her Pakistani accent transformed, the way that all rock 'n' roll lyrics have the power to do, so that she sounded more like me than herself. "It really is a very catchy tune. Very optimistic. Have you ever heard it, Saira?"

I was laughing. "Well, now I have!"

Big Nanima shook her finger at me, threateningly, but I noticed that her toes were still tapping and she hummed the rest of the song to herself before saying, "The words still run through my head. Mocking me sometimes, when we seem to take backward steps instead of forward. But I do believe them. That things—in the world—really are getting better. That song played on the radio, on the *Hit Parade*, the day I sat in one of the cars, with my brother and sister-in-law, on the way to the airport. My other brothers were following us, with their wives, in their own cars. It was 1967. We were going together—the whole family—to pick up Zahida, your *nanima*. She was on her way in from London for a visit. I was so happy, I remember! And the words of the song were so appropriate. Only that morning I had thought those words to myself, looking around at the faces of the young women in my classroom, reveling in their good fortune. Every year, since I had come back from England, our enrollment was increasing. School and college had become standard expectations for well-brought-up girls—a prerequisite, almost, for a good marriage, rather than an obstacle to it.

"My good mood lasted all the way until we brought Zahida home, to our eldest brother's house—the boys lived separately now that our parents were gone—when we realized that this visit of hers was not the family reunion we had all looked forward to. She told us what Kasim Bhai had said and done. That her marriage was over. I looked at my sister's tear-stained face and saw that she was no longer the beautiful young sixteen-year-old who had cried out of remorse so many years before. She was a mother—a grandmother—now!

"But the years faded away as I watched her wrestle with the magnitude of what she had lost. Zahida was—bewildered. She had been everything she was supposed to be—an obedient daughter-in-law, a dutiful wife, a caring mother, a pious woman—and she had lost everything. I—who had been none of those things, done none of what I was supposed to—not out of choice, granted—had everything, compared to her. She was still my younger sister, and—oh, what I felt for her! How to even explain it?

"You will know, Saira. You have a sister, too. That bond, the one between sisters—it is second only to the one between a mother and a daughter. My brothers still did not realize—they hoped that our brother-in-law would come to his senses. But I knew better. I knew that Zahida could not go back to India—not without facing a kind of humiliation I would not wish on an enemy, let alone my own flesh and blood! I would not—could not—wish for my sister what I had managed to escape for myself. A life of dependency. Living off of obligation. So, I asked her to live with me. I had plenty of room to spare.

"Zahida moved in here. She moped around for several weeks, still in shock. And then, finally, I raised two delicate subjects that sparked the arguments that would rage between us for all the years that we lived together. One—I told her to divorce Kasim. Why should she stay married to him? *Chee!* After what he had done to her. Yet, in some kind of misguided attempt to save face, Zahida refused, saying what I know she did not in any way believe! That eventually, Kasim would leave his English girl and come back! Hah!" Big Nanima shook her head, still disgusted by her sister's assertion.

"And the other argument?"

"Ah! Well, within weeks, Kasim Bhai sent her a letter and a check, saying he would continue to send them on a monthly basis for her support. Zahida sent the check back! I understand why she did it—pride. But there is no shame in accepting what someone *owes* you. She *insisted*—claiming that if Kasim no longer claimed her as his wife, in name and fact also, then she had no claim on any benefits that arise from the title. Every month it flared up between us. Like clockwork, whenever the check arrived.

"The whole thing rippled down to affect the children, of course. Your mother and your *khalas,* out of loyalty to their mother, refused to accept any gifts from their father, though he tried to send *them* checks, too, on birthdays and when their children were born—you and Ameena, also. When Zahida and Kasim Bhai were both gone, the girls relented. It was quite a large amount they all stood to inherit. All of them, except your mother. Who never took a cent, not while her parents lived, and not after they died."

We were quiet together for a while. I stood up to look at the pictures again, and then walked around the room before I came to stand before Big Nanima. "I always knew you were a teacher. A professor. But I guess I never realized what an accomplishment that was."

Big Nanima smiled. "An accomplishment? Maybe in my time it was. But, for your generation—getting an education, making a contribution to the world you live in—that is your right and your duty."

Again, I looked around the room. "So—this house? It belongs to the college?"

"Yes. I'll have to leave it behind when I retire."

"What will you do then?"

"I have a little flat that I bought for my retirement. I'll live there."

I thought of the uneasy companionship that Nanima and Big Nanima had established. "Alone?"

"Yes. For as long as I can. That is my fear for the future."

I raised my eyebrows, questioning.

"That eventually I will become too old or sick to care for myself. May God take me from this life before that day ever comes. But I have to be prepared for the worst. Because I have no children to rely on. It should have been me, you see. Instead of your *nanima*. I always hoped that I would be the one to go first. Because she was not alone. She had three daughters to go to when the time came."

"You're not alone, Big Nanima."

"In the end, Saira, we are all alone. Some of us more than others, perhaps."

I put my hand in hers, like I had when I was younger.

FIVE

⁓᎑⁓

Most of the rest of my stay in Karachi centered around the drama of anticipation that I felt at the thought of finally meeting the Englishwoman for whom my grandfather had left my grandmother. Despite the behind-the-scenes trauma that she and her children caused before their arrival, my family treated the Foreign Guests—as they had been dubbed—with a gracious, formal kind of welcome that quickly thawed to a genuine, if hesitant, warmth. Because Belle was clearly thrilled to be among us, throwing herself into the festivities of Zehra's wedding with a carefree kind of abandon that was hard to resist—though I tried to, for longer than most of my relatives. Belle's presence was the reason for my mother's absence, and I resisted her smiles and laughter—at first—out of simple, biological loyalty.

The fact that Belle and her children were put up at a hotel instead of at the house of one of my relatives—an insult the import of which she could not have known in a cultural context where hospitality is defined by even giving up one's bed for one's guest if called for—made my initially aloof stance imperceptible, because she was not a part of the day-to-day preparations for the wedding, which we were all so involved with. When I did finally fall victim to her charm, I was bolstered, in my defeat, by knowing that Big Nanima, who had resisted Belle with as much effort as I had, fell soon after me.

Zehra's *mehndi* ceremony was the first of the official wedding functions and for ladies only. It took place in Lubna Khala's magically transformed garden—the lawn was covered with beautifully woven carpets laid under a colorfully patterned canopy. Chairs lined the perimeter for elders to sit on. Lanterns lit the place, casting an Arabian-nights flavor over the whole affair. A low platform was set at one end of the garden, decorated with strings of flowers and pillows, where Zehra would sit with her bridegroom—the only male invited—wearing traditional yellow. In front of it, one of my second cousins would play the *dhol*, the two-sided drum, to accompany the songs that all of the girl cousins, myself included, had rehearsed until our voices were hoarse—songs whose lyrics included friendly insults we had prepared especially for the family of Zehra's groom, who would have prepared similar insults to lob at our side.

When the evening began, I watched from a sullen distance as Belle—a middle-aged, heavyset woman whose waistline rivaled Big Nanima's and who looked much older than my mother and her sisters, despite their being, as I knew, all close in age (nothing like the beautiful bombshell I had pictured in my mind)—was invited to perform the *rassams*, the ceremonies, which included taking out *sadaqa*, alms, and the symbolic application of henna to Zehra's betel leaf–covered palm. The real henna application would take place the next morning, when the henna applicators, who were servicing the guests now, would come to spend the day working on the intricate designs that would adorn Zehra's hands and feet.

"That is an honor she is not even conscious of." Big Nanima was standing beside me and her comment was mumbled under her breath, meant only for my ears.

It was the only opening I had been offered by anyone since Belle and her children had arrived in Karachi. "Do you think Mummy was right not to come?"

Big Nanima's head tilted to one side. "Right? I don't think this is a question of what is right or wrong. I think Shabana made a decision with her heart. Right and wrong are questions of the mind, separate from emotions, which can be slippery to live by."

I frowned, not understanding. Big Nanima put her hand on my cheek, laughing a little. "Don't listen to me, Saira. I'm being a little emotional myself and not making any sense. Belle was your grandfather's choice of companion. He loved her. That is the simple truth of it. Your mother, Lubna, Jamila—they each had to adjust to that truth in the best way that they could. Jamila was the only one who knew him in his second life. Maybe this"—Big Nanima nodded to the circle in which Zehra sat, surrounded by my aunts and Belle and her daughters—"is not a bad thing. Maybe it's a kind of healing that they have all longed for. Something that Shabana needs to stop running away from, too." Big Nanima sighed. "But my loyalty is to only one person in this story. To Zahida. My sister. The woman that Kasim Bhai abandoned without a backward glance. So I am not the right one to consult in this matter, Saira. Because my heart sees that woman laughing with your cousin, with my sister's granddaughter, and all I feel is that this is Zahida's place she occupies, just as it was Zahida's husband that she loved."

My cousins called me away from Big Nanima's words, then, to tell me Jamila Khala wanted us to perform the first of the dances that we had prepared, before dinner was served. The floor was cleared as guests scooted back to the edges of the carpets to give us room to dance, all of the female cousins, all of Nanima's granddaughters together, except for Ameena, moving barefoot, in synchronized rhythm, to the sound of India's latest film hits. The hems of our long *kameezes*—heavy with gold and silver *dabka*—swung, emphasizing the sway of our hips and the flash of the colors we wore—vivid reds, fuchsias, royal blues. We twirled and circled and squared off while the other guests whistled and clapped and took our measure, thinking of sons and nephews who would need wives in the coming years. When we were done, the smell of *tikka*s and *kabab*s, of saffron and spice, was our invitation to dinner—laid out on silk-skirted tables under another festively decorated canopy at the side of Lubna Khala's garden. That was when Belle sought me out. By the time I saw her coming, it was too late to escape without being obvious.

She had gone through the buffet already and stood next to me as I went down the line, her plate piled up with food to a height that began to explain the roundness of her figure. "What rhythm you have, Saira! Your grandfather would have been proud to see you here, dancing with the other girls."

She had caught me off guard—speaking to me as if she knew me—and I didn't know what to say. So I smiled, the kind of smile that only lifted the corners of my mouth. Saying nothing, I took a chicken leg from the chafing dish filled with *tikka* pieces, and hoped she would go away.

But she didn't. She balanced her plate, carefully, in one hand. And took my hand with the other as we reached the end of the buffet, where I had stopped—and was now unable—to pick up a fork.

Belle put her plate down for a second, unwilling to release me. She picked up a fork and put it on my plate, took up her own again, and tugged at me as she said, "Come, love. Come and sit with me while we eat." She led us to two chairs cozily set up in a corner of Lubna Khala's garden. I looked around to find an excuse to escape, hoping someone—an aunt, a cousin—would issue me a summons that I would have to respond to. But no one seemed to notice my captive state.

I looked back at Belle, watched her stab a piece of *Bihari kabab* on her plate with her fork and place it carefully into her mouth. She didn't chew for a moment, just savored the flavor, with her eyes closed, and said, "Mmm—this is heavenly! I can't tell you how much I'm enjoying the food here in Pakistan! It's my first time here, you know."

"Is it?" I didn't care if it was or not.

She nodded, her mouth—which she had indulged again with another fork-stabbed piece of meat—too full to speak. My own food was getting cold, the grease on my plate visibly starting to congeal. But the way she was eating—with so much simple plea-sure and delight—made my mouth water. With an inward shrug, I started in, too, following her example and beginning with the *kabab*. We ate together, in silence, for a while. Then Belle, hav-ing worked her way around her plate, issued forth a loud sigh, and burped, ever so softly.

She laughed. "Excuse me! Oh! That was delicious!" Her eyes were fixed on me, as if waiting for me to agree. When I didn't, she said, "You know, Saira, I would have known you for Kasim's granddaughter anywhere. You look just like him."

"I do?"

"Oh, yes! Hasn't anyone ever told you that?"

I shook my head. Belle studied my plate for a moment, long enough for me to wonder whether she hoped I would offer her some of the food on it, since her own was now scraped clean. But I didn't.

She looked back up at me and asked, "How is your mother? I was so sorry to hear that she wouldn't be coming to the wedding. I would have loved to have met her."

I felt obliged to respond, "She couldn't—um—come," failing to do so with any grace.

"I've heard so much about her, you see. About all the mischief she got into as a child. Kasim would never have admitted it, you know, but Shabana was definitely his favorite child."

"She was?"

"Oh, yes! Without a doubt!" Belle's smile was bright, loud, sincere.

I blinked. And this time, when I smiled back at her, it was without effort. She took my hand back in hers, making my smile fade immediately.

"I've been looking for a chance to pull you away and get you all to myself."

"You have?"

She nodded happily. And then looked away, toward the flower-studded stage where Zehra sat with her soon-to-be husband, Shahid. My own gaze followed hers as she said, "How I wish Kasim were here—to see all of you, his granddaughters, dancing together! All of you except your sister, of course. Ameena."

It was odd, to hear this woman—a stranger, with a British

accent—talking about my mother and my sister as if she had
some claim on them. I pulled my hand away from hers.

Belle didn't seem to have noticed. She asked, still looking at
Zehra, "Does she look like you?"

"Who?"

"Ameena?"

"Oh—no. She looks like my mom."

Belle nodded. "Who looks like hers."

"How—how do you know that?"

Belle laughed at the look on my face. "From your grandfather, love. He told me she was very beautiful."

"Oh." I watched Zehra for a moment. I saw Belle's daughter, Tara, who sat beside my cousin. Her niece. She leaned in and
said something in her ear, something which made Zehra crack up
with laughter. Before I knew what I was doing, my mouth was
open and I was asking *her,* "How did you meet him? My *nana?*"
I said the last word a little defiantly, the emphasis serving as a
declaration of sorts.

Belle gave me a measuring look and asked, gently, "What
have you heard?"

I already regretted the question—for too many reasons to
list. "Uh—something about a park?"

"Yes. At Hyde Park. At Speakers' Corner. Have you ever
been there?"

I shook my head.

"Your grandfather—your *nana*—you know he was in London, with your grandmother, waiting for Zehra to be born? Can
you imagine? And now she's all grown up—about to be married
herself!" Belle sighed, deeply content. Then, her eyes met mine,
her nose wrinkled just a little bit in distaste. "I know what you're

thinking—what everyone thought. That he was going through some kind of midlife crisis. And I just happened along, at the right time and place—or the wrong one, I suppose, depending on your point of view. All I can tell you is what he told me himself.

"Your grandfather was not an unhappy man. Before he met me. But those days in London—I think those were the first days he ever really had to himself. Walking about in the park. It was spring. And all those lovely clichés about London in the spring—they're all true. He was enchanted. By the flowers, the soft blades of grass sprouting from the earth. The song of the birds that he actually *listened* to—for the first time in his life—instead of just hearing it in the background. He would hang about for hours at Speakers' Corner, listening to new voices and ideas. It was toward the end of the sixties, you know. Really exciting.

"Well, one day, he was standing there, listening to an especially excited speaker at the Corner—a rabid feminist, between you and me—who was demonstrating her point—something to do with the bondage of patriarchy and its partner in crime, capitalism—by burning a bra." Belle laughed. "I don't think your granddad had ever seen a bra being thrown about in public before. He was all stiff and proper, his lips pursed, like he'd just sucked on a lemon, shaking his head, in his three-piece suit, umbrella in hand. He looked more like an Englishman than any of the hippies around him. He turned to go, embarrassed, I think, by the display of ladies' undergarments, when I saw—I'd been standing right beside him, watching him out of the corner of my eye, laughing to myself a little, I have to admit—that he'd dropped his wallet. I picked it up and grabbed hold of his arm, saying, 'Excuse me? I think you dropped this?'

"Well, he turned around and saw me, giving me one of those head-to-toe looks that men give and think we don't notice." Belle winked at me as she said it, and I felt my face flush at the "we" she'd tossed my way. "I don't think he quite liked what he saw—I was a regular hippie in those days myself, wearing a pair of tattered old jeans, beads and shells around my neck, a roach clip in my long, dirty hair, and, to top it all off, no bra to speak of. Because his lips pursed up even more tightly as he took the wallet from me. I thought he looked a bit worried, as if he were resisting the urge to check if all his money was still there.

"I laughed and said, 'It's all in there, I'm sure. You can check, if you like.' And then he was embarrassed, as if I'd read his mind or something. He thanked me and stood there, pretending to listen to the woman who was still going on up there, shrieking like she was mad, raining spittle down on the lot of us. And then, she nailed him, with spit, right on the nose." Belle was laughing loudly now. "I felt so sorry for him—he looked so absolutely disgusted by the whole thing. I reached up and wiped off his nose with the sleeve of my jacket.

"I reckon he thought we'd crossed a line or something. Of intimacy, I suppose. Because, next thing I knew, he was introducing himself to me. And off we went to tea. We talked—about everything under the sun. And I saw that I'd been wrong about him. He wasn't prim and proper at all. He was charming, full of life and laughter. Interested in everything I had to say—staring at me, open-mouthed, for half the hour, as if I were a creature from another planet."

"Did he tell you he was married?" I knew it was a rude thing to ask, but I couldn't help myself, and—I suppose—I wasn't afraid of Belle's opinion of me the way I had been of Razia Nani's.

Belle gave me a long look. And I knew, somehow, that she wasn't angry. "Yes. Almost as soon as we sat down in the tea shop, actually."

My face burning, I said, "I'm sorry. It's none of my business."

Belle took my hand. Gave it a squeeze. And then let it go, perhaps this time sensing my discomfort. "No, love. You have nothing to be sorry about. It's—it's not easy to understand what happened—and I'm not sure how to explain it without muddling it all up. That day—over tea—well, it was very clear that there was something there. Between us. In the end—I don't know why I did—but I gave him my number. Told him to give me a ring. Knowing that he wouldn't, of course. It's not something I'd ever done before. Chatting up married men—especially older married men—was just not in my book. Not normally.

"Your granddad told me what happened when he went home that afternoon—that your aunt had begun labor and she and your grandmum were already at hospital. Zehra popped out later on that night. He was ecstatic. Hung around the next morning at hospital, showering cash all over the staff, handing out jewelry to his daughter. But he was getting in the way there, hushed out of the room whenever the sisters brought the baby in to be nursed, or the doctor came to check stitches in places he didn't want to think about. He decided to go for a walk. And ended up at the Corner—where I was mooning about, hoping to see him, without admitting it to myself, of course.

"I saw him before he saw me. I came up to him from behind, put my hand on his shoulder. He turned. Our eyes locked. Without a word, we went back to my place. And—well—things happened. He told me he was a granddad now. Asked me why I was with him. I told him I'd answer that when *he* did. And there we were. In the middle of something totally unexpected. Nothing was the same for either of us. Nothing could be.

"When Kasim went home that night—after spending the rest of the evening at hospital, holding Zehra in his arms—your grandmum found a button on his shirt missing. He thought for sure he'd caught it now. But she just sewed a new button on, like the good wife that he'd always taken for granted. He told me that he felt sorry for her. Isn't that awful? I almost cried when he told me, I felt so dreadful for her. He did, too, for what it was worth. He knew, you see. What his own role was in the life she led. She was his wife. He'd been her husband. They were married before they'd ever gotten to know each other—or even to know themselves. And that was fine. Before. But it wasn't anymore. He knew that it was over. You see, for Kasim—for your *nana*—there was never any choice in the matter. It was the same for me. And because *he* had changed—had been reborn—the people who depended on him, who were *what* they were, *who* they were, because of him, would also have to be reborn—to recreate themselves. And while he felt badly about his part in their past, he could no longer be responsible for their futures." Belle stopped talking to take stock of what I was thinking. I don't know what she saw on my face. But her next words made me jump. "Have you ever heard 'Getting Better'? By the Beatles?"

Very slowly, I nodded.

Belle started to sing, softly, under her breath. And then said, "That song was playing on the radio in those days. When your granddad and I met. In it, the man says he's changing his scene. That's what your granddad did. He changed his scene. He *had* to." There was a long silence that I didn't know how to end. "What bothered him most was losing touch with his family. We had Jamila, of course"——she said Jamila Khala's name with an *er* at the end of it——"and her children. But he longed to see your mum and Lubna. And all their children. Especially when we started to have children of our own."

Reminded of my mother, who had slipped my mind toward the end of Belle's story, a question popped out of my mouth before I could even acknowledge it in my head: "Did you—did he take you dancing?"

Belle lit up. "All the time! He taught me—ballroom dancing, I mean. Speaking of dancing!"

Someone had put on some music and I jumped out of my seat, seeing my cousins starting to collect again for another performance, wanting to get away from Belle before anyone noticed us tucked away so intimately in that corner of the garden. I turned to her and stared down at her shoes for a moment, unable to think of what to say. Finally, I mumbled, "It was—uh—nice— talking to you."

"It was lovely! Now away with you. The girls are lining up already!" She was laughing at me.

I carried a lump of guilt around in my throat for the next hour after dinner, when the dancing resumed. The choreographed numbers shifted into free-form. Jamila Khala danced with Zehra. Lubna Khala danced for what looked like the first time. Belle's daughters got up and moved in time to the music, joining in with the rest of us, their nieces. Then, out of the corner of my eye, I saw Belle approach Big Nanima, the only close relative still seated, and pull her up out of the chair she was sitting in. Big Nanima shook her head at first, sternly. Then she smiled a little, then laughed at something Belle said to her as she pushed her up into the center of our circle and danced with her until we were all breathless from dancing and giggling at the strange sight of them together.

When the music stopped, I heard them laughing together, Belle saying, "You're a terrific dancer, Adeeba!"

I heard Big Nanima's answer, too, a little breathless: "Well, don't tell anyone, but I used to go dancing a lot. In London, when I lived there many years ago."

SIX

❧

Razia Nani and I left Karachi—the image of Belle and Big Nanima dancing together still vivid in my mind. Razia Nani, dissecting the details of Zehra's wedding, took great pleasure in calculating the value of the jewelry and gifts that had been exchanged between the bride's family and the groom's. As we got closer to landing, I prodded her attention away from the wedding that had just taken place and to my father's family, with whom I would stay in London.

"He's a big shot, your Ahmed Chacha. Very rich and important."

I listened closely, because I didn't know Ahmed Chacha as well as I knew my mother's family. On past visits to London, I usually stayed with Jamila Khala. But she was still in Karachi, basking in the afterglow of success that a daughter's wedding affords.

Razia Nani was still talking. "He married well, your Ahmed Chacha. A banker's daughter. Nasreen. A very nice woman. Though their children are another story! *Oof!* Rude and disobedient. They never greet their elders properly and wear outrageous clothes."

My twin cousins, Mohsin and Mehnaz, were assigned the task of retrieving me at the airport. As I emerged from customs with Razia Nani, my eyes searched the faces in the crowd gathered, waiting to greet arriving passengers. The air felt crisp and impersonal—not like the cloying, humid breath of hot air that wrapped around me like a sheet of plastic as soon as I had disembarked in Karachi. But the view, in some ways, was not all that different. The skin color, the facial features, and the languages I heard spoken among the majority of the people lined up before me were all familiar. Brown. *Desi*—though most were dressed in Western clothes and many spoke English with British accents. The British, after all, were not the only ones who left India after Independence.

I found my cousins in a hazy waft of smoke. Mehnaz was leaning, one foot up, against a pillar outside of the terminal building. Mohsin's face was hidden behind a camera, its focus trained on one of the Sikh women who worked at Heathrow, comprising the whole custodial staff, whose uniform was *desi*—a *shalwar kameez*, complete with *dupatta*. A cigarette dangled, defying gravity, from his lower lip. Mehnaz saw me first and lifted a finger to point, mumbling something under her breath, something apparently amusing, which made Mohsin's lips lift, nearly relinquishing their hold on the cigarette. He clicked his picture and lowered the camera as they both took steps forward to meet me.

"Well. 'Ere you are, then!" said Mehnaz cheerfully, as she stubbed her cigarette out under a heel that looked like a lethal weapon. "'Ow are you doing? 'Ad a good flight, did ya?"

The only way, as an ignorant American, oblivious to the subtle differences and nuances among working-class English accents (yes, I knew they existed; I had, after all, seen *My Fair Lady* at least a dozen times), that I could describe Mehnaz's accent would be as "cockney." Years later, I felt an acute sense of betrayal to discover that she, and Mohsin, too, for that matter, had attended very upper-crust schools in London . . . the kind that made class (and, in desperate times, money) an entry requirement and accent an exit one. The kind that meant that her accent was about as authentic as Audrey Hepburn's. But I have to admit, I admire the effort that dropping all of those *h*s must have required.

I turned to say good-bye to Razia Nani again. Another of her sons was standing to the side, head lowered in shame from the scolding his mother had given him for being late to pick her up. She gave each of my cousins a disapproving once-over before asking, doubtfully, "Are you sure you will not come and stay with me, Saira? I'm not sure if I should let you go home with these—uh—children." Mohsin had his camera up again, pointing it at Razia Nani, playing with the huge lens as if he were focusing a slide under a microscope.

I said, "No, thank you, Razia Nani."

With one more suspicious look at Mohsin and Mehnaz, Razia Nani nodded and left.

Mohsin, who had not yet said anything to me, cradled his camera to his chest with one hand and picked up the bigger of my two bags, shoving it onto his back with the other hand, like the porters that I had seen so many of at the airport in Karachi. Except that this porter had purple streaks of color in his longish hair, through which I could see a silver peace sign hanging from one ear. He wore black, drain-pipe jeans. And thick, clunky combat boots.

When we got to the car, Mohsin packed and smashed my things into the "boot" and handed the keys back over to his sister.

"Bollocks! I drove 'ere! You drive this time, Mo!"

Mohsin's hand did not retract, fearfully, as mine would have at Mehnaz's forceful tone. He merely shook his head, still mute, and jingled the keys even closer to her face.

"Bloody 'ell! Stupid, bleedin' 'art joey! The air'll be just as polluted whether I drive or you do!" Mehnaz turned to me, her words still punctuated by exclamation points, to explain, "Mo 'ere is going to save the whole bloody world! By not driving! 'E doesn't mind if I do, though! Bloody fuckin' 'ypocrite!"

"I can't help being a passive participant in the desecration of our planet. But at least I'm not an active one." Mohsin's words were delivered in a carefully neutral monotone, as if to make up for the distinctive language of his sister.

Mehnaz snorted in reply.

The miles from Heathrow into the posh London suburb where my uncle lived whirred by as Mehnaz drove, maybe to punish her brother and maybe by habit, like a crazy woman convinced of her own lone sanity. The horn was sounded every few miles or so, accompanied by colorful—and I mean that literally—commentary about the other drivers she encountered.

"Bloody dirt-colored Paki! Go back where you bloody came from!

"Did you see that bloody yellow Chinker?! Oy! Lady! Open your bloody eyes, would you?!

"Hey, white boy! Watch what you're fuckin' doing! Oh, yeah? Well, fuck you and your whole bloody fuckin' racist country!"

I shrank back in the tiny space of the back seat, in horror, grateful that the windows were rolled up and hoping that no one could actually hear her. Once, when I must have moaned out loud, Mohsin looked back at me, white-knuckled and knock-kneed. He nodded his head in the direction of his sister and rolled his eyes, then held his camera up and shot a picture of me. I tried to smile, but it was too late. He laughed, silently, and turned his head back again to look straight ahead.

He took a few more pictures from the passenger seat of the car on our way home.

I asked, "Do you always carry your camera around? Everywhere?"

Mohsin nodded. "I have to, don't I?"

"You have to?"

"To bear witness."

I shook my head, thinking I'd misheard him—his accent was clearer than his sister's, but it was an accent, still, to my ears.

When we finally turned into the driveway of my uncle's house, my aunt came out of the house to greet us, no doubt alerted to our arrival by the screech of brakes in the driveway. She embraced me, told me how nice it was to see me and how happy she was to spend some time with me. Mehnaz, mumbling something about a phone call she had to make, disappeared into the house. My aunt was just beginning to list all of the places she wanted me to see when Mohsin interrupted.

"Why don't you ask Saira what *she'd* like to see, Mum? She's a big girl, you know. She might have some ideas of her own."

I looked up sharply, searching his face for any trace of sarcasm. Not finding any, I bit my lip, thinking. The obvious light bulb came on, "Well, I *would* like to see Hyde Park. I mean, I've heard about Speakers' Corner, you know? But I've never been there."

Mohsin gave me a measuring look.

His mother said, "Hyde Park? Yes, we can go there. We can go there tomorrow, after Madame Tussaud's. It's a wax museum. You'll see all the famous people there. The Chamber of Horrors also. Very scary. Just what you youngsters enjoy. The next day, we'll go to Bekonscot. It's a miniature English village. Small, small houses. Small, small gardens. Small, small trains. They move, also, from station to station. So cute. You'll love it!" She clapped her hands together in excitement.

"Oh, yeah. I remember that place. Jamila Khala took us there. A long time ago. When I was little," I added, hoping to get out of the childish excursion.

"Oh? You've been there already?" The disappointment in her voice was clear.

"But I'd love to go again, Nasreen Chachi," I said, trying to be polite, hoping she would notice the lack of enthusiasm in my voice.

Mohsin heaved one of my bags up onto his back.

"*Beta!* Don't carry that like a *junglee*! You'll hurt your back! Come, why are we standing outside? Come into the house and I'll get you something to eat. Come, come, you must be hungry. I bought some nice shepherd's pie, frozen, from Sainsbury's. I'll just pop it into the micro. And chocolates. Lots of chocolates. Everybody loves English chocolates."

I followed my aunt into the house and paused, for a second, at the entrance to the living room. There it was—Ahmed Chacha's bar, well stocked with an assortment of bottles that held fascination for Ameena and me, raised in a house where alcohol was strictly forbidden. We had asked Mummy about it on past visits. She had pursed her lips and shaken her head, her disapproval too strong for words. Ameena and I had marveled at how two brothers, our father and Ahmed Chacha, could be so very, very different from each other.

Controversy erupted a half-hour and two servings of ready-made shepherd's pie later. Mehnaz came into the kitchen, wearing a leather miniskirt that would have made my mother faint. Her heels were even higher and deadlier than before. She had on more makeup than seemed possible. I saw my aunt's face as her eyes fell on her daughter, and slid out of my seat to sidle over to the other side of the cavernous kitchen, where I tried to look busy and involved with the task of washing my plate.

"Mehnaz! What do you think—?!" My aunt paused, remembering, perhaps, that I was still in the kitchen. Her voice was a notch more controlled as she continued, "What are you wearing, Mehnaz? Are you going somewhere? Because I wanted us all to be together tonight. We're going out for dinner. Taking your cousin to a restaurant. As soon as your father comes home." Her tightly held composure slipped, just a little, when she said, "Which will be any minute. Please go up and change your clothes."

"Oh, sorry Mum. Can't. Going out tonight. I'll be 'ome late. Don't wait up for me." Mehnaz's voice was cool, casual.

"Mehnaz, no! We're all going out together!"

"Sorry, Mum, I told you. I've got bloody plans, don't I? And I can't bloody well change 'em!"

"Plans? Cancel them, I'm telling you. Now! Before your father—" she was interrupted by the sound of the front door slamming.

"Sorry, Mum. Got to run." Mehnaz slipped out the back door before her mother could answer and just barely before my uncle came into the kitchen.

He walked in, put his briefcase down on the table, and came toward me, hand extended for a handshake. "Hullo, hullo, Saira. Welcome, welcome. So nice that we'll get some time with you. How was the wedding?"

"Very nice, Ahmed Chacha. Everyone in Karachi sent you their *salaam*s." My voice strained with the effort to conceal my part, as witness, in the scene that had just taken place.

"Good, good. Well, your aunt and I—and your cousins, of course—have been looking forward to your visit. Isn't that so, Nasreen?"

"Oh, yes! We were just talking about where we should go to eat dinner." I could hear the same strain in my aunt's voice.

"Well, Saira? What are you in the mood for? Pakistani food? You've probably had your fill these past weeks, eh? Chinese? Italian? There's a lovely little French place close by. Whatever you like, okay?" My uncle clapped his hands and rubbed them together, as if to indicate his readiness for anything. "Nasreen? Where are the children?"

"Uh—" My aunt was interrupted by the arrival of one of them, Mohsin, who had earlier disappeared. "Here's Mohsin. And Mehnaz is—has gone out. She had plans."

I saw my uncle's lips purse and then curl into a miserable attempt at a smile, something that came out looking more like a sneer. "Plans?" He gave me a quick look and said, "Oh, well. We'll just go without her, shall we? In"—he glanced down at his watch—"a half an hour?" He looked up at each of us for confirmation.

My aunt said, "Yes. That's perfect."

Mohsin didn't say anything.

And I, ignoring the weight of the convenience food I'd just

consumed, nodded my agreement. "Ummm—can I—uh—just freshen up a little?"

Nasreen Chachi said, "Of course! Let me show you up to your room."

The house was huge. I started to wonder, for the first time, about how little I knew about this uncle and his family. The wealth on display, like art in a frame, was not inherited. At least not by my uncle, because what wealth would have passed to him from his parents, presumably, would have also passed on to my own father. I knew, from hearing my father and mother talk, that Ahmed Chacha had a very good position at a local, Pakistani-owned bank. A bank, I had learned from Razia Nani, that was founded by his wife's father. His reputation, Razia Nani had informed me, as a hardworking man of integrity is what had earned him the attention and sponsorship—and eventually the daughter—of the rich, self-made man he considered his mentor.

Nasreen Chachi left me at the door to the guest room, where my bags—thanks to Mohsin—were already propped up against the wall. I went into the private, attached bathroom that Nasreen Chachi had pointed out and stopped to stare, for a moment, at the bidet sitting next to the toilet, wondering what and how the use of what was basically a seatless potty could be. I shrugged and contented myself with the use of the equipment I was familiar with. The fixtures in the bathroom were crystal and gold. Gaudy, but faithful in the fulfillment of their purpose—function and the demonstration of immense wealth.

The bedroom was a little too pretty—a Laura Ashley kind of décor with ruffles and floral prints everywhere. I unpacked my nightgown and my toothbrush and (I couldn't help myself) opened all of the drawers and closets to find any evidence of past guests. Disappointed, I turned and left the room, stepping out on the landing to hear the sound of raised, angry voices, muted and unclear, carrying up from the kitchen on the floor below. I decided some tactful delay was in order. I circled the landing, peeking into open doors. One of them—wide-open already, I swear—was in rather horrendous disorder. The panties and bras strewn about the floor, pop-star posters hung haphazardly about the walls, and stench of stale cigarette smoke declared its owner to be Mehnaz. I passed on, finding myself strangely uncurious as to what snooper's treasures I might find there.

Another room, similarly aromatic but otherwise tidy, was a bit more interesting. Standing at the entrance, where the door had been left only slightly ajar, I could see that the posters on the wall were of people—with the exception of one of John Lennon—unconnected with the music industry. Malcolm X. And Martin Luther King Jr. A picture of Gandhi. And others, whom I did not recognize. Some I learned of later. Cesar Chavez. Ho Chi Min. Ché Guevara. There were books everywhere, some of them stacked on an old-fashioned shipping trunk located at the foot of the bed, dilapidated and worn, a precursor to the modern luggage located in the guest room I occupied.

As I stood there, hovering on the threshold between curiosity and voyeurism, I could hear the voices from below, drifting—louder now and less muffled, still fading in and out—up the stairs.

"—I don't care what she said, you should have bloody stopped her—bloody—ungrateful—slut—girl! After all I've given her—a car—everything she asks for—still—no gratitude—shameless—absolutely no shame!"

"But, Ahmed—she—friends—important—plans—can't

expect—" Nasreen Chachi's voice did not come up as clearly as her husband's and slipped out of hearing completely as I took a step into the room that was, of course, Mohsin's.

Ahmed Chacha's furious reply was still audible, if less distinctly so. "Friends—friend—scandal!" Then my uncle seemed to shift focus. "And you—Mohsin—bloody nonsense—how many bloody times—to get rid of that bloody earring—cut your bloody hair—and that color—purple bloody hair—no more of this bloody nonsense—no son of mine—walk around town like a bloody—what are they called?—a bloody punk! Grow up, Mohsin—be a man—for—sake!"

Inside the room, I saw the other wall, opposite the posters, which I had not been able to see from the doorway. It was covered with photographs which drew me further into Mohsin's space so that all I heard now was Nasreen Chachi's pleading tone and Ahmed Chacha's correspondingly angrier one. The subjects of the photographs were all people—a few smiling, most of them somber and sad, their faces smudged with dirt, hair matted, and clothing ragged. Some of the pictures, with their telltale background flashes of red—double-decker buses, post boxes, telephone booths—were taken in London. Many—with the gaudier background blaze of multicolored, tassel-swinging rickshaws and buses, the latter marked with Urdu script—were from Karachi. There were children in these pictures—rummaging in garbage heaps. Horribly deformed beggars, too—immediately familiar to me from the sight of them on the streets of the city I had left merely hours ago. I studied them all. So hard that I forgot I was trespassing. So closely that I failed to hear the silence that had replaced the angry voices downstairs, the tread on the stairs, the owner of the room making his entrance.

Mohsin was behind me before I detected his presence, startling me so that I jumped and whirled to face him, embarrassed at having been caught on the voyeur side of the threshold that had beckoned. He stood quietly, hands in his pockets, his shoulders hunched as if stuck in a shrug.

I stuttered and stammered out a lame explanation: "I—I saw the—the posters. And then—I came in to look and saw—these pictures. I'm sorry. I shouldn't have. Come into your room. Without permission."

Mohsin finished the shrug and freed his hands from the confinement of his pockets. He took a few steps and stood beside me, looking up at the pictures that had been the source of my entrapment, as if for the first time, not saying anything, yet seeming to give permission to continue what I had begun.

I did, taking my time over each photograph. After a while, I asked, "Did you take all of these?"

Mohsin nodded.

"They're—really good. I mean—I don't know anything about photography, but—I—" I broke off, still visually ensnared by the evidence of his talent.

"You—? What?"

I dragged my eyes from the wall to find him looking at me with an expression that was intense and difficult to read.

"I—can't look away."

Mohsin's expression lightened as he nodded again.

"What did you say before, Mohsin? In the car? When I asked you whether you always carry your camera around? You said you *had* to?"

"Yes. To bear witness."

I had heard him correctly, but I still didn't understand. I

opened my mouth to ask what he meant at the same time that I heard Nasreen Chachi calling to ask if we were ready to leave.

When we went back downstairs, Nasreen Chachi was as effusively cheerful as before and Ahmed Chacha was jovial—even more so after draining the little glass of amber liquid that he refilled once before we left for the restaurant.

Dinner—at the French restaurant that my uncle had recommended—was uncomfortable. Little aftershocks of my uncle's earlier outburst—which I had to pretend not to know about—reverberated throughout the evening. My own discomfort became acutely personal when my uncle began the meal by offering me wine.

When I refused, as politely as I could, he said, rather forcefully, "Oh, I insist, Saira. What is French food without French wine, after all? Don't worry, we won't tell your parents." His conspiratorial wink made me feel somehow disloyal. I refused again, pointing out that I was underage.

"Oh, they won't care here. We come to this restaurant quite often. And they're not as strict about such things here in England as I believe they are in America. No? Not even a taste? You're sure?"

"She already said no, Dad," said Mohsin.

My uncle, whose cheeks were glowing red and whose upper lip shone with moisture, smirked and said, "Ah, yes! My son. Defender of the faithful. And the oppressed. The weak and the poor." Ahmed Chacha turned back to me and said, with no less sarcasm, "So! My brother has done a good job raising his daughters, eh? Good Muslim girls? Obedient? No boyfriends, eh, Saira? No, of course not. No, no. No drinking either. Very bad—drinking is a very bad habit. No justification for it. None at all." He took another sip of his wine. "Clearly, it is forbidden. And you, Mohsin? No wine today, eh? Keeping your cousin company? Very good. Good boy. A gentleman. A gentleman with bloody purple hair!" Ahmed Chacha laughed heartily and then looked around with some surprise to find no one laughing with him.

The food, I remember, was really very good and quite adequate compensation for the awkward, slightly drunken, company of my uncle. When we returned home, I was yawning frequently enough to legitimately excuse myself for the night. But I must not have been as tired as I thought because I heard, again, the raised voices from downstairs, confirming that the pause before dinner had been for my sake rather than because the argument had been over.

I must have fallen asleep at some point. Because I was awakened again at what seemed to be an outrageous hour by the screech of a car outside, doors slamming, and feet stomping around downstairs. The voices resumed their loud business—with even more fury now—indicating, in contrast to the silence of moments before, that they had stopped temporarily sometime after I had fallen asleep.

The next day, thankfully, was a weekday and my uncle left early, in his chauffeur-driven car, for the bank. My aunt was up early, too, to serve breakfast to Ahmed Chacha before beginning a round of phone calls—social calls, by the sound of them, involving the circulation of news: death, birth, marriage, and scandal had to be assimilated and circulated to audiences eager to be informed.

Mohsin and I had our breakfast together in silence before he disappeared, camera in hand, telling his mother he'd be back at noon to spend the day sightseeing with us. It was eleven o'clock before Mehnaz shuffled downstairs with huge black circles under her bloodshot eyes, which—it took me a moment to realize—were the residue of last night's makeup binge. Then, when Mohsin returned and Mehnaz had showered and dressed, we were finally off. The lack of any conversation in the car that Mehnaz drove—rather sedately, in what was surely uncharacteristic deference to my aunt's request—was a welcome change from the noise of the night before.

I must admit that I was not as old or sophisticated as I would have liked to claim, because I enjoyed Madame Tussaud's museum immensely. Especially the famous Chamber of Horrors. Mehnaz and Mohsin started off coolly, taking pains to prove how above sightseeing they both were. Eventually, though, Mehnaz descended enough to direct some of her deadly sarcasm—in kinder, gentler form—at me, so that I felt, perversely, less of a stranger. Mohsin shared his coolness, putting me on the right end of his humor as he mocked the more pompous expressions to be found among the famous wax faces. He teased me, too, tapping my shoulder from this way and that, mercilessly, in the Chamber, even managing to scare me once as I paused before one of Jack the Ripper's unfortunate victims, catching me and my tonsils with his camera as I screamed. Nasreen Chachi laughed with her children, scolding them only a few times, whenever they lit up what they called cancer sticks, which they both did at every chance they got.

Our next stop was Hyde Park. I remember resenting the constant chatter of my aunt as we walked, at a leisurely pace, in the direction of Speakers' Corner. It would have been nice to walk around alone and in silence, absorbing the atmosphere, trying to relate the setting with my grandfather and his twenty-year-old little love story. I did try—looking around, staring at faces in some kind of ridiculous attempt to find something familiar. Of course, I didn't succeed. The whole venture was a bit disappointing. The soapbox speakers seemed to have less to say than their hecklers. And both were few in number.

Mohsin echoed my thoughts: "Pretty pathetic, isn't it? But it gets exciting when things are happening . . . some big deal that gets everyone riled up. Must have been something else in the sixties." His voice had turned wistful.

I looked at him sharply, wondering if he had guessed the nature of my interest in this London landmark.

Mehnaz spoke before I could ask, rolling her eyes as she said, "Not that again, Mo." She turned to me to explain, "Mo 'ere is obsessed with the sixties. Reckons 'e would 'ave made a fine 'ippie. A flower child, eh, Mo?"

"It just would have been nice to live in a time when you felt you could have actually made a difference, that's all." Mohsin sounded defensive.

"Yeah, well, they bloody didn't, did they? I mean everything's even shittier now, innit? Or at least that's what you're always going on about . . . about 'ow bad everything is, 'ow evil the government is." Mehnaz turned to me again. "Especially *your* government, Saira. Bloody Yanks! Just can't keep their 'ands off of anything, can they? Or at least that's what Mo 'ere is always saying." She said this with a wink and then settled back, arms crossed, to watch whether the match she had just struck would catch.

But it didn't. Mohsin just grinned back at her and said, "Well, I wouldn't want to hurt our American cousin's feelings, now, would I?"

I didn't rise to the bait either, grinning at Mehnaz's ruefully deflated expression.

When we headed home, Mehnaz, driving more carefully than ever, said, "Mum? I thought it would be nice if we came back tonight to the city for dinner and a movie at Leicester Square. I'm sure Saira would enjoy 'erself. Yeah, Mohsin? There's that movie you've been wanting to see. What do you say?"

"Oh, Mehnaz. I don't know. I'm tired and I'm sure your father would rather have dinner at home tonight." Nasreen Chachi was rubbing her bare feet, marked with the lines of the leather lace-ups she had worn and complained about all day.

"Well, that's good, innit? 'Cause I didn't *mean* you. I meant us. The *youngsters*." She was rude, but still had not utilized any exclamation points. Her tight grip on the steering wheel was a sign of the effort she was exerting to contain her natural volume level and tone.

"Oh. You and Mohsin and Saira? Mmmm . . . I don't know. I suppose it would be all right." Nasreen Chachi was clearly not keen on the idea. "But Saira is younger than you, Mehnaz. I'm not sure what her parents would say. Why don't you go to the local cinema near the house?"

Mehnaz's efforts failed for a moment. "Because it's not the bloody same, is it?! Who wants to spend an evening in the bloody boring suburbs?! I mean," she dropped down again, hastily, "you did want Saira to see the sights. And Leicester Square is one of them."

I jumped in. "Oh, my parents would be fine with it, Nasreen Chachi. We've gone out before. In London, I mean. With my cousin Zehra. Just us kids, without any adults. They won't mind if you don't."

"Well, I guess it will be all right. Yes. Yes, it will be nice for you all to spend some time together. Just make sure you watch out for your little cousin, yes?"

"Oh, we will. Don't worry." Mehnaz winked at me again and I was thrilled at the prospect of a real night out. Mohsin, however, remained rather expressionless.

Later, having escaped Ahmed Chacha—who dismissed us with a cheery wave of one hand and a clink of ice in the glass he held with the other—and as soon as we got back into Mehnaz's car to head for the city, she said, casually, "Right then, I've just got to make a stop on the way into town. To pick up a friend."

"Then you can drop Saira and me off at the tube station. We'll go into the city on our own." Mohsin's voice was cold now, instead of neutral.

"Suit yourself." Mehnaz sounded unsurprised and still remarkably cheerful.

"I will. Suiting you, too, obviously."

"'Ey, I 'ave nothing to 'ide! Come or don't come. I don't bloody fucking care one way or another." She looked into the rearview mirror, catching my eyes. "Sorry, Sai. 'Ope you don't mind?"

I had no idea what she was pretending to be sorry for. So I didn't answer. A few minutes of daredevil driving later, Mehnaz dropped us off at the station.

Before descending underground, Mohsin paused to take a picture of an old, homeless woman who sat on the sidewalk across the street, outside of a McDonald's restaurant. She was dressed, unseasonably, in a coat and hat, the holey gloves on her hands as dirty as the skin that showed through. In her winter layers, she looked big, a wide triangle shape of fabric propped up against the brick wall behind her. She was muttering to herself, the look in her eyes manic. Many people walked by her without seeming to see her there at all—the way I would have if Mohsin hadn't stopped to take a photograph. I understood, suddenly, what Mohsin may have meant. Bearing witness. I looked up to see that he had taken his picture already and was waiting for me.

"Do you recognize her?"

I frowned.

"There are a few pictures of her in my room. She sits there every day. Same exact spot. Rain or shine."

I stared at the woman for a moment and then turned away. We descended the station stairs and boarded the tube into the city. Having expected some kind of explanation about our split from Mehnaz, I was disappointed when Mohsin slumped down in his seat, put his head back, and conked off for a noisy nap.

When we got into the West End and switched lines to get to Leicester Square, I took advantage of his wakefulness to ask him, "What was all that about? With Mehnaz?"

"As if you didn't know. Mehnaz has a boyfriend. An *English* boyfriend." He was genuinely amused by my question.

"But I didn't. I didn't know. How could I know?" I was earnest, now, not wanting him to think I had been feigning my innocence.

"Then you must be one helluva deep sleeper." I must have given him a blank enough look to make him reconsider. "Okay, so you're one helluva deep sleeper. She has a boyfriend. Our father doesn't approve. They fight about it every night. He threatens to disown her. She threatens to run away. And so on and so forth. Typical East-meets-West sob story."

"We could have gone with her. I wouldn't have told anyone."

I knew that I sounded sulky, but I couldn't help it—the resentment, one I was used to, of being younger than and therefore not privy to, welled up inside of me. "I would have liked to meet her boyfriend."

"I told you that my father doesn't approve."

"Yeah. So?"

"Well, neither do I. Not of the fact that she has a boyfriend. But of who he is." His tone was edged with controlled anger that I somehow knew was not directed at me. "And I didn't fancy spending an evening in their combined company."

"Oh." There was nothing more that I could say.

The set of his mouth softened a little as he looked down at me. "Besides, bad as Mehnaz can be, her boyfriend is even less wholesome. I don't think your parents would approve of you hanging around with the likes of him." He smiled, suddenly, a wry expression with which I was becoming familiar. "Plus— this way—I get to bully you into watching the movie I want to see and I don't have to worry about some bloody wanker telling me to watch some ninja movie instead."

A thought occurred to me and I couldn't help but ask, "And you?"

"What?"

"Do you have a girlfriend?"

He laughed. "No. No, I definitely don't have a girlfriend."

When we arrived at Leicester Square, it occurred to me to ask, "What movie are we going to see anyway?"

"A new one by Attenborough."

"Attenborough?"

"Sir Richard. The guy who made *Gandhi*."

"Oh." I thought of the poster in his room.

"It's called *Cry Freedom*. You'll like it, I think. It's about South Africa. About Steven Biko, one of the heroes of the antiapartheid movement. I've been waiting for it to come out. Do you mind? I suppose we could go see something else, if you'd rather."

"No. That sounds good."

It was the first political movie that I had ever seen. And it affected me deeply. I was still sniffling a bit as we exited the cinema.

Looking politely away as I wiped my nose on my sleeve in a gesture I tried and failed to make delicate, Mohsin asked, "I gather you liked the film?"

"I loved it. Didn't you?"

He shrugged. "The movie was supposed to be about Biko. Attenborough marginalized him. Made the white guy the hero. The journalist."

"I didn't think of that."

"So? What do you feel like eating?"

I shook my head, looking around at all the little shops— which were closed now—and restaurants, which weren't.

"There are some nice little restaurants here. Or we could just get some takeaway and eat and walk around."

"That sounds good."

He walked us to a little stand that sold savory crêpes, folded into paper cones designed specifically for what Mohsin had proposed. As we waited for the man to serve us, Mohsin caught me by surprise, asking, "What were you looking for at Hyde Park?"

I took my eyes away from the batter the man at the stand had spread into a circle on the griddle and met Mohsin's eyes. I stammered out an answer, trying to buy myself time to think about how much I should say to this very perceptive cousin of mine, "Umm. I wasn't looking for anything. I just wanted to see what it looked like. I'd heard so much about it."

He frowned. I watched him try to scan in between my words for a moment. The crêpe man handed me my cone, overflowing with cheese and mushrooms.

Mohsin wouldn't let it go. "What had you heard about it?"

For some reason, the urge to talk about my grandfather with Mohsin was suddenly overwhelming. "Well, I was thinking about my grandfather. My mom's dad—" I hesitated.

But Mohsin was already nodding his head. "Ah yes, randy old Kasim Saeed."

"You know about him?" I shouldn't have been surprised.

"Of course I know about him. He's legendary, isn't he? People still talk about how he fell for that woman. And left your poor old grandmother at the side of the road. But I still don't see the connection."

I had lost him.

"Hyde Park?"

"Oh! That's where he met her."

"Aha! I should have known. A fourteen-year-old girl wouldn't be interested in political rhetoric, would she? No, it was romance. Much more in character." The crêpe man handed Mohsin his food and we turned and walked away, blowing on our crêpes before each of us ventured a bite.

My mouth was still half-full when I said, in my own defense, "I really did want to see Speakers' Corner. I wanted to hear them talking. And see where—how—it could have happened."

More polite than I, Mohsin chewed his food and swallowed before saying, "Well, that's a good question, isn't it? He had courage, your grandfather, you've got to give him that. Takes some balls to go against your culture and take a stand for your own happiness."

I nodded my head, taking another bite and agreeing with the words that Mohsin put to my own feeling.

"But then, it was basically a selfish kind of courage, wasn't it?" He pointed his crêpe at me to emphasize his words.

I bristled at them, as offended at the accusation as if he had made it against me.

But he continued before I could express my offense, "What do you know about your other grandfather? Our grandfather, I mean. Roshan Qader?"

"About Dada?" He nodded, taking another bite out of his crêpe. "I don't know. He died after Ameena was born. He had two sons. Ahmed Chacha and Daddy. And—that's all, I guess."

"That's a shame. There's a lot more, you know. A lot more you should know. Like, he had three wives. And the last two were sisters."

"What?!"

He laughed to see my eyebrows shoot up to somewhere in the vicinity of my scalp. "Relax. None of them at the same time."

My brows came back down in a frown.

"The first wife died giving birth to their second child, a girl, called Gulshan. The daughter died a few years later. But they had a son, too. Dawood. Dawood Chacha. The second wife, my grandmother, died of typhoid when my father was only six months old."

"*Your* grandmother? Dadi wasn't your grandmother? So Daddy and Ahmed Chacha are only half brothers? I didn't know that!"

"Yeah." Mohsin was grinning. "Your grandmother was his last wife, *my* grandmother's elder sister. My grandmother was half his age, younger than Dawood Chacha—her stepson. Yours was only a few years older. Dawood Chacha died during Partition. No wife or kids." Mohsin paused, thoughtfully, for a moment. "But Dada never saw us either. Mehnaz and me. Even though we were born before he died."

I nodded my head, urging him to go on.

"He had courage, too, you know. Real courage, different from your other grandfather's. The unselfish kind."

"What do you mean?"

Mohsin cocked his head to one side. "How could you not know any of this? Doesn't Nadeem Chacha—your dad—ever talk about him?"

I shook my head.

"Well, I guess that's not so surprising. Neither does mine."

"Then how do you know anything about him?"

"I know because I've made it my business to know." Mohsin leaned in closer to me as we walked around the Square. His face was more animated, less cool than I had yet seen it, excited by the news he was about to share.

"Did you know that he worked with Gandhi?"

"Gandhi?" I thought, again, of the poster in Mohsin's room. "What—how—?" I gave up, not even knowing where to begin with my questions. "No. I didn't know."

"Yup. Dada was very involved in the Independence movement. He did everything. Went on strike. Civil disobedience. Went to jail even. He got beaten by a *lathi* once. Nearly died. But he just went right on fighting—for justice, for freedom. That kind of commitment takes courage."

"Just like Biko." There was awe in my voice.

"Yes. Just like Biko."

"Tell me more."

"I can do better than that. I can show you."

"Huh?"

Mohsin pointed at the paper cone in my hand, the contents of which I had devoured without even being aware of it. "You finished? Let's throw these in that rubbish bin over there and go then. I'll show you what I'm talking about when we get home."

SEVEN

W E DIDN'T TALK at all on the way back to my uncle's
house, because jet lag caught up with me and it was my
turn to fall asleep to the gentle rock and roll of the underground. I
glanced across the street, at the McDonald's, as we emerged from
the station and found the old homeless woman was still there.

"Does she sleep there? On the sidewalk?"

Mohsin frowned and glanced at his watch. "No. She's usually
gone by this time."

"Where does she go?"

Mohsin shrugged.

"Have you ever spoken to her?"

"Not really. I bought food for her once or twice."

"So—you don't know anything about her?"

Mohsin shook his head.

Struck by an impulse, spontaneously and without thinking, I
started to cross the street, but looked the wrong way before I did.
The bus that came from the right—from the wrong direction, in

my American head—would have flattened me if Mohsin hadn't pulled me back out of the street in time. The bus driver—a *desi*, I saw, from too close as the bus slid past, blowing the bangs off my forehead—honked angrily. I paused, my heart thudding, but only for a moment. I looked right before attempting to cross again. Mohsin followed, his lifesaving hand still gripping my arm tightly for fear of what had almost happened. Safely over, I stood in front of the woman awkwardly, my actions uninformed by any specific plan or thought. Slowly, the old woman looked up, muttering to herself, her neck craned at an uncomfortable angle that made me kneel down beside her.

I heard her words—directed at me, I was surprised to realize, and not herself as I had supposed. "Dat vas wery dangerous. Seely girl."

She had a thick accent that ruled English out as her native language—Eastern European, I would have guessed—and bad breath, one among other malodors that I was beginning to detect.

"I looked the wrong way."

"Seely girl. You veel be hurt. Looking the wrong vay."

I nodded, surprised to see how focused her gaze was on my face.

"Do you have a home?" I asked.

"Home." Her eyes brightened, as if the word had reminded her of something she had forgotten. "Eet ees time to go home." Suddenly, the mountain of the woman's form began to move upward. She was muttering to herself again, as far as I could tell, speaking words—harsh, guttural sounds—of a language I didn't recognize. When she stood, she lost some of the stature that her seated form had afforded, and I was surprised to find her height to be less than mine. Muttering to herself a little more, she gathered the belongings which she had hidden under the spread of her coat—grocery bags filled with mysterious treasures. Then, she looked beyond me and pointed, with a gloved finger, at Mohsin.

"Dat boy. He take peektures of Magda."

"Yes. Is that your name? Magda?"

"I vant. Peektures of Magda."

Mohsin, who had remained silent thus far, cleared his throat. "I'll bring you pictures."

"Yays. Dat veel be nice. Peektures of Magda. Like moowie star. Wery glamorous." She smiled, revealing gaps where some of her teeth used to be.

She turned and left us, shuffling away slowly as Mohsin and I stared after her for a few moments before turning, ourselves, to leave.

The house was quiet when we got home. I looked at the clock on the mantel in the living room and saw that it was just past midnight. The hour, I remember, made me feel terribly grown up.

"Do you think Mehnaz is home yet?" I whispered, worriedly.

"Nah. Her car's not in the drive. She won't be home for hours." Mohsin sounded unconcerned.

"Won't your parents be mad?"

"They would be if they were awake. But they're not. They won't wait up tonight. They think she's with us." Mohsin stood with his hands in his pockets for a moment, before asking, "Do you want some juice or something? I'm getting some for myself."

"Yes, please." He turned to go to the kitchen. But I stopped him. "Mohsin? You don't have to stick to juice because of me. I mean, I don't care if you want a beer or something," I said, as nonchalantly as I could.

He laughed and shook his head. And I was vaguely relieved when he came back with two glasses of orange juice. He beckoned me upstairs and into his room. He put his glass down on the desk in the corner and waved me over to the bed as he seated himself at its foot, in front of the shipping trunk I had noted with passing interest the day before. He swept its surface clear of books before opening it to remove, with some solemnity, another book of some kind, well-worn and leather-bound, with papers sticking out of it, like bookmarks.

"What's that?"

"This." Mohsin put his palm over the cover of what he held, caressing it a bit. "This is Roshan Qader's journal."

My eyes widened. "Dada's journal?"

Mohsin nodded.

"Where'd you get it?"

"I found it in the trunk. Hidden away in a corner of the attic."

"Inside the trunk?"

"Along with a bunch of papers—letters and newspaper clippings that he collected." Mohsin sat down next to me and opened the book to the first page to show me the date. January 21, 1921.

"He started it right after he got out of jail. The first time. He was at Amritsar in April of 1919, at Jallianwalla Bagh, defying British orders that banned public meetings." Mohsin was tracing a finger down the first page of the journal, but my eyes were on his face. "The general in charge ordered the troops to fire on the crowd, peaceably assembled, without giving them any warning to disperse. Hundreds were killed. More than a thousand wounded. And our grandfather was arrested. He was only nineteen. But he was already married. To Fauzia. Who was pregnant with their first child, Dawood, our dads' half brother."

"We had another uncle." It finally dawned on me, what Mohsin had told me at Leicester Square, what he was telling me now.

"Yes. Dawood Chacha. He was born while Dada was in jail. They beat him up pretty badly and then kept him there for a long time. When he got out, Dawood Chacha was already two years old. And Dada—the rest of his life had begun. A life of service. His own family always came second to it. The same choice that all great men—and women—have to make." Mohsin stroked that first page. "This journal reflects that commitment. It's mostly about his work. With only a few references to personal things along the way. Dry stuff really, a bit over *your* head, I should think. No sex and romance. Not like your *other* grandfather's story."

The superior grin on Mohsin's face prompted me to punch him in the arm. "I care about other stuff, too. Keep going."

Mohsin shrugged. "You can read it yourself, if you like." His casual tone didn't match the white-knuckled grip with which he was suddenly holding the journal, and I noticed his hand had retreated, possessively, rather than extending to match the offer of his words.

I had to hide a superior smile of my own. "I will." I thought of my mother's stories. Of Big Nanima's and Belle's. Their voices echoed in my head, along with Razia Nani's. Here were more family secrets that no one had ever bothered to share. That my father had a brother and sister I had never heard of. That my grandfather had been beaten and jailed by the British. "I'll read it later. But—you tell me the story first." The next smile, a little sheepish, I couldn't hide, feeling like a little girl begging for a bedtime tale. "I like the way you're telling it. Makes it more alive."

Mohsin smiled at me and punched me back, gently. But I could tell he was happy to oblige. He cleared his throat ceremoniously and started talking again. "I don't know why, but our grandfather and his first wife, Fauzia, didn't have any other children for a very long time. But—a little over ten years later—she was pregnant again when Dada decided to join the Salt March. The British government had a monopoly on the manufacture of salt. So Gandhi decided to march to a coastal village called Dandi, to take salt from the sea. To thumb his nose at British rule— though he probably wouldn't have put it quite that way. To show that Indians refused to recognize the authority of the Raj. Civil disobedience. Peaceful resistance. *Satyagraha.*" Mohsin turned a few pages of the book he still held in a slightly more relaxed hand and pointed out the date. March 4, 1930. "Dada mentions—in passing—that Fauzia was very upset about him leaving her to go on the march. 'Regretfully, I took my leave of her amid a torrent of tears. Despite all of my efforts to persuade her of the rightness of my decision, Fauzia could not understand why this march with Gandhiji was so important. She remembered Jallianwalla Bagh. So did I, but with a very different effect.' By the end of the march, Dada was in jail again. This time, for less than a year. He received this telegram in prison." Mohsin handed me a fragile piece of yellowed paper, addressed to Roshan Qader in April of 1930.

REGRET TO INFORM YOU FAUZIA DIED IN CHILDBIRTH STOP
YOU HAVE A HEALTHY DAUGHTER STOP

My hand shook a little as I handed the telegram back to Mohsin. I watched him tuck the piece of paper carefully back into the page where he had taken it out from and looked up to find him watching me with a face I couldn't read.

I felt compelled to say something. "That's—that's so sad." The words were inadequate, I knew. "So—he—he wasn't really there for her, was he? In jail when she gave birth the first time. In jail again when she died."

Mohsin shrugged. "He did what he had to do."

"He shouldn't have gone on that march." I said what I was thinking out loud without meaning to.

"He *had* to go."

"No he didn't. He *chose* to go. There's a difference."

"Sometimes there is."

I stared at Mohsin. I knew what he was thinking. "*That's*—not—the same."

"No. It's not. Dada left *his* wife—"

"His *pregnant* wife!"

"Yes. She was pregnant. But he left her—only temporarily, mind you—for something important. Something bigger than himself. Your other grandfather—Kasim Saeed—he left *his* wife, threw her away like trash, for nothing but his own self-ish—" Mohsin broke off. Now, it was his turn to look a little sheepish. "Sorry, Saira. He's your granddad. And it's none of my business after all."

I shook my head and blew out a noisy breath of exasperation

as I said, "I'm not defending him! I just—oh, just get on with the story!" I heard my own tone and added, meekly, "Please."

Mohsin laughed. "All right. Well—" He broke off to look back down at the little book for inspiration. He thumbed through quite a few more pages. "Dada got back home almost a year later. Dawood Chacha and the baby—her name was Gulshan—were with Dada's mother, our great-grandmother. Dada writes that Dawood Chacha took his mum's death hard."

"How old was he?"

"Just eleven. Dada sent him off to school when he got back from jail."

I felt my forehead crease with judgment.

Mohsin shrugged. "It's the way things were back then."

"What about the baby?"

"She didn't know her dad. And, well, the way things worked in those days, Dada's mum was pretty much in charge of her care. In the beginning, anyway. Until one night, soon after Dada returned from prison. He wrote about it." Mohsin was holding the journal out to me, a finger running under a couple of lines of close, old-fashioned handwriting. "The baby—Gulshan—approached him, toddled her way over to his knee as he sat and worked on an article he was writing. It was the first time she ever looked at him as someone familiar. Not a stranger. She called him 'Papa'—here's the bit, here."

I scanned the words quickly.

"It's only a few words, I know. But when you read the whole thing—and you see how little there is of anything sentimental—you realize how much that moment and the next one he wrote about must have meant to him. That night, Dada heard Gulshan, who slept with her grandmother, crying and fussing. He knocked at his mother's door and asked if everything was all right. She was teething. And his mother was tired. She handed Gulshan over. The baby looked up at her father. Said 'Papa' again. He took her to his room, put her down beside him in his bed, and she fell asleep in seconds. From that moment on, Gulshan became Dada's constant companion—climbing up on his lap when he wrote or read letters, received and reciprocated social and business calls, traveling with him by train or horse and carriage as he crisscrossed the subcontinent, busy with so many projects that it would make your head spin. I know that because so many of the letters that he received later—after—made reference to little Gulshan as her father's 'sweet little shadow'—that was how one of Dada's friends put it.

"Two years later, when Dada was about to leave, with Gulshan, on another trip, she came down with the measles." Mohsin rifled through the journal again. "'Dr. Khan having reassured me of the routine nature of her malady, I have reluctantly decided to leave Gulshan behind with Majee while I engage on this journey. I have explained the importance of our mission to Gulshan, whose understanding I have noted as being that of a child well beyond her years. Still, seeing her so weak with fever, my heart is unsettled at the thought of parting from Gulshan, who grows more like her mother every day.'" Mohsin paused.

I knew what would come next, but had to brace myself in order to bear it.

"A few weeks later, Dada had reached Wardha, on his way to Segaon, when this telegram caught up with him, two weeks too late." Mohsin handed me another yellowed piece of tissue-thin paper.

GULSHAN GRAVELY ILL STOP

RETURN HOME IMMEDIATELY STOP

NOT MUCH TIME STOP

I stared at the words for a long time before handing the paper that captured them back to Mohsin.

He said, "From what I could figure, looking through the dates, Gulshan was already dead by the time Dada got this. It was meningitis—a secondary infection from the measles." Mohsin put the telegram away, as carefully as he had the first. He paused for a moment, noting the moisture collecting in my eyes. Then he turned the pages again, putting the journal down on the table in front of us. "Um. Six or seven—maybe eight years—after Fauzia died, Dada married again. Her name was Shaheena. He had one son with her. My dad. She died of typhoid a few months after he was born. Dada was there for her death. He describes it in the journal. 'I arrived home last week after a month's absence to find Shaheena lying motionless, eyes half-open, weak with fever. I knew the truth immediately, that Shaheena was on her deathbed, recognizing the symptoms too well, those insidious signs, the final stages of typhoid. She was a wonderful wife, a partner, supportive of all of my efforts for the poor. Daily, she made the trip to the *jhugee*s down the road, carrying baskets of food and clothes to distribute to those in desperate need. She befriended the humble occupants of those hovels, laying aside the class hierarchies that divided them from her. It was what killed her, in the end.

As a guest in the tin-roofed, straw and mud huts she visited, she never refused the refreshments they offered her, loath to give offense. Refreshments made of water, the disease-ridden, infested water that comes with poverty. I mourn her loss, remembering her cheerful good-byes, so frequent as the nature of my work took me away from her so often. My work—seeking to eradicate the conditions that killed Shaheena, the poverty, the class divide, the horrible discrimination of caste. Her death strengthens my determination, because too many suffer the same.'

"Dawood Chacha must have been twenty-one—older than his stepmother was. Then, only a few weeks after my dad's mum passed away, Dada's mother sent a marriage proposal on his behalf to Shaheena's family. She decided that this time, the baby—Ahmed—would have a mother. Not like Gulshan. So, she arranged her son's marriage to his sister-in-law. Amna. Your grandmother. My dad's aunt."

"That's—that must have been weird."

Mohsin tilted his head. "Not really. It made sense. Your grandmother, Amna—Dadi—well, she was getting on a bit in years. In her mid-twenties already. What would have been considered an old maid. And Dada's mum probably figured it was the best thing for everyone."

"Have—has your dad ever talked about it? About being raised by a stepmother? Who was also his aunt?"

"Never. I never even knew until I read Dada's journal. So it must have all worked out for the best."

"I guess." I shrugged off my doubt and fixed my eyes back on Mohsin, expectantly.

"Right. Well—" Mohsin's voice trailed off into a moment of silence. And then became suddenly certain again as he resumed his narrative on a different note, less personal than the trajectory we'd followed until now. "The day did finally come—the day Dada and Gandhi and the whole Independence movement had been struggling for—for so many years. But the way it happened took them all by surprise. The way the negotiations ended, no one was prepared really, not least the British themselves. They withdrew in a pretty nasty kind of way—like parents who've given in to a tantrum. They clicked their tongues, washed their hands of the whole Subcontinent, and left it all cut up in pieces, giving it up in a way that was designed for failure, handing power over in bits. And the Indians responded in kind, acting like children, fighting furiously over those bits and pieces.

"Gandhi—the Great Soul of India's independence—greeted the day with fasting and prayers, mourning all the riots and bloodshed, begging the people to stop. It wasn't a time for celebration. India was divided—in heart, in mind, in soul, and in blood. That's not what all those great men had worked for. Muslims in the middle, like Hindus and Sikhs in the west and east, they all had decisions to make. For Dada, there was never a question."

Mohsin picked up the journal, rustled forward through the pages, and then set it back down on the table, between us, his finger tracing the words he then read aloud: "'It is wrong, horribly wrong, to support the creation of a nation founded on the religious identity of its majority. My brother, who has decided to leave India, to migrate to Pakistan with my mother, his wife, and his children, believes this is a time to be pragmatic. That what is right and wrong is less important than what is safe and practical. To no avail, I have tried to persuade him that what is right and wrong is always of paramount importance. To stray from principle in the interest of expedience is the road to disaster. The struggle to know what is right, to condemn what is wrong, to fight for the former and against the latter, has been the whole purpose of my life. For me, there is no point in being safe if one is wrong. This nation is founded on a sense of unity and brotherhood that transcends ethnic and religious affiliation. His, the nation he chooses, has sealed the pact of discrimination and separatism in a way that will set precedents for the future that I tremble to contemplate. He is afraid for his children, that in India they may become an oppressed minority. Whereas I would wish, a thousand times more, that my children wear the yoke of oppression, striving bravely against it, than to join the ranks of the oppressors. A thousand times!'" Mohsin's eyes, when he looked up, were shining. "Isn't that amazing? To think that *our* grandfather wrote those words? Every time I read them, I—I'm in awe. The bloody irony of it! Of what he wrote and how things ended up with his sons! You—you see what I mean, don't you, Saira?"

"No—they—? What do you mean?"

"I mean my dad. And yours. They did just the opposite of what Dada wished for, didn't they? They turned their backs on their country, the country he helped to liberate—both of them chasing after the oppressors—the Empire—that Dada worked to get out from under for so long. Instead of sticking around and doing what needed to be done. Like their brother did."

I didn't say anything, I couldn't, in anticipation of the answer I knew was coming to my next question. "What happened to Dawood Chacha?"

"He—he became a journalist."

I took a deep breath and held it.

Mohsin nodded. "He died—was killed. Murdered by an

angry mob while reporting on the riots in Calcutta in 1947. My dad was eight then, yours only three."

I wanted to say something, opened my mouth to begin, but no words came.

Mohsin cleared his throat and read again from our grandfather's journal: "'Dawood's death was the sharpest blow in a series of them. Amna, who was more of a sister to him than a mother, wept bitterly when we were given the news. Ahmed and Nadeem, both of them so young, met their first conscious experience with death bravely as I myself have learned to do over the course of my life. I am mourning, like all of India mourns, for its sons and brothers, daughters and sisters. Yet there is consolation in knowing that Dawood's life was a worthy one, that the loss of it can be tallied in the column of other sacrifices for the cause of justice. He was an optimist whose hope for the future was ever eternal, a light shining brightly in the darkness of the barbarous violence that rages on throughout our nation. To the children, to Amna, it falls to me to explain that to honour Dawood's memory and the memory of all those who suffer still, we must fight on, never wavering before the forces of injustice.' He goes on a bit here. And then, 'Curiously, when I think of Dawood, alone and beaten in that crowd of degenerated humanity, I think of his sister, my little Gulshan, and their mother.'" Mohsin pulled out a flimsy piece of newsprint. "This is one of a couple of clippings that Dada must have cut out and saved."

I took it from him. And skimmed through the words without reading them. I can't even remember the headline, my eyes caught and held by the small letters of the byline. Dawood Qader.

Mohsin spoke on. "Four months later, Dada wrote, 'I have

borne many losses in my lifetime—two children, two wives, so many comrades. Never have I faced a moment so bleak, never have I shuddered with such convulsions of despair. After so many little victories, mixed in outcome, to be sure, it seems that all is lost, that the forces of injustice have finally won.'"

"What was he talking about?"

"Gandhi's assassination. But Dada followed his own advice. He didn't waver from his purpose." Mohsin paused and then licked his finger, using it to turn more pages as he said, "Over the next ten or twelve years, Dada had his finger in all kinds of projects—women's literacy programs, workers' rights bills, child labor laws, health clinics, housing development.

"My dad grew up. He went into law. Dada was very proud of him, when he graduated. First class, first. He went to work at a law firm—the senior partner was an old friend of Dada's. He started out doing research and writing briefs for the senior barristers. And then he tried his first case. From what I gather"—Mohsin was still thumbing through the pages of Dada's journal—"he didn't do too well." There was an unsympathetic note of humor in his voice—one that came at my uncle's expense. Mohsin stopped turning pages. "Dada wrote, 'The boy is more like his father than he would care to admit. Ahmed's courtroom delivery lacks fire. My own lack of oratory skill kept me happily occupied behind the scenes for all of my life, a foot soldier in all of the projects I involved myself with. Yet Ahmed cannot reconcile himself to the lack of glory that such a role might entail. He has taken it to heart and is dejected, despite all of my efforts at consolation.' Eventually, my dad found his niche. In an area that Dada did not approve of. Tax law. Specifically, loophole-hunting. 'Ahmed has become a first-class lackey, finding ways to enrich the very robber barons I have worked against all of these years, helping them to hold on to their ill-gotten gains, to increase their excesses, instead of sharing with the sweat and blood that earns it for them.'

"My father became indispensable at the firm, generating huge amounts of money from rich, corrupt clients. They must have fought about it. A lot. Until, finally, my father ran away to England. Where he'd been offered a job at a bank, Saif Bank, owned by one of the robber barons Dada had no respect for. A Pakistani banker." The corners of Mohsin's mouth curved up. "My other grandfather. Dada and Dad broke off all communication." Mohsin bent his head again. "'With disgust, I wash my hands of the boy. In vain have I reminded him of his duties and obligations. He has been seduced by power and wealth and has turned his back on all that matters.' Dad married the boss's daughter—my mum—a year later. There's a letter here, from my dad. Informing Dada of his engagement, inviting Dada and Dadi to a reception that was to be held in Bombay. The main wedding was in Pakistan. *Your* parents met each other at the reception in Bombay."

I nodded. "I know."

"And Dada must have attended, too. Because my dad sent him this really angry letter afterward." Mohsin had pulled out another piece of paper. "Let me read you a bit." Mohsin took a second to scan down the page. "This is the line that gets me— 'Given an opportunity to make peace, to let bygones be bygones, you, sir, chose to make a mockery of yourself and our family by turning up at the wedding in rags.'" Mohsin was chuckling as he folded up the letter from his father and put it back into the pages of the journal. "Can you imagine? Showing up in rags?" He shook his head. "God! My dad must have blown a bloody fuse!"

Then the smile faded from Mohsin's face. "Within a year or two, your mum and dad were married. And they went off to America."

"My dad came to America to study medicine—to make a better life for himself and my mom—!" I spit the words out, trite as they were, the product of years of public school social studies indoctrination about the strength of a nation built on immigrant stories like my parents'. But I was struck, for the first time, by the implication of what they meant from another perspective, from that of my grandfather and Mohsin.

"They had medical schools in India."

"But—he wanted to specialize—the opportunities—he—"

"Yeah, yeah, yeah. Guess there were no sick people in India? And that's why he never came back? Like he promised his dad he would?"

"He—? How do you know—?"

"It's all right here. In this letter Nadeem Chacha wrote to Dada. From America, shortly after your sister was born." Mohsin pulled a blue airmail envelope out from near the back of the journal. He handed it to me.

I held it, noting my father's handwriting on the outside, the return address in Los Angeles. After a long pause, I pulled out the tissue-paper letter it contained and read the letter.

September 14, 1969

My dear Papa,

I hope this letter finds you in good health and bright spirits. I apologize for the infrequency of my correspondence and know that you will be wondering at my reasons for writing now.

Shabana and the baby are well. You will have heard of the

138

continuing scandal in Shabana's family. Her father remains in England. Her mother has shifted to Pakistan permanently. The situation is awkward, to say the very least.

I am nearly finished with my residency, which is progressing well. I have decided to follow up my residency training with more practical experience. I feel that the opportunities here, the chance to work with the very latest techniques and technologies, under the supervision of some of the best doctors in the world, will be invaluable and unavailable back home.

I want to reemphasize my commitment to return to India, to carry on the legacy of service that you have inspired. Employment here will only enhance my ability to do so. In addition, I will be earning a significant salary, when compared to what I will be able to earn back home. Such savings will be especially important for us when Shabana and I return home to establish our household now that we have begun our family.

I know that you might not agree with my plans, but I hope at least that you understand and believe that my motivations are not based solely on monetary consideration. With this in mind, I have accepted an offer of employment, to begin upon graduation, at a highly reputable hospital and in practice with a first-class medical team, which will afford me a wide range of experience and help to maximize the further development of my skills. Shabana and I have set a limit of five years for our time here. I hope you understand this decision. It has not been made lightly.

Shabana sends you her salaams.

Affectionately,
Nadeem

I looked up at Mohsin, a million stray thoughts rushing through my head. It was the first time I had ever considered my father as a whole person. A person who was born and lived and made choices before there was a me, before he was my father or Ameena's. I thought about other choices he might have made. About what those other choices might have meant for me and my life.

I shook my head to clear it, remembering Big Nanima's words: *There's no if. There is only what is. What was. What will be.* "What about Dadi?"

"She was already dead. Right after your parents were married."

I nodded, having suspected as much already. "How long after this did Dada die?"

"He died a couple of months after receiving that letter from your dad. Just after Mehnaz and I were born." Mohsin turned the pages of the journal again. And pointed to the date on the page where he stopped. December 15, 1969. "That's our birthday. Mine and Mehnaz's. A few weeks before he died. See what he wrote?" He pushed the journal into my hands for the first time, forcing me to read the passage for myself:

On this day was born my grandson, Mohsin. An auspicious birth, he brought with him a sister. It is on your shoulders, my son, that I rest all of my hopes for the future. Do not fail me in your efforts for what is right and what is just. Bear witness to their opposite, to evil and injustice, which are one and the same. Bear witness so that they may not be committed with impunity. Whatever path your journey takes, do not succumb to the seduction of indifference to suffering, which authorizes evil.

I looked up, stunned. I muttered, "Bear witness—bear witness. That's what you meant. Mohsin—this is—this is awesome."

"It is a bit, isn't it?" Mohsin cleared his throat.

"He must have been so lonely at the end. After a whole life of sadness and sacrifice."

"Yeah. Like something out of a tragic play."

"I see my son is filling your head with nonsense, Saira." Mohsin and I both started, hearing the voice intrude on us from behind. We turned, hearts racing, to see Ahmed Chacha standing in the doorway to the room, another glass of ice and amber liquid in hand. His eyes rested on the journal I held for a moment, before he entered the room and walked toward the window, parting the curtains to take a look at the driveway in front. "Mehnaz is not in her room. Where is the car? Where is your sister, Mohsin?" His voice was controlled. But there was a steely note to it that made me pity Mehnaz.

"She met up with some friends. Saira and I came home on the tube."

Ahmed Chacha was still standing at the window, holding the edge of the curtain. "You let her go?" He used his glass to point at the clock on the mantle. I saw that it was past 1:00 AM. "Is this any time for a young girl to be out on her own?"

"I'm not her keeper."

"No." Ahmed Chacha sneered, waving his arm at the letter and journal in my hands. "No. Not hers. You're much too busy preserving the past, I see, keeping the memory of long-forgotten nonsense alive. Much more important than your living, breathing sister." Ahmed Chacha turned to me and shook his head, "You see, Saira, what a contradiction my children are? One is obsessed with ancient history, taunting me with irrelevancies of the past—the other bent on flouting the obligations of her culture and heritage with no regard for her own future."

"Maybe she'd care more about her future if you gave her something to be proud of from the past." Mohsin had stood up, as if to back up his verbal challenge with a physical one.

"Something to be proud of? You think that your grandfather is something to be proud of? A man who abandoned his own family, time and again, for some useless crusade of justice? What did he ever accomplish? Nothing! I was only a few months old when my mother died—a horrible, untimely death that he was responsible for. What kind of husband sends his wife into the slums to her own death? That is not what makes a man, Mohsin. A man is someone who provides for his family and protects them. It is easy to talk of ideals in the abstract when you are young. When you have nothing to lose. My father was not in this position. His obligation was to his family."

Mohsin didn't say anything. But his silence was no concession. I knew I was witness to an argument that had not just begun.

Ahmed Chacha sighed. He took a sip of his drink and shook his head. "Your fixation with impractical notions of justice is all right now. But eventually you must grow up and become a man."

"A man like you?"

"Don't you sneer at me! Don't you hold up that poor excuse of a father as an example of light to your impressionable young cousin! My father was a fool who chased after an imaginary, utopian world. He lived in his head, with a bunch of ideals for company—useless ideals that feed no one and which make the world dangerous. I swore that I would never be like him—that I would work hard. In the real world. To provide. You have never felt the lack of a single thing in your life, you and Mehnaz, you spoiled brats! Yet you would criminalize these things—making wealth a crime instead of the blessing that it is, like some damned communist!"

"First of all, your premise is wrong. Dada lived in the real world, too. He faced up to it. Instead of shrugging his shoulders, hiding his head away in the sand, grabbing what comfort he could for himself."

"Faced up to it? He wasted his life!"

"Not the way I see it."

"Tilting at windmills. You think any of these damned fool ideologues ever actually achieved anything?"

"That's not the point. It's the journey they took that mattered. The destination is the same for all of us."

"None of that mumbo-jumbo abstraction, if you please! You think the British ran away because of a little brown man in a loincloth and his friends? The British left because it was in their interest to leave. That is how the world works. That is how change happens. Self-interest. To work against one's own interest for some imaginary cause of justice is to be a fool."

Mohsin shook his head. "You tell yourself that. If it helps you to sleep at night. I don't want any part of it. I don't want to eat the food I've snatched out of the hands of others."

"Then go hungry, you fool!"

I don't know where the argument would have turned next. The sound of a car on the drive, the flash of headlights through the crack of the curtains shifted my cousin's attention—and his father's. A few seconds later, we heard Mehnaz enter the house. Ahmed Chacha left the room to meet her at the door, and another loud argument began. She stomped up the stairs, her father trailing after her, both of them yelling and screaming back and forth.

Mohsin and I stared at each other for a long moment. I looked down, in surprise, to find Dada's journal still in my hands.

"You said you found this—the trunk—in the attic?"

He nodded. "Last year. It has loads of other stuff in it—Dada's—that someone had packed up and shipped over to my dad. He never even bothered to open it." There was quiet outrage in Mohsin's voice, and disgust. "There're pictures in there. Pictures of his first wife. Of my grandmother—my real grandmother. And Dadi. Little Gulshan. And Dawood Chacha. Our dads, too, from when they were kids. And letters. From so many people, some of them famous. In India, you know. Letters from my dad. That one you read from yours. And this diary."

"Can I see them all?" I asked, standing up—yawning and stretching—my body betrayed again by the adverse effects of jet lag.

Mohsin smiled. "I'll show you the rest tomorrow. You can take some of the pictures with you, if you like. Until then—" He took the diary back from me, thumbing through it again until he found what he was looking for and said, "Here's a picture of him. Our grandfather. He must have been in his twenties when that one was taken."

It was small, the size of a passport picture. And black-and-white, of course. Even so, the resemblance was eerie.

I was quiet for a long moment, studying the picture, before saying, "Mohsin? You know you look just like him?"

"I did notice a resemblance."

"But then, you *are* just like him, aren't you? I mean in more ways than looks?"

"You think so? Well, there are some very significant differences. Trust me." He was laughing, amused at something he didn't share.

I turned back to face the wall of photographs, looking for and finding Magda. Magda in winter, Magda in the rain. Mohsin had taken pictures of her—as he had that evening—from across the street, from an angle close to the ground, at the same level she sat. The legs of passersby were in some of the shots, in motion, on their way here or there. One shot showed someone stopping to drop some money into her lap. Another showed a child, eye-level with Magda, tugged along by the hand of an adult, dragging his heels as his eyes connected with the old woman who smiled at him shyly.

"I wonder where Magda is right now. How she lives. What her story is."

"Magda. It's funny, that," Mohsin said. "I never knew her name until tonight. Until you talked to her. Most people don't see her at all—not as a person."

"I wouldn't have seen her either. If you hadn't stopped to take her picture."

"But that's all I ever did. She was just an image—something I saw from behind the lens of my camera. Now she has a name. You have a way about you, you know. Cousin Saira. A way of drawing people out. You pay attention."

"But we still don't know anything about her. None of the details of her life."

"We know her name. That's something."

EIGHT

I CAME HOME FROM that summer in Karachi and London—head swimming with the voices of a reconstructed past, full of a self-importance I couldn't wait to share—only to find that my family had been busy arranging the future in my absence. Ameena's future, at any rate.

At the airport, after a quick hug, my mother began, "Your sister is engaged! To a doctor! He's an Indian boy, finishing up his residency in San Francisco. From a very good family in Bombay. We are so excited! We didn't want to tell you the good news on the phone. So we decided to wait and surprise you. Isn't it wonderful? It will be a long engagement, of course. Your sister is still very young. Two years at least—though I suppose it all depends on how long we can keep them apart, eh Ameena? Well, Saira, aren't you going to congratulate your sister?" Mummy was breathless from excitement. I was breathless from shock, looking from one dearly missed face to another for some sign that my mother had developed a rather disconcerting sense of humor in my absence. There was none.

Ameena wouldn't meet my eyes. But her fair skin was suffused with a flush of pink that I took to mean only one of two things: she was either embarrassed, or she had a fever. I touched her forehead, when she leaned forward for a hug, and drew the obvious conclusion on finding it cool and dry. My father just grinned, punctuating my mother's continuing monologue with an occasional nod of pride and pleasure.

"It happened only three weeks ago, just after you left town. Can you imagine? Three weeks ago, when we came to drop you at the airport, we didn't even know the boy . . . and now? Now, we have a new son-in-law . . . a new son. Ameena has a fiancé! Don't worry, Saira. I know you must be dying to meet him. He is coming tonight, flying in from San Francisco for the weekend. In fact, he comes every weekend that he can and stays with his aunt who lives in Diamond Bar. Though he spends the whole of the weekend at our house. His poor aunt—you know her, Saira, she is Nilofer Auntie, she's the one who introduced Shuja to us—she complains that she hardly sees him when he comes. Of course, it is not *her* that he is coming to see, is it, Ameena? He's been waiting for you to come home, Saira, is dying to take Ameena out. But I told him they had to wait for you to come back. So that you could play chaperone. Won't that be fun? You'll get to eat with them at all the fancy restaurants he wants to take Ameena to, lucky girl. And movies, too. Though I told him, G-rated movies only. I don't want him to be getting ideas. Ameena is a very good girl, aren't you, Ameena? And Shuja will only love you all the more because of it.

"Doesn't your sister look beautiful, Saira? She's lost some weight, I think. But it only makes her features sharper, more delicate, *nah*? Of course, there's a lot of work to do. Shuja's relatives are gathering here next month, coming from all over the States, for the *mungnee*. Nilofer Auntie is here, of course. She is his father's sister. He also has a *khala* in Florida, a *chacha* in Chicago, and another one in Houston, isn't that right, Nadeem?" My father nodded, tapping his fingers on the steering wheel. "We decided to wait for them before celebrating the official engagement. And for you, of course! Ameena could not have celebrated her engagement without *you*, Saira. Shuja's parents have both passed away, both when he was still a young child. The poor boy, all alone in the world. He was raised by one of his uncles. But now he has us, eh?

"So you will get to meet your brother-in-law tonight. Let's see, what will you call him? *Jeejaji?* Or just Shuja Bhai? We should ask him what he prefers. Oh, Ameena, I am so proud of you. I hope you know what a lucky girl you are."

We suffered in this way the whole long drive home. My mother, I decided, had morphed into some kind of Indo-Pak version of Mrs. Bennet. Ameena was typically quiet. The shy, blushing-bride routine would come naturally to her, I decided, recalling Jane with some bitterness. So, who was I supposed to be? Lizzy?

More like Jo to Ameena's Meg, I decided later, during dinner. I disliked Shuja on sight. Resented his intrusion on my homecoming. The conversation was carried by my mother and Shuja, and I couldn't decide who puckered up more at the mutual butt-kissing that was its main ingredient. My mother had taken pains over the meal, one of her second-rung dinner-party menus—I assumed she had already served Shuja her best dishes in the first few weekends of motherly-in-law joy—served on her best china, in the formal dining room. A far cry from the serve-yourselves-from-the-pots-on-the-stove usual.

Just as my resentment peaked at the realization that no one had even asked about my own adventures in Pakistan and London, Shuja flashed a white-toothed, wolfy smile at me and asked, "So, Saira? How was your trip?"

I swallowed the food in my mouth, along with the hostility that rose up in it, to say, in a clipped and teeth-gritted voice, "Fine."

"You went for your cousin's wedding? That must have been fun."

My mother, not liking the flash in my eyes, interjected smoothly, "Not as much fun, I am sure, as Ameena's and your wedding will be. Saira was so excited when we told her the good news. She couldn't wait to meet you, Shuja. Which reminds me—we were trying to decide what Saira should call you? Shuja Bhai or—?"

"Oh, I think just Shuja is fine. Anything else would be too formal. Don't you think so, Saira?"

I gulped, again. And nodded.

Shuja put his linen napkin down beside his plate and pushed himself slightly away from the table as he said, "That was delicious. As usual. Mummy."

My eyes rounded. And though his use of the word sounded awkward and artificial to me, no one else seemed to think so.

My mother nodded, flushed with pleasure. "I'm glad you liked it, Shuja. You are a pleasure to feed. Always so appreciative. Of course the best is yet to come. Ameena has made some *ras malai* for dessert."

Shuja smiled with pleasure, shooting goo-goo eyes at my sister, which tickled my esophagus unpleasantly.

Mummy was still gushing on about Ameena's cooking skills,

which I hadn't known she possessed: "She's just learned how to make it. It was a very good batch. Don't forget, Ameena, to give Shuja the *ras malai* that you kept aside for Nilofer Auntie, when he goes."

While Mummy and I cleared the table of food and debris, my father frowned and fidgeted, a sign that I wishfully interpreted to mean that he was as sick of this phony charade as I was. I saw how impatiently Daddy waited for Shuja to finish the tea that Ameena made for him—I noticed she hadn't needed to ask how much sugar to add—drumming his fingers on the table in front of him. I realized my mistake as soon as the last sip was supped, when my father whipped out his Scrabble board so fast that I thought he must have had it ready, lying in wait, under the table.

"Oh, Nadeem! Poor Shuja has played with you every time he has come. Leave the poor boy alone!" My mother shook her head and puckered her lips again at the object of her sympathy.

"Oh, I'm sorry, Shuja. If you'd rather not play—?" My father let the question hang, clearly disappointed at the prospect of missing out on a game.

"Are you kidding? I've still got to pay you back for that sound beating you gave me last time! No, really. I'd love to play. Dad."

I watched, sour-mouthed, as my father smiled warmly and began to set up the Scrabble board. Ameena, I noticed with some satisfaction, looked slightly annoyed with both of them. But my spirits waned again when Shuja looked up and smiled into her eyes, mouthing *just one game,* making her blush and smile prettily as she helped me finish clearing off the table and sat down to watch the game with a look of melting adoration that was as hard to miss as it was to swallow.

I trudged around the house for the next hour or so, as repelled by the family scene taking place in the dining room as I was fascinated. Finally, Shuja got up to leave. My parents hovered solicitously in the foyer, declaring how nice an evening it had been, how much they looked forward to seeing him again the next, and how happy we all were as a family to have him be a part of ours.

Then, Ameena cleared her throat and said the first words that I remember her uttering that evening. "Um. I'm going to walk Shuja out to his car."

"Of course, of course, *beti*. Drive carefully, Shuja. *Khudahafiz. Khudahafiz*."

"*Khudahafiz*."

"*Khudahafiz*, Mummy, Dad. 'Bye, Saira."

"Uh—'bye."

The door shut behind them. And my parents were still for a moment. Then, as if tired from the effort of having sustained so much smiling pleasantry all evening, their expressions returned to normal: their teeth faded back inside of their mouths, they slouched forward as they released the stomach muscles they'd been holding in and allowed their backs to assume the natural curve that holding themselves up had forced them to straighten, and their voices, as they began to speak again, lost the polished, musical tone that had been affected for the duration of Shuja's presence.

Turning back to go finish up in the kitchen, my mother exclaimed, "Oh no! Shuja has forgotten the *ras malai* for Nilofer Auntie. Run, Saira, give him this before he drives off." I obeyed without thinking, running to catch up. It took me a moment to register what I saw when I did. Shuja had his arms locked around my sister, one of his hands running up her back and then down again, lower and lower. His mouth was on hers, sucking all of the air out of her, it seemed. They must have heard my footsteps, but it was Shuja, not Ameena, who recovered quickly enough to push away before I reached them. He was grinning at me, his teeth flashing by the light of the streetlamp. Ameena looked dazed, her eyes unfocused, her breathing ragged.

Shuja saw the package of dessert in my hand. "Did I forget that? Thank you, Saira. So sweet of you to run out and give it to me. You should go straight to bed. You look tired enough to be seeing things. Jet lag can do that, you know." He was still grinning.

"Come on, Ameena!" My voice was shrill and scolding. I sounded like she usually did, I realized in surprise. "Mummy and Daddy are waiting."

Ameena didn't look at me as she turned back to lean into Shuja. "I'll be there in a minute, Saira. Go back inside."

"No. Come with me." I didn't recognize myself. Hadn't recognized anyone since I came home. I blamed Shuja for that, and my voice became even shriller as I repeated, "Come with me, now!"

Shuja gently pushed Ameena in my direction. "You'd better go, sweetheart. I'll see you tomorrow."

Ameena held on to his hand. "Will you call me? Tonight?"

He laughed, indulgently. "I'll call you. Go now, little one. Go with your sister. 'Bye, Saira."

"Hmph!"

His laughter, the sound of his rental car door slamming, and the rev of the engine followed us into the house.

I WAS THE frequent, if unwilling, chaperone for my sister and Shuja during the course of the next year. Shuja flew down every chance he got. Sensing my recalcitrance—it was hard to miss,

I'm sure, with all the sulking and sniping that I subjected him to—Shuja expended a great deal of effort on wooing and winning *me* over, something he found totally unnecessary with my besotted sister. I went everywhere with them. Restaurants, movies, amusement parks, shopping malls. I took my role as chaperone very seriously, more for the perverse pleasure that thwarting Shuja's lustful advances on my sister afforded me than anything else. It was a strange position to be in—the reluctant witness to their Mummy-approved romance. They managed to escape my presence every once in a while—times when I would agree to go off shopping by myself, sit alone in a theater watching an R-rated movie while they sat through non-lust-inducing G-rated ones, or stand in lines for rides that Shuja and Ameena preferred to sit out. I didn't want to think about what they did then.

My bias against Shuja was so strong that it took me quite some time to see what my sister might have seen in him. That while he was neither tall nor short, he carried himself in such a way as to convey that he was present, occupying space. That the firm features of his face, regular and symmetrical, gave an impression of quiet strength. That the line of his mouth, the frame of his jaw in repose, indicated him as someone who knew enough of pain and loss to be able to recognize it in others with sympathy—a good quality, I suppose, in a doctor.

He had a sense of humor that was impervious to the withering looks of scorn that I threw at him constantly. Strong enough, in fact, to penetrate the most strongly armored of sulks. I laughed often, unable to maintain my defenses against the barrage of one-liners that he threw my way. But it was a reluctant kind of laughter—resentful—earned by extortion, and both he and I knew that it didn't really count in the battle we were waging.

All of this escaped my notice, so diverted was I by the sight of those fumbling hands, those air-sucking lips, whose assault I'd witnessed on my first night back. It was impossible to believe that Ameena, goody-goody Ameena, who would normally avert her eyes at the steamy sex scenes that daytime soap operas and night-time dramas were so full of, could actually endure and enjoy such indignity. Ameena, who until now had been more than happy with the more cheesy than sleazy kind of romance, which she consumed voraciously in the form of the Harlequin romances that I found stashed away in the bathroom cabinet and under her bed. Stories about virginally pure heroines, like Ameena, who sat around wait-ing for knights on white horses, or Porsches, to rescue them. Now, it seemed, she no longer needed those novels. As she was making room for the trousseau of clothing and accessories that she was amassing in preparation for her wedding, I was witness to the day, soon after my return from Pakistan, when Ameena cleaned her room out from top to bottom—tossing the Harlequins into a huge garbage bag the way other newly affianced women might toss out letters and photographs from former lovers.

What I eventually found most objectionable about Shuja per-sonally was that he really wasn't. Objectionable, that is. Over the next few months, I was forced to admit it—no matter how hard I tried to find evidence to the contrary and regardless of those first, biased impressions—my future brother-in-law was a nice guy. It is funny to think of it now, of how childish my resentment was, though it is not difficult to explain. Shuja—a virtual stranger—had descended on my home and family like a tornado, whipping up change everywhere in his path. *My* sister was now *his* love-struck fiancée. *My* parents were now *his* adoring parents-in-law. He claimed them as his own. But he was nothing to me.

Nothing but an unwelcome interloper. The reason, I believed, that no one ever did get around to asking me about my trip to Pakistan. A couple of days after my return, I had tried to raise the subject of Belle with Mummy.

"Chh, Saira! I didn't go to the wedding precisely because I am not interested in *that* woman."

"Yeah—but how do you think I felt when I found out—from Razia Nani?! That Nana was alive for all those years—that he'd left Nanima for someone else?"

Mummy had been silent, scrubbing the pot she was washing with unnecessary vigor.

"I met her, you know. Belle. Don't you even want to know what she's like? And your sisters and brother?"

"Chh! What has any of that got to do with you, Saira? Nothing! Nothing to do with you—now go on and—and—polish the silver in the dining room. Last time Shuja was here, I saw how tarnished it has become—I was so embarrassed! What will Shuja think of us?!" The conversation had been over before it even began.

I had also tried to ask my dad about his father, about the fact that he had lost two wives before marrying Dadi. This was awkward. Speaking to Daddy was always a special occasion in itself. He felt it, too, and looked at me for a long, quiet moment before asking, "Why do you ask?"

"Mohsin told me about it. And that you had a sister who died before you were born. And a brother who died during Partition."

My father had said nothing.

"Is it true, Daddy?"

"It is."

"Do you remember your brother? Dawood Chacha, right?"

He had shrugged. "Not really. I remember feeling sad—seeing my father cry, which I had never seen before." Daddy had shrugged again, dismissing the subject in a way that made me feel the futility of ever bringing it up again.

The past and what I had learned of it seemed irrelevant to both of my parents. Only the present mattered. Our house became the set of a sitcom and Ameena was the star. All Mummy could talk about was Ameena. Ameena and Shuja. Their engagement was Mummy's personal triumph, the confirmation of the worldview she had so carefully tried to cultivate. Ameena, only eighteen, was engaged to be married to her very own Prince Charming—the just reward for being such a good, obedient daughter.

"What about college?!" I had asked, some days after polishing the silver. "I thought Ameena was supposed to start college this fall?"

"Yes? What about it?" My mother had been amused by the outraged tone of my question. "She will go to college as she had planned to do."

"But—if she gets married in two years, she won't finish, she'll be moving to San Francisco—doesn't that matter?"

"Of course it matters. She'll transfer—and continue her studies after she is married. We've discussed all of that with Shuja. Really, Saira, I don't know why you are so worried. Shuja is a good boy. Should we pass up a good proposal so that Ameena can finish college first? Why? That makes no sense. There is no choice here that Ameena is being forced to make. She can have both things—a good husband and an education."

I knew what I was worried about. That "we" that Mummy had uttered. *Should* we *pass up a good proposal . . . ?* We. I didn't say anything more about it. But it was a sour proposition to have to contemplate—that there would be any such "we" in my future. That my marriage—that any part of my adult life—would be determined by "we." I thought of Big Nanima, living alone in her little house. That's what I wanted for myself. Space. Freedom.

Something Ameena seemed only too happy to relinquish—despite all of my efforts to convince her otherwise. I told her about Big Nanima, about how she had gone to England to study.

But Ameena had only clicked her tongue in sympathy for Big Nanima—*poor, lonely Big Nanima*—who had never been blessed with the good fortune that Ameena was embracing with gratitude. "It's wonderful—the way she's made the best of her life. But—it's not like she had a choice, is it? I mean—no one would choose to be alone. To not have a family, to not be a mother."

"I would!"

"That's what you say now, Saira. You'll change your mind. You'll see."

I tried to tell her about Nanima, too. I thought that if she knew the details of that particular fairy tale, the truth about our grandparents' marriage, about how it ended, she might become aware of the risks involved in trying to live out her own.

"I already know about Nanima."

"You know? About Nana?"

"That he left her? Of course I know."

It was not the answer I had expected. "How—who told you? Mummy?" Jealousy reared up like bile in my throat.

"No. I've never discussed it with her. I don't think she likes to talk about Nana. Nanima told me."

"Nanima told you?"

"She told me—last time I saw her in Karachi—that he left

her. For another woman. An Englishwoman. How did you know about it?"

"I met her—the woman that Nana fell in love with."

"*Fell in love with?* That sounds—that's not the way I would put it."

"No?"

"No. That makes it sound like—like he couldn't help himself. Like he had no choice."

"Maybe he didn't."

Ameena frowned, as what I had told her seemed to register. "You—met her? When—how could you have met her?"

"In Pakistan. At Zehra's wedding."

"What?! Why didn't you tell me? How could she—who invited *her?*"

"Her daughter—Nana's daughter—is Zehra's best friend. They were all invited."

"*Nana's daughter?* He had a daughter with that woman?"

"Two daughters. And a son."

"I—but—I don't believe you! How could you not have told me all this?"

I didn't know how to answer her question. But I tried anyway. "Since I came back from Pakistan, from Zehra's wedding—the only time I ever spend with you is when Shuja's around. You—you're always so busy—mooning around all the time, sighing over *him,* planning out his next visit. And with Mummy. Making shopping lists for your trip to Pakistan." I sounded pathetic, whiny. Mummy and Ameena were going to Pakistan at Christmas, to shop for more jewelry and more clothes than they had collected already.

"A trousseau fit for a fairy-tale princess," my mother had declared her goal to be. "It will be the same for you, Saira. When your time comes. Lovely clothes and jewelry. A loving husband. And a lovely life ahead of you." It was her way of softening the blow—I wasn't invited to go with them on that trip. "We are going to be there for a whole month—you're only off from school for two weeks, Saira. Hardly worth it. Besides, you were just there. Don't pout, Saira. Your lips droop enough as it is."

"Aw! Poor Saira!" Ameena was laughing at me.

My back stiffened, rejecting her sympathy for me the way I had already rejected her pity for Big Nanima. "So, I guess Nanima didn't tell you everything, did she?" I crowed, eager to fill in the gaps of her knowledge.

"I guess not. She never told me that Nana had a whole other family. What was she like? The 'other woman'?" The quotation marks hovered in the air.

I wrinkled my nose a little, still oddly reluctant to admit the truth of what I had seen. "She was—charming. That's the perfect word. Everyone was kind of pissed off about Belle being there, at first."

"Belle? That's her name?"

I nodded. "But then she charmed everyone."

"You talked to her?"

"She talked to me. Told me I look just like Nana." A thought occurred to me then. "Do you think that's why Nanima didn't like me?"

"Nanima liked you! She loved you!"

"Not the way she loved you."

Ameena didn't say anything to this. "What were the kids like?"

"Nice, I guess. I didn't really interact with them. Zehra and

Tara—that's the oldest daughter—are very close." I paused, re-membering Razia Nani's fingers. "The second oldest is Adam. And the third one is Ruksana. She's younger than me."

Ameena shook her head, muttering, "That just blows me away." I saw the realization dawn on her face as she said, "They're the reason Mummy didn't go to the wedding?"

"Mmm-hmm."

"They're her sisters. And her brother."

We lapsed into silence.

Then, "Saira?"

"Hmm?"

"You don't like him."

It wasn't a question. And the use of the pronoun didn't ob-scure her reference. But when she said it—just like that, as a mat-ter of fact—I knew it wasn't true. But I wasn't ready to admit that yet, maintaining a silence that I knew to be stubborn.

"He makes me happy, Saira."

My throat suddenly filled. I had to wait for a few moments before saying, "I'm glad. I'm glad you're happy, Ameena. I—it's not that—he—he's a nice guy. It's just that—everything is dif-ferent. You—you're going to be married."

Ameena nodded, managing to contain her happiness—for my sake, I realized—so that her face remained sober. Sober, with sparkling eyes. The expression that cameras would capture, later, at her wedding.

"Shuja had an idea, Saira. He noticed—who couldn't?—that all you talk about is Big Nanima—how she went away to col-lege. I'm guessing that you want to be able to do the same?"

I nodded slowly, warily.

"You know Mummy will never let you go."

"It's not fair—it's what I want more than anything—"

"I know. You have a few years, still, to convince her. So—Shuja and I thought—we could work on her, too. After we're married. You should think about applying to schools in the Bay Area. You'll be far away enough to not be *able* to live at home. And close enough to us so that it might make it easier for Mummy. To let you go."

My eyes widened at the thought. "You think—you think she'd let me—yes, of course, if *Shuja* said so—" I trailed off on a note of renewed resentment.

"It was his idea, Saira. He understands how you feel."

"I—I'm sorry. It's not that I don't like him, you know. Not really. He's impossible not to like. That's one of the things about him that irritates me so much."

"One of the things? You have a list?" Ameena was laughing. She suddenly seemed so—mature. So grown up.

"Ameena? Are you sure?"

Her smile faded. She took my hands in hers. "Yes, Saira. I'm absolutely sure."

"But—how can you be? So sure?"

Ameena shrugged. "I don't know. It's—I just am. That's all."

We were both quiet for a long moment.

Then, I pulled my hands away from hers, tucked them behind my head, and asked, "What does it feel like? To be kissed?" I laughed to see my sister blush. She didn't answer me. But I found out for myself a few months later.

NINE

∿

WHEN I STARTED high school in the fall, a month after Ameena's official engagement, I became a disgustingly dedicated student. Big Nanima's story had done that for me, given me a focus for achievement that I may have lacked before. The way I saw it, high school was a stepping stone leading to where I was determined to go, where Ameena had given me reason to hope I could go. To college. Away from home.

I decided I would be the ideal college applicant. Taking the exhortations of our school guidance counselor very seriously when he told us to demonstrate leadership and well-roundedness beyond the classroom, I signed up for every extracurricular activity I could. I was in the Spanish Club, the Young Scientists' Club, and the Speech Club. I was on the school newspaper, the yearbook, and the literary magazine, too.

Just after the winter break, when Mummy and Ameena were still in Pakistan, the drama teacher announced that tryouts would be held for the spring production of *Grease*. As a lowly freshman, I had no hopes of getting in the play. But I tried out anyway, for the role of one of the Pink Ladies. Wary of what my parents would say, I hoped to get the role of Jan—Jan of "brusha-brusha-brusha" fame, whose sexless, side-role status would, I hoped, be cute enough to overcome the objections Mummy would raise to the idea of me performing on stage with boys. I ignored the little voice in my head—the Mummy-impersonator—that said, *What about the dance scene? Even Jan has to dance with a boy!*

A week before Mummy and Ameena came back, Mr. Jenkins, our drama teacher, posted the audition results on the door of the school auditorium. I was one of the last of those to elbow my way forward to see them. I stood and stared at the list of cast members for a long time, unable to believe what I saw. My name was up there, next to the name of the character I was slated to play. Rizzo. Rizzo the anti-virgin. Rizzo of "false alarm" fame. Who had to swing her hips—no, her pelvis!—around in the Sandra Dee number. In her underwear. Who went around with not one, but two guys. Two guys!

I don't know how long I stood there, rooted to that place. Eventually, I turned, hearing congratulations from other students, all older than me. I saw Mr. Jenkins standing in the hallway, surrounded by excited students who were asking about scripts and rehearsal schedules. I waited until they'd dispersed, before approaching him, dragging one foot in front of the other for what felt like an interminable distance.

"Mr. Jenkins?"

"Saira. Congratulations!"

"Uh—thanks. I—I wasn't really trying out for the part of Rizzo."

"I know. But you've got it!" He hadn't noticed yet that he was much more excited than I.

"But—I—"

I saw Mr. Jenkins's eyes narrow. "You know what an honor it is? For a freshman to get such a major part?"

I think I tried to say something but could only produce a strange sound from somewhere deep in my throat. I nodded emphatically to compensate, to let him know that I understood.

"You nervous?"

"I'm—terrified!"

He laughed. "That's not how you came across at the tryouts. Don't worry. You'll do fine."

I nodded again. And backed away from him, unable to say what I knew I should. That there was no way I could play Rizzo. That I wouldn't live long enough to do it anyway, if my mother found out.

I went home. And fretted. Sometime in the night, as I stared up at the ceiling of my room, tracing the crags and crevices that were cast by the shadows of my bedside lamp, it hit me. What Mr. Jenkins had tried to convey. This wasn't a bad thing. It was something to be proud of. But there was no way I could find to convince my mother of this. I thought about not telling her at all, but discarded the idea pretty quickly—there was no way I could *not* tell my mother I was involved in the play. Because between now and spring, I would have to stay after school, even beyond the hour or two for which she had grudgingly granted permission to accommodate my extracurricular fervor.

"Why?" she had asked. "Why do you have to join all of these clubs, Saira? One club, two clubs I can understand. But you have to stick your nose into everything that's going on in school? I don't like it. I don't like you spending so much time there, away from home. Ameena didn't join all of these clubs. She was a good student also."

But telling Mummy that I was *in* the play wasn't possible either. Because then she would ask what role I was playing and what that role called for. So, I decided, I would tell her that I was the stage manager, that I had to be there for all of the rehearsals. She had never had reason to doubt my word before.

A week later, when she and Ameena came back from Pakistan, she accepted my story with only a sigh and a grumble—and signed the blank permission slip distractedly, without question. She had other things on her mind. Ameena and Shuja had asked permission to be married in the summer, a year ahead of schedule. There was a wedding to plan—"a million things to do!" My deception was easy to carry out.

I stayed after school until five o'clock every day for two and a half months. I learned my lines. Got over those first few days of paralyzing shyness. Mastered the Sandra Dee number. And worked on my solo. I kissed Kenickie—only stage kisses, true. But kisses all the same. And danced with the Scorpion. Every day for two and a half months.

A whole new world opened up for me. We in the cast were a kind of family. We'd pass each other in the hallways, we who had been strangers before, and smile, wave, hug. We were a federation of very divergent states—a microcosmic cross section of the often contentious population of our school. There were jocks among us, and cheerleaders. Band geeks and science freaks. There were people like me, people who were too lowly, too anonymous, to even be noticed by those who were more easily typecast into the clearly defined factions that formed the makeup of our daily lives in high school. We were all the objects of Mr. Jenkins's perverse sense of humor—pawns that he cast against type, turning shy, repressed, insecure teenagers into flamboyant sluts on the stage. Nerds were cast as icons of cool while a famous pothead became a jock. All of us were given the opportunity to walk in each other's moccasins in a play that provided the perfect context for such role-reversals. *Grease,* with all of its stylized reinforcement of classic American stereotypes that still held true at the end of the eighties, became a deep metaphor for life for all of us.

I loved playing Rizzo. I loved her rebellious nature, loved that she was the smartest character in the whole play. Someone who knew and understood the social order of Rydell High better than anyone else—all of its rules, which she flouted in the pursuit of happiness. She suffered the consequences, but it was a price she was willing to pay. She was nobody's victim. I borrowed Rizzo's cynical view of the world and made it a part of who I would become.

Those days of preparation, practice, rehearsals—those were the high points of my life so far. Any fears I may have had about these two worlds colliding—the world at home, Mummy's world, with the world at school, which was my own—were completely submerged in a heightened kind of awareness of myself as something more than what I had been before.

But they did collide. As I suppose I knew they would. In the process, I hurt my mother by my deceit. At a level that I think she never quite recovered from.

Mummy asked, a few weeks into rehearsals, about coming to see the play.

"You don't have to come, Mummy. I'm just the stage manager."

"But you've been working so hard, Saira. We want to see it, too. To see the stage and the costumes you have been working on."

I had paused, not wanting to protest too much. "I'll get you tickets."

She smiled, satisfied.

A few weeks before the play, at the dinner table, on an evening when Shuja was in town, she asked again, "Did you get the tickets for your school play? Because Shuja and Ameena said they would like to come, too. I hope it's not too late?"

Again, I had paused. Just for a second, before slapping my hand on my forehead. "I totally forgot to even get *your* tickets! Oh, no! I—I think they're all sold out. I'm sorry."

The second had been long enough. I had seen the glimmer of a suspicion born in my mother's eyes. But it was gone, aborted, before its first breath could be drawn and I was witness, for the first time, to the power of parental denial. Curiosity stifled out of fear. "Sold out? Oh, Saira! We all wanted to see it."

"I'm sorry. Next time."

She was looking down at her plate, forming her next bite, and didn't look up as she said, "Yes. Next time."

I looked away from her, guiltily, to find Ameena watching me, her eyes squinting. She opened her mouth to say something and then closed it again.

I wasn't surprised when Ameena pursued the subject again later that night. She'd been out of high school for less than a year, after all, and knew that tickets for school plays were usually still available at the door. She came to the doorway of my room a little while after Shuja left, stood with her hands on her hips for a moment, and then entered, closing the door carefully behind her before asking what she had refrained from asking in front of Shuja and my parents: "Saira—why did you lie to Mummy?"

Having anticipated this conversation since dinner, I had already decided to come clean with Ameena—to throw myself at her mercy. "I had to. I—I'm in the play, Ameena."

She blinked. "In the—*in* the play?!"

I covered my face with my hands and spilled it all out, the whole story. How I had tried out for the part of Jan, how Mr. Jenkins had cast me as Rizzo. I looked up at her as I revealed this, the most shocking part, and saw her mouth fall open and stay that way for the rest of my explanation.

All the way until I asked, a little desperately, "Are you going to tell, Ameena? Are you going to tell Mummy?"

"I—I don't know what to say, Saira. I can't believe it—you— you know she's going to kill you!"

I buried my face again. "I know! I know! But I can't drop out now. There's only two weeks left before the show! I can't drop out—I—the whole school would—I would die, Ameena!"

"Either way, Saira, you're dead!"

"Ameena—you know I *can't* drop out. You *know* I can't."

Ameena's silence gave me hope.

"You won't tell, will you? You can't! Please, Ameena! I—I promise—no more plays! Just let me get through this one. I promise."

"I—Saira—it's not just about staying out of trouble! How *could* you?! You—Rizzo, Saira? *Rizzo!* She's—she's a slut! The whole play—*Grease*—the whole story—it's—so inappropriate! What is Mr. Jenkins thinking, anyway?"

I forgot all about my own dilemma and the need to be contrite and hollered out, in defense of Mr. Jenkins and in defense of the play, "What?! What's wrong with the play? It's a great play!" as if I had been personally attacked.

"A great play?! It's horrible! Cheap and immoral! And degrading! To women!"

"Huh?"

"Yes! The main character—Sandy. She's a nice, sweet, innocent girl who has to go and dress like a slut to please the man she loves. And somehow that's supposed to be liberating."

"That's not what the story is about!" I was thinking of my part, of Rizzo. And I felt my hackles rise.

"Yes it is! What it boils down to, anyway."

"But—you can't! You can't boil it down like that. I mean, there's so much more to it. It—it's about Adolescence! And Innocence!" I could hear my own capitalization. "It's about America and Individualism—and the Struggle against Authority—and Freedom, to be your own Person!"

Ameena laughed scornfully. "So—Sandy becoming a slut in the end—like those other girls—that's about being her own person? Pleasing her boyfriend? Becoming what *he* wants her to be?"

"But—but—"

"That's the scariest part about what you've done, Saira! You've lied to Mummy. You're playing the part of—*Rizzo*! And—you don't even understand what you've done! Mummy— if she knew—she'd be right to be furious! That play goes against everything she's ever tried to teach you, everything she wants you to be! Where's your sense of—decorum? Of shame? You— don't you care about what's right and wrong? Or is it all about having a good time? That's what that play is about! Having a good time! Who cares about what you give up—about honor and principles!"

"Ameena! It's a play! Just a play!"

Ameena's mouth was open, ready to respond, when the door-knob to my room jiggled. We both knew it was Mummy, coming to investigate what all the commotion was about. I shot a plead-ing look at Ameena, muttering, "Please, Ameena. Please!" just as Mummy made her entrance.

"What are you two arguing about? The shouting! The screaming! Is this any way for two young ladies—one of them engaged to be married!—to carry on?!"

My eyes were still fixed on Ameena, desperation dripping down my face.

She gave me a long, serious look before answering Mummy, "We were just discussing the school play." I closed my eyes and braced myself. "I think it's a stupid play. And Saira thinks—*Saira* thinks it's a good one!" I opened my eyes to see if what I heard could be believed. Ameena was—was she? She wasn't. She was not going to tell Mummy. I nearly fainted in relief as Ameena changed the subject to ask Mummy a question about what des-sert she had decided on for the wedding. They both turned and left the room, Ameena shooting me a hard, disapproving look as she did. But she didn't bring up the subject again. And I thought I was safe from Mummy's wrath.

A stupid thought to hold, as it turned out. But I have to admit, selfishly, that I was relieved at the timing of when Mummy finally found out the truth—on the last day of our four performances, when it was already too late for her to stop me.

She told me later how she came to know. At the grocery store, from a neighbor who had seen the show the night before. Mrs. Garner raved about my performance. Telling Mummy that my solo, "There Are Worse Things I Could Do," was better than the one in the movie.

I was on stage when I saw my parents in the audience, during the last scene, out of the corner of my eye. I froze for a second and then stumbled instead of skipped with Kenickie down the stage as we all ramma-lamma-lammaed our way around in apparently random choreography for the big finish.

When the curtain came down, after we made our bows and huddled together backstage for our final embrace, Joe, aka Kenickie, asked me what had happened.

"Are you okay? Your legs, like, buckled under. I had to drag you through the rest of the number. What happened? Stage fright finally get you?"

No, it wasn't stage fright. This was our last night of four performances and the words hadn't even crossed my mind. "I don't know what happened. Weird, huh?"

He was shaking his head, laughing, still high from the whistling, wooing, and standing applause that our audience of parents had lauded us with. Our audience of parents, my parents among them.

I don't know what Mummy had told Daddy about Mrs. Garner's revelations, have no idea how she felt when one of the ushers must have handed her the program, sponsored by DeWolfe's Garden Shop, with my name near the top of the right-hand column of the cast list. They had both seen *Grease* on television and knew what the play was about. Had enjoyed it from afar, as something removed from their lives and their daughters'—a strange and exotic view of American life that had nothing to do with their understanding of what adolescence should be about, a waiting game until real life began with a bang, with a wedding, when love and sex and responsibility would be woven together, tightly, in a contract designed to avoid paths that led to immorality and shame, heartbreak and despair. None of which they wanted me to be touched by.

I had seen other parents attending the play on the previous three nights of the performance, beaming up at their children, proud to see them on the stage taking on personalities that were familiar to them and amusing. Not foreign and terrifying, as mine must have been for Mummy and Daddy.

I hid backstage for as long as I could. But when I came out to face them, I found my parents had already gone home. Straightening my shoulders in a completely false pose of courage, I climbed the ladder of my own shamelessness to new heights, going to the cast party that was scheduled for that night, enjoying myself, laughing with the family that was about to break up, instead of going home to face the wrath of my real family waiting—in a state of anger I didn't even want to imagine—at home.

Stephanie Reardon—who played Sandy and lived up the street from us—dropped me home that night, as she had every evening during rehearsals. I said good-bye to her cheerfully, masking the knot in my stomach as I had masked all of my turmoil about being in the play from my fellow cast members.

When I let myself in the house, I found my father in the living room. He was alone, sitting on his recliner, hand on the remote, watching television. Whenever we watched television together, that hand hovered on the clicker, ready to switch channels in case a love scene happened upon the screen. His reflexes had slowed as Ameena and I grew older, not quick enough for my mother, who would yelp out a warning anytime anything suggestive came on, something she no longer objected to our seeing alone but considered inappropriate for a father to watch in front of his daughters.

When he saw me, he clicked the television off and tucked the footrest of his recliner back under the seat. He looked at me for a long and silent moment. And then said, "Your mother has gone to bed."

I didn't know what to say. I was relieved, even as I acknowledged my relief as temporary. I was not afraid of my father. Because he was a man of few words, his reprimands were not long-winded like my mother's. I knew I had merely to listen for a few minutes before he would move on.

"Your mother is very upset."

"I know."

"You lied to her." Maybe realizing that he should include himself in what I had done, he added, "You lied to both of us," though, technically, I had not. Because my father had always had so little to say to us, to Ameena and to me, I rarely had anything to say to him either. So I had not lied to him. Because I had not told him about the play to begin with, knowing that what news of my life and of Ameena's my mother thought he should know, she relayed to him, keeping him updated on a need-to-know basis only.

"I'm sorry, Daddy."

"Why did you lie? Why did you hide that you were in the play?"

"Because I knew Mummy wouldn't let me do it. I didn't want that part. Not in the beginning. I just wanted to be in the play. But Mr. Jenkins cast me as Rizzo. He thought I could do it. He thought I'd be good. It was a big part, Daddy. But I knew you and Mummy wouldn't approve."

"So you lied."

I nodded.

He nodded back. "That is not an excuse to lie. Just to get what you want. That's one of the worst reasons a person lies."

"I know, Daddy. I'm sorry. I really am."

"You were good."

I looked up, now, from the properly contrite posture I had assumed, eyes on my shoes.

"But you should not have lied. That was wrong. And you will not try out for any more plays."

I nodded. I felt like I was getting off easy.

But he went on. "I told you that you could have Ameena's car when she is married. I have changed my mind."

It was the least of what I had expected. I ran through the last few months in my head. The experience of being in the play, of being liberated as Rizzo. And it was a price I would have paid again if I had to.

So, the punishment had been doled out, but the confrontation with my mother was still ahead.

But my father wasn't done. "This happens, Saira. Your values and our values—they won't always be the same. But that is not an excuse to lie to us. And as long as you live under our roof, you are obligated to follow our rules, to live by our values, not yours."

I stayed quiet for a few moments more, absorbing his message. Then I braced myself. "Is Mummy really asleep?"

"She went to bed." My father sighed. "But I don't think she's asleep. I don't think she'll be able to sleep tonight. You can go to her if you like. I'll be up for a little while longer. Watching TV."

"Where's Ameena?"

"She's gone to a wedding with Shuja and Nilofer Auntie's family." My father glanced at his watch. "They should be dropping her off soon."

My parents' bedroom was dark. I had to squint to find the outline of a lump on my mother's side of the bed. An angry, stiff lump that had its back to me.

I whispered, "Mummy?"

No answer. But, as my eyes adjusted to the lack of light, I saw a balled fist flex a little. Not the relaxed, limp hand of someone asleep.

"Mummy? Can we talk?"

Still no answer.

I entered the room fully now. Walked over to her side of the bed and stood looking down at her. I saw something flicker in the area where I guessed her face was. The whites of her eyes.

"Mummy, please. I'm sorry. I'm really very sorry."

I knelt down on the floor beside her bed, put my arm around her shoulders. She pushed me away. And sat up, taking a deep breath as she reached for the lamp beside her, turning it on. As the light clicked on, so did her face. Out of her mouth came a stream of hot words that must have been burning up the inside of her mouth while she had held them in.

Some of them were familiar words, uttered with a vehemence and bitterness that were new. Others, which I'd never heard from her before, were hurtful. "Get out of my sight, you shameless, shameless creature! You slut! Whore! Dancing around on stage, half-naked! *Randi!* Slut! This is what I have raised, oh, God forgive me! What did I do, what did I do to deserve this humiliation, oh, God, it must have been something terrible to deserve this! Kissing boys—in front of the whole world! Slut, whore! In front of the whole town! Where will I show my face, *Ya Allah*, she has left me with no face to show to anyone!" It went on like this for quite a long time, my mother alternating between utterances of recrimination spat against me while her hands slapped at my shoulders, and appeals to God, which she would raise her face to offer to the ceiling with hands raised.

If I was thinking at all, it was that if I sat there and took it quietly, for long enough, she would run out of anger to hurl in my direction, she would spend her way back to some kind of normal, sane demeanor in front of which I could beg for forgiveness. But her screams just got louder.

And then, abruptly, she was silent. She had heard, through her screaming, what I had not. A car door slamming, the opening of the front door. We both listened to the sound of voices that rose up from downstairs. Shuja's and Ameena's. Shuja greeting my father, asking after Mummy and me. Saying good night. The front door opening and shutting again. The car in the driveway pulling away. After which, Mummy resumed her raging as if she hadn't stopped.

Ameena came in the room. She approached the bed and pulled me out of Mummy's striking range. "Mummy, shhh. Mummy— please stop. I—I'm sorry, Mummy."

"Why are *you* sorry? Sorry to have a slut for a sister? Who brings shame down on all of us?"

"Shhh, Mummy. Stop. I—I'm sorry because I didn't tell you."

Mummy was struck dumb, fully retreating back into the cushion of her pillows. Then she said, softly, "You knew? *You* knew? About the play? That Saira—that Saira was in the play? You *knew* and you didn't stop her?"

I spoke up, to defend Ameena. "By the time she knew, it was too late."

"You be quiet, you shameless creature!" Mummy shouted at me again, holding her hand up against me and my shamelessness. She turned back to Ameena, deadly calm again. "You let her do this? How could you, Ameena? How could *you*?" Mummy put her hands up to her face and sobbed into them, muffling her words. "What have I done to deserve these daughters?"

"I'm sorry, Mummy." Ameena was crying. "I should have stopped her. But it was too late. She—she was in the play. She couldn't drop out of it. I—I should have stopped her. I know that. But I didn't."

Mummy sobbed and sobbed.

Until, finally, my father came in the room and ushered me and Ameena out of it, saying, soothingly, to all of us, "*Bas, bas, bas.* Enough. Go to your room, Ameena. Saira. We'll all talk it over in the morning. Leave your mother, now, with me. She's too upset. Go. Shabana, *bas, bas, bas.* Stop it now, Shabana. You'll make yourself sick. Stop it, *jaan, bas.*" He was stroking her back when I left, holding her head to his shoulder, calming her down, finally, having removed the offensive sight of me and Ameena.

Ameena tackled Mummy the next morning. She tried to explain. What it meant to be in the play. That it was considered an honor. That she had been caught between telling her what I was doing and understanding the need for me to fulfill the commitment I had made to Mr. Jenkins. My mother shook her head, not understanding what Ameena was trying to explain.

Shuja came over again that night. When he asked me about the play, about how the show had been, I looked up at my mother, meeting her eyes for the first time that day, before saying, "It was okay." After he left, all seemed well between Ameena and Mummy.

Not so between Mummy and myself. We tramped around the house in mutual evasion for the next few days.

Until a week later, when Mummy came to my room.

I put the book I was reading down and watched warily as she entered.

She sat down on the edge of my bed. "I'm ready to talk now, Saira. About what you did."

It was the sign of sanity I had hoped for on that first evening, when my mother had turned into someone else, someone I didn't know. Which is how she must have felt seeing me on that stage. "I'm sorry, Mummy."

"What are you sorry for, Saira?"

I had thought about that and decided the truth was called for. Though I wasn't sure she would be able to handle the truth. "I'm sorry about lying to you, Mummy." But I didn't say I was sorry about being in the play.

She took my hand. "That is what I am most hurt about. That you deceived me. That you lied. I don't think you've ever done that before. Have you, Saira?"

"No, Mummy."

"It's the worst thing you could have done. If you had told me the truth—"

I interrupted her, "If I had told you the truth, you wouldn't have let me be in the play."

She shook her head. "That's not true. I wouldn't have stopped you from being in the play. But there were other parts you could have taken. Instead of doing what you did. I wouldn't have liked it, that's true. To have you dancing around on a stage. With boys. But the role you played, pretending you had had sex with so many boys, thinking you might be pregnant, making fun of good girls, and dancing around in your underwear"—she was getting agitated again, her voice getting shriller—"how could you, Saira? How could you behave like that? In front of every-one? Weren't you ashamed?"

"It was a play, Mummy. I was acting. Everyone knows that."

"You kissed a boy, Saira. Your father is the only man I've ever kissed. Shuja and Ameena have not kissed yet." I had to resist the urge to snort. "And will not until they are married. You're only fourteen years old and you've kissed a boy. On a stage, in front of the whole world. If people hear about this, if *our* people hear—who will marry you, Saira? A girl who kisses strangers? And who will believe that you don't have boyfriends, that you're a good girl? I'm not sure if I believe it myself anymore. Not when I saw you on that stage, behaving so shamelessly. If you are such a good actress, how do I know you are not acting with me?"

"I'm not, Mummy. That was a play. That wasn't real."

"But how do I know what is real, Saira? How can I ever trust you now? You've lied to me, betrayed me. How do I know now, ever, if you are telling me the truth or telling me another lie?"

A battle began inside of me about what to say next. About this question of truth and lies, which I had known would be asked of me, for which I had an answer ready. The answer I gave her, finally, to try and make her understand: "You lied to me."

"What?! When have I ever lied to you?"

"About Nana. You told us he was dead. But he wasn't. He was alive, all the way up to the week before Nanima died. He was alive and you told us he was dead."

"You think that's the same thing?"

I knew it wasn't. "No. I didn't say it's the same. But it was a lie."

My mother closed her eyes, shook her head in disbelief.

I pressed on, "You never even asked me about it—about meeting Belle. About how I felt when I found out. And when I tried to tell you, you wouldn't listen."

"I didn't ask you—I didn't listen—because I didn't want to know. I still don't. I refuse to discuss that with you." Her actions matched her words. She stood up and walked out of the room.

We never discussed the play again, the whole argument absorbed into the urgent preparations for the wedding that was soon to take place.

TEN

ο◡ο

ALL OF MUMMY'S family came to celebrate Ameena's wedding, except Big Nanima, who was busy working on the production of a television drama, an adaptation of Dickens's *David Copperfield*, which she had written. Madness pervaded our home as the family reunion that was supposed to have taken place the year before at Zehra's wedding (and which didn't, because of Mummy—who did not invite controversial "foreign guests" to *her* daughter's wedding) took place here, in our home in America, where there were no servants to order around, no drivers to hustle people back and forth to sightsee and shop, and plenty of guests who were accustomed to both. I remember feeling invaded and under siege. Saris were burnt on the ironing board by people who had never had occasion to iron, teacups piled up every few seconds on tables and counters and in sinks, bathrooms had to be scoured out every half-hour (by me, most of the time). The washer and dryer were in perpetual use. And once, someone—trying to be helpful—ran the dishwasher using regular dish soap, causing a flood of foam in the kitchen.

The wedding itself was cultural schizophrenia. The house was crammed full of aunties and uncles and cousins, an Indo-Pakistani oasis of exotica, overflowing with music, spicy foods, loud laughter, and the late-night hum of conversation, which intrigued the neighbors, who peeked out of windows surreptitiously as they nosily bore witness to the bustle that our home could not contain. They must have wondered at the four mini-vans parked in front of the house, rented to provide transportation for the nuptial militia that is required to get a *desi* wedding off the ground. I felt like a member of the Addams family and made Ameena laugh at my metaphor, snapping my fingers to punctuate the "ba-da-da-dum" I sang whenever we saw the neighbors' curtains rustle. Most of them, our neighbors, were invited and delighted to attend, looking stiff and foreign at the backyard *mehndi* and, later, at the hotel reception—their suits and dresses drab next to the flaming colors of the saris, *ghara-ra*s, *shalwar kameeze*s, and *sherwani*s that my relatives upstaged them with. They stayed close together, the white people, Ameena's friends among them, along with my father's colleagues and friends of Shuja's, like a group of wide-eyed tourists, amazed at the strangeness of the natives, a little afraid of getting lost, as if they really were in a foreign land.

Ahmed Chacha and Nasreen Chachi came, too, the last to arrive, just one day before the first of three wedding functions. Mohsin and Mehnaz were with them. Mohsin was more or less the same, the purple hair having been replaced with green, peace sign still dangling from his ear, camera in hand. My mother's lips pursed at the sight of him, something that tickled the slightly wicked sense of humor that I was developing as I waded deeper into adolescence. Mehnaz, however, made Mummy smile and cluck with approval.

I could see why, once I managed to recognize the stranger who stood beside Mohsin. She was modestly dressed, devoid of makeup, her hair styled conservatively in a sleek bob. She offered demure *salaam*s to my mother and father, a cheerful hug to me and Ameena. I studied her closely, barely able to keep my mouth from hanging open, looking and listening for some sign of a barbed tongue tucked into a cheek, a pointed arch of a brow, a curl of a lip, anything to indicate an act at my parents' expense, or hers, failing to find any. My eyes met Mohsin's, flashing a question at him, which he answered with a slow, mocking smile.

Mehnaz kept it up the whole drive home, all of us squashed in one of the four infamous minivans. She spoke sweetly, in perfect Queen's English, all of her *h*s intact. Mohsin studied the scenery earnestly while his sister gushed with Ameena over the wedding plans, asking eagerly about color schemes, henna patterns, and wedding songs. Ameena and Mummy were both happy to launch into descriptions of what had been their whole and sole focus for months. Nasreen Chachi fell asleep in the car. Daddy and his brother discussed the weather and the stock market. After a long battle with traffic, we dropped this other branch of the Qader family off at a hotel near our home—something Mummy shamefully lamented but that couldn't be avoided, given the crammed, no-vacancy state of our own house by now. So I didn't get a chance to ask Mohsin about how Mehnaz had been transformed into a Stepford wife-in-waiting.

Nor would I, for the next few days. Not until Ameena's wedding reception, by which time I had yet seen no sign of return of the old Mehnaz. I saw Mohsin sneak out of the reception hall, onto the adjacent terrace, just as dinner was being served, and guessed the reason. I followed him and found him lighting up. Alone.

"Mehnaz doesn't smoke anymore?"

Mohsin shook his head.

"What about her boyfriend?"

"She dumped him."

I took a moment to digest this. "What's happened to her? Did your dad put her on tranquilizers?"

Mohsin shrugged his lips—a totally failed attempt to smile, which made me feel oddly worried. I watched him take a drag on his cigarette.

"Mohsin?"

He shrugged his shoulders this time, as he exhaled a stream of smoke and said, "Mehnaz and I—we've always had this weird, competitive thing between us. Since we were little. Which one of us learned to read faster, to ride a bike, swim. We'd see who could eat more ice cream. And how fast. Who got better marks at school. It was—it wasn't something we ever talked about. Then, later, it was which one of us could be more rebellious. Which one of us could piss our father off more."

"She was winning, big-time, when I last saw you."

"Yeah. Well. She's given up, hasn't she?"

"Given up?"

"Thrown in the towel. Decided to go straight. And narrow."

"Oh. Why?"

"Because she knows she can't win."

"She can't win?" This was heading somewhere I wasn't sure I wanted to go. I thought of Mehnaz, about her boyfriend. I briefly entertained the hope that Mohsin's confession—for that was what I felt was coming—would be nothing more than just such an admission. He had a girlfriend. I looked up to find him watching me. And the look on his face made me abandon that hope. "What is it, Mohsin?"

He didn't say anything for a moment. When he did, he looked away and seemed to want to change the subject. "You remember Magda?"

I frowned and nodded warily.

"She's gone."

"Gone?"

"I haven't seen her in months. After that night—last summer—when you talked to her, I used to stop and ask how she was doing. She'd answer sometimes. Sometimes, she'd just mumble to herself. I gave her copies of the pictures I'd taken of her. She thanked me for them. And then—I haven't seen her since Christmas. I don't think she was well. I asked the people who work at the McDonald's—they didn't know who I was talking about. The people at the newsagent's next door—a *desi* family—they haven't seen her either. No one's seen her. I think she might be dead."

I didn't know what to say. I hadn't thought of the old homeless woman since I'd seen Mohsin in London.

"I had copies of those pictures of her framed. I've brought them to give to you. If you want them."

"Of course I want them."

He lapsed back into a heavy, awkward, frustrating silence.

It was my turn to shrug. I think I turned to leave, mumbling something about getting some food, when Mohsin stopped me with a hand on my shoulder.

"You really want to know?"

I turned back around. "If you have something to say, Mohsin, just say it."

His eyes were on the glowing tip of his cigarette, fast approaching the filter. As if addressing it, he said, "In England, we call these fags. I believe the word means something different here." His eyes moved to lock with mine. Then he threw the stub down. I watched him grind it under his shoe and heard him say, explicitly, what he had already implied: "Saira. I'm—queer."

"I figured you'd tell her eventually." Mehnaz had appeared out of nowhere, her beautiful *gharara* caressing the ground as she crossed to close the distance between us. "Though I don't think little Saira knows what you mean." She stopped to appraise my incredulous face, and added, without needing to, "He means he's gay. A fruitcake. Homosexual. A poof-ta."

I looked from her to her brother, unable to decipher the cryptic tension that flowed between them. Then I put it all together, what Mohsin had told me, and said, "Mohsin's gay. Okay. And that's why you've decided to be the perfect daughter?"

She laughed, acknowledging the point I had scored. "We can't both get ourselves disowned. Who would Mum and Dad leave all their lovely money to?"

I saw Mohsin laugh—out of the corner of my eye; I was having trouble meeting his gaze. I'm not sure what I felt. Confused, I suppose. Putting gay and Mohsin together in a sentence felt strange, somehow wrong, because the word was a derogatory epithet in the typical suburban high school that I attended. Even if the label was his choice, I felt uncomfortable about its association with someone I cared for and admired.

But I think I understood the honor implied in his confidence in me. "They—your parents don't know?"

"Mo's still alive, isn't he?" Here, finally, was the Mehnaz I knew.

I wanted to say something profoundly accepting to my cousin. But I had no idea what that should be. I was still trying to think something up when we were interrupted again.

"There you are!" My mother called from the glass door that connected the terrace to the reception hall, out of breath as she had been for days. "Come in, all of you. It's time for the *joothachupai*."

We followed Mummy back into the hall, and the rest of the wedding proceeded as normal. I took my place among a gaggle of giggling cousins, stealing one of Shuja's shoes. Mehnaz took the other. And Zehra—whose wedding had been the setting for an old family scandal come to life—took the lead in negotiating with Shuja and his friends over how much money he had to pay in order to receive his shoes back so that he could leave the hall respectably, with his bride on his arm.

Mohsin's quiet declaration—the seed of future scandal that would explode and reverberate over long-distance phone lines throughout the family when he would come out two years later—faded in the noise of music and laughter. It took me a day to formulate all of the questions I fired at him—the whats, whys, hows, and so on—of what his sexuality meant. The details that I needed to understand who he was and why that would make him an outcast later. Another outcast, like my grandfather, whom I was supposed to shun and would not.

Ameena's *ruksati*, the traditionally tearful good-bye that she bid us as she departed from the reception hall—with a significantly poorer, shoe-clad Shuja—signaled the end of the evening. Daddy's eyes were moist when he put his hand on Ameena's head in a clumsy farewell gesture that smooshed her hairdo. Mummy sobbed as she embraced Ameena, the daughter who had fulfilled all high hopes and expectations. I did, too, for that matter, the daughter who would not.

ELEVEN

 ❧

FOR THREE YEARS after Ameena was married, I was the only child. That was difficult. There was no one else for Mummy to focus on. And after what had happened with the play, she made a point of being vigilant, wanting to know where I was and what I was doing at every second of the day. Then, I got into Berkeley. And through the miraculous powers of influence that Ameena and Shuja wielded, I was allowed to go—despite the dire warnings and strongly worded resistance of my mother.

"She's difficult enough to control already! What will become of her with so much freedom? Drinking and dating and drugs, I warn you, Saira, if you do any of these things, I will never forgive you and neither will God! Keep yourself pure, Saira, and chaste, until we find you a good husband, like Shuja, who will love you and take care of you as well as he does of Ameena. O God, I implore You to send us a good boy for Saira, so that she is engaged and settled quickly and safely! Promise me, Saira, that you will remember who you are, remember what we expect of you. No drinking. No dating. No drugs."

Of course, I broke all of those promises. The rebellion began almost immediately.

Alcohol came first. Then pot. Dating. And then sex. Sex, not love. All of them—while pleasant enough, with some practice—turned out to be highly overrated.

The morning after the first night I had sex was bad. Shivering with chills, I felt sick and feverish, my stomach clenching and unclenching with each breath. The guy was still asleep, the smell of last night's beer and tequila heavy in the fetid air he exhaled. I felt cheap. And used. Like the wilted, dirty condom on the floor next to the bed. I knew love had nothing to do with what had happened in the tangle of sheets that he did not wash as often as he should.

By then, I was corresponding regularly with Mohsin, the only one who could understand the gravity of the choice I had made, a choice that meant the loss of a morning-after discussion with my mother—something I knew I would have been entitled to, because I eavesdropped for quite some bit on the one that took place between Ameena and my mother—the choice not to save my virginity for the sanctity of a wedding night.

But what had happened could not be undone. This choice was exclusive to others and I had made it with eyes and arms wide-open. Until now, the journey I had consciously diverted from the directions my mother had given me had been on a parallel route. Three right turns was all it would have taken to get me back on her one-way street. Now, I was going in a different direction—and Ameena's footprints had never marked these sands.

Mohsin offered me support without judgment, calling me

long-distance from some squalid location in Africa—where he was taking photographs of starving, balloon-bellied children—when I wrote to him about my exploits.

"Did you enjoy yourself?"

"It was okay."

"It'll be better next time."

And it was.

But the best thing about college really was what I was there for. The classes, the professors—some of the male ones I had intense crushes on, unlike the postadolescent boys I merely slept with. I attended my own classes and anyone else's that sounded good, read required books and others that Mohsin recommended. I was majoring in history, but had no idea what I would do after graduation. Except that it wouldn't be what my mother planned and prayed for.

After my first year away, I came home resigned to going backward in time under my parents' roof. Mummy moped around the house with me, obsessed with the idea of getting me married. I had reached the age when Ameena was married and that seemed to make Mummy a little desperate. I shudder, now, to think of how my mother, trying hard and failing to be subtle, got the word of my availability—accompanied, I learned later, by a full-size, glossy headshot—out on the proverbial "street" where *desi* families gathered and speculated, assessed and collated young people into the "happily ever after" that getting married was supposed to promise. A couple of inquiries had been made and I'd even been forced to meet a prospective marital candidate. I blew him off as best I could, but he proposed anyway. Mummy was ecstatic. Until she saw my reaction.

"Oh well. If you don't like him, then you don't like him.

Nothing to be done. But—he was handsome, Saira. You have to admit. An engineer! With a good income! Maybe if you met him again—no? Are you sure? Absolutely sure? Okay. I understand."

Two weeks into summer, Mummy suddenly decided that we should go to Pakistan. I had my suspicions about what her motives were—feeling uncomfortably like a worm on a hook, about to be cast.

"Is this going to be some kind of husband-hunt, Mummy?"

"No! Of course not."

I knew she was lying—but decided to go along so I could see Big Nanima. And Mohsin, who was back in London, conveniently en route.

Soon after we got to London, I was fuming. Mummy had tried to hide her motives for going to Pakistan from me. But not from anyone else.

"I don't understand why you're taking this trip in the first place, Shabana. Everyone knows that all of the Prince Charmings of India and Pakistan are in America anyway. Earning the status-symbol degrees that their fathers wish they could have earned, giving their mothers something to brag about to their friends at their tea parties and club dinners. Haven't you looked for a good boy there?" Ahmed Chacha was stirring the tea that Nasreen Chachi had just handed him as he addressed my mother, that old familiar smirk still there, swimming just under the surface charm of his voice.

"That's true, Ahmed Bhai, but the boys' mothers are all back home, aren't they? And the sons will be home, too, at this time of year," Mummy said to her brother-in-law.

"What a good girl you are, Saira! To go along with your

mother and father on a trip like this. You must be eager for marriage. Well, I'm sure you'll have no problem finding a good boy. Who could resist our little Saira? And the green card that comes with her, eh?" The smirk had surfaced. It glinted at me through his teeth.

I wasn't fourteen anymore and wanted him to know it. But I resisted the urge to reply with a snarl. The smile I flashed at him did involve the baring of teeth, however, as I tried to change the subject: "How is Mehnaz?"

Nasreen Chachi was standing near the tea trolley. She glanced at her watch before picking up a plate of samosas to offer around. "She called a few minutes before you all arrived. And will be here any minute. She and her husband. With the children. She was quite eager to see you." Mehnaz had married a parent-approved Pakistani a year after Ameena's wedding and had two children already.

I didn't ask about Mohsin, since I probably knew more about him than his parents did. He had been out of the closet, and out of the family, for two years. I looked up to see Ahmed Chacha watching me, brow furrowed, seeming to guess where my thoughts had wandered.

A heartbeat of awkward silence reigned until Nasreen Chachi said, smoothly, "And Ameena? How is she?"

"She and Shuja are well."

"No children?"

"No."

There was more awkward silence as we all waited for the bowl of *gulab jamun*—which had replaced the plate of samosas—to make the rounds.

Then Nasreen Chachi said, enthusiastically, as if she'd just remembered something important, "Shabana, you must look up my friend Hawa in Karachi. Her son is a lovely boy. Studying business at Harvard—or was it Yale? I can't remember."

I watched Mummy pull out the little black book in which she had begun to collect names and contact information for people who might help her on the hunt she was on. (It really was a little black book!) I fixed my eyes, over Ahmed Chacha's shoulder, on the old bar that stood in the corner of the living room and felt my tongue run longingly along the rim of my lips as I read the labels for expensive bottles of whiskey, cognac, and other stuff I would have killed to have a little of. I wasn't sure how I'd make it to Pakistan without doing bodily harm to my mother.

The doorbell rang, and in seconds we were knee-deep in the noisy antics of Mehnaz's two boys. The room bustled with activity, and clumsy attempts at conversation were now unnecessary.

Under cover of all of this commotion, Mehnaz leaned close to say, "You're here 'til the end of the week? Mohsin wants to see you. Can you meet him day after tomorrow at Hyde Park? Speakers' Corner? At noon?"

I looked around nervously and nodded, wondering what excuse I'd give to get away from my parents.

But my cousin had thought of that. In a cozy voice, loud enough to be heard above the howls of her children, Mehnaz said, "Shabana Chachi, I was just telling Saira that I'd love to take her shopping. Day after tomorrow." Mehnaz turned to me smoothly, pointedly, "Shall we meet at noon? At St. John's Wood Station?"

I nodded again and saw my mother do the same, happily absorbed in my uncle's grandchildren, patting their heads a little wistfully. Pestering Ameena to provide her with grandchildren had become a hobby.

A little while later, in the minicab that took us to the tube station, I couldn't help but wonder out loud why my father and his brother had so little to say to each other. "Daddy? You and your brother—you're not very alike, are you?"

My father shushed me, pointing with his head in the direction of the Sikh cab driver seated in front of us. I smiled to myself, thinking of Razia Nani and the awful time I had restraining the urge to shush her the last time I had been in London, on my way to Karachi—realizing for the first time where my own theory of diminished *desi* degrees of separation may have originated. When we got out of the cab at the station, I looked across the street at the place where Magda had sat. There was no one there now.

I turned back to my father and tried again, "You and Ahmed Chacha are very different, aren't you, Daddy?"

"What do you mean?"

"You don't seem to have much to talk about. Is it because you're only half brothers?"

"We never thought of ourselves as half brothers! We're brothers. *Bas.*"

"But, you're so different. You wouldn't have thrown Mohsin out in the cold if he were *your* son. Would you?"

Daddy shrugged.

Mummy said, "Really, Saira. Out in the cold. As if his grandfather hadn't left him a nice pot of money."

"Yeah, but he's still been kicked out of the family."

"It's true that your Ahmed Chacha has been very harsh—but it is not something that anyone could have expected him to accept easily."

I ignored Mummy and focused back on my father. "And

you don't seem to have anything to talk about. With Ahmed Chacha."

Daddy shrugged his shoulders. "We don't have much in common, I suppose."

"Ameena and I don't have much in common. But we still talk. We're still close."

"That's different, Saira. You're sisters. It's different with men," Mummy said with a smug tone, one I had noticed before, when she'd brag about how close she was to her sisters, despite the miles that separated them.

Our train pulled in and we boarded.

MY MOTHER'S SUPERIOR assertions were tested the next day, when I woke up to the sound of an argument taking place between her and her sister. It was still raging when I shuffled into Jamila Khala's kitchen after brushing my teeth hastily and washing the sleep out of my eyes.

"*Oof,* Shabana! Stubborn, stubborn, you've always been stubborn! He's been dead for so many years! Today of all days—enough is enough! I insist that you come with me!"

"I will not, Jamila!"

My father came into the kitchen, apparently oblivious to the sounds of shouting that I had woken to, placed an empty teacup in the sink, and said, "That was excellent tea, Jamila. You should teach your sister how to make tea the way that you do." When no one answered him, he looked up and around, took in the stony expressions on the faces of his wife and sister-in-law, the puzzled look on my face, and made a hasty retreat, mumbling something about what a good cricket game there was on television.

"Who are you trying to punish, Shabana? A dead man? You're only hurting yourself with this grudge you won't let go of. Everyone has made their peace. Lubna went to the *kabrastan* last time she came. Just go and say *Fateha* at his grave, Shabana. For your own sake. Let go of the past."

"I cannot. For Amee's sake, I cannot forget. You may have forgotten what he did to Amee—you and Lubna also, keeping up with that woman and her children, treating them like family—but I will not!"

"*Oof-ho!* You act as if it was you he abandoned! What he did to Amee—that had nothing to do with any of us, Shabana. You were not even there. You had gone to America already, begun your life with Nadeem. He didn't leave you. He left Amee."

"He left Amee and forgot all about me, Jamila. You don't know what it was like for me—alone in a new country, dying from homesickness, waiting for them to come and visit, when I heard what he'd done. How can you know what I felt? As if I had lost both of my parents. Especially later, when I became pregnant. You had Amee and Aba with you when you delivered Zehra. When I had Ameena, I had no one. No friends, no family. Just Nadeem and me in that hospital full of strangers. Ameena was two years old before I was able to go and visit Amee. In Pakistan. He threw Amee out of her home and I lost mine, also, because of it. Pakistan was never my home. But he left me no home to visit in India."

"Oh, Shabana. You never gave him a chance. He wrote to you so many times. You never answered his letters. He talked to me about it, was so hurt that you never wrote to him. He was human, Shabana. Only human. And that is why you are so angry with him. Because you thought of him as perfect—you worshipped him, Shabana! More than any of us ever did. That is why you have to come with me today, on his birthday. I only go to his grave twice a year. On his birthday and on his death anniversary. And I think that your being here, in London, in my house, today—it's like it was meant to be, Shabana. I will not take no for an answer."

"You have no choice. I am not coming." Mummy turned to me. "Go get ready, Saira. We'll go shopping while Jamila Khala is gone. I have to buy some chocolates for everyone in Karachi, a sweater for Big Nanima, and Lubna Khala wanted me to buy her some bras from Marks and Spencer. Ask your father if he wants to go with us."

Having measured the mood of his wife on his brief foray into the kitchen, my father had decided to make a day of it in front of the television and declined to come with us. I decided to brave the scowl on Mummy's face, to go with her, in the hope of hearing more about the subject that had—after so many years— finally ruptured open in my aunt's kitchen.

It turned out to be a strangely portentous decision on my part. If I hadn't gone with Mummy, she might have gone shopping alone or not at all. And then what happened, a reckoning of sorts, which Mummy had tried to duck out of, might not have taken place.

Mummy and I got on a bus to the West End. We sat down-stairs with a clear view of all of the passengers who got on and off at each stop during the long ride into the city. At one stop, a young woman got on the bus. She flashed her pass to the driver as she boarded and stopped short in the aisle when our eyes met.

"Saira?"

I had seen her already, without registering the vague sense

of familiarity that had tickled my mind. I knew who she was as soon as she said my name.

"Ruksana?"

She had to move over, leaning in closer to Mummy, who sat in the aisle seat, to let another passenger pass. I was farther away, by the window.

Five years had passed since I'd last seen her. But I knew who she was. Mummy's youngest sister. The one who looked most like the father they shared.

"Oh my God! How long has it been? What are you doing here? Is this—your mother?"

I looked at Mummy, wondering, for a second, if she knew who stood beside her. The pursed lips, the pinched eyes gave me my answer. I didn't know what to do.

Ruksana had answered her own question: "Shabana? Oh my God! Can you imagine? What are the odds that we'd meet like this? Are you staying with Jamila?"

Mummy's lips tightened even more, hearing this stranger refer to her sister with such familiarity.

I stepped in, finally. "Yes. With Jamila Khala. How are you? And Tara and Adam? And—how are you all?"

"Very well. I—this is ridiculous—we can't talk here! Let's get off of this bus and go get some tea or something."

I looked at my mother, who sat, staring at Ruksana, still frozen.

Tentatively, I said, "Mummy?"

She didn't look at me, her eyes still on Ruksana. "You look like him."

Ruksana reached her hand down to take my mother's. Then she moved her hand to press the yellow stop request button, ringing the bell, saying, "I know just where we'll go—they have the best scones, freshly made. Very English." She was smiling when she took my mother's hand again, leading her off the bus when it stopped. I followed them, listening to Ruksana, who chatted on as we walked, "He would have been seventy-seven today. And this is the best birthday gift he could have asked for. I wish Tara were here, and Adam, too. She's in Paris, with her husband and kids. And Adam's off in Greece. On holiday. Here we are." We had reached a quaint little tea shop, which Ruksana led us into. She ushered us over to a table by the window and sat us down, both Mummy and I pliant in her managing wake. "I was just on my way home from college. I live there, at college, but I wanted to be with Mum. So that she wouldn't be alone today." A young woman came to take our order. "Right. We'll have—is tea all right for everyone?" I nodded. Ruksana glanced at Mummy, took in the blank expression still on her face, and turned back to the server. "We'll have a pot of tea for all of us to share. And some scones, please. And can I have a few extra for takeaway? Thanks." Ruksana turned and looked at me as the server walked back to the counter. "I still can't believe it! To just bump into you like that on the bus!" She turned to my mother, taking her hand again. I saw my mother flinch just a little, not enough for Ruksana to notice. "I can't tell you how thrilled I am to finally be able to meet you. And today of all days—like it was meant to be! Now, I finally get to see the sister who was Aba's favorite daughter."

Still tongue-tied, Mummy shook her head slightly.

"Yes, you were! Mum always said so and Aba never denied it. Do you know that all of our bedtime stories, the ones that Aba would tell us when he tucked us in at night, they were all about you and Jamila and Lubna? He told us about the little kitten that you rescued, do you remember it? Mothi was its name, wasn't it? And the time that your cousin Masood bought a little chick but was too scared of it to hold it. Aba said you were the one who ended up taking care of it. And then Masood finally screwed up the courage to hold it one day and it jumped out of his hands and a crow swooped down and caught it and devoured it all up in just a few minutes. Aba said you cried and cried, Shabana. And we all cried, too, just hearing about how upset you were.

"Oh—Tara is going to be so jealous! That I'm the one who met you first. She's the one who's good at keeping up with everyone—asking about you and Saira and Ameena from Jamila. She's been back to Pakistan twice more since that trip when you were there, Saira. Did you know she's married to a Pakistani? Like Lubna. It was quite a dramatic thing—the way they had to fight his family. They're very conservative and didn't like that Tara is half-English. But she won them over in the end. And now she's become quite a good Muslim—she reads the Quran—I don't think any of us ever picked up a Quran the whole time we were growing up—and fasts in Ramadan and prays five times a day and everything. She's more religious than her husband is!" Ruksana laughed and I had to laugh, too, without really finding anything that she said to be funny.

She talked on and Mummy and I sat, both of us forming separate impressions of the plump, vivacious young woman who sat across from us at the small table now laden with a pot of tea, cups and saucers, and a plate piled high with scones. Her skin was darker than Mummy's, a shade of gold that set her apart from the other white, English patrons in the tea shop, but which still did not look *desi*. Her eyes and short, straight hair were only slightly lighter than the dark, dark brown of ours. She was wearing a camel-colored skirt that ended just above the knee, sensible-looking shoes and stockings, and a ruffled blouse topped with a blazer that matched her skirt, all combined to create an effect that was a little older than I knew her age to be and yet very attractive all the same.

I realized that Mummy and I had both said nothing since we'd first seen her on the bus and that one of us had better start talking so that Ruksana wouldn't start to doubt our social abilities—something she obviously had no problem with.

"Um—so, Tara's in Paris? On vacation?"

"No—she lives there. Has lived there for the last three years. The kids speak better French than they do English. They speak Urdu, too. Better than I do." The corners of Ruksana's lips turned down wryly in an expression that was disconcertingly similar to one I had seen on my mother's face.

"And Adam? What does he do?"

"He works with a public relations firm here in London. Political consulting mostly. I think he's assigned to Labor nowadays, but it's a fickle business and I know he's done work for the Tories, too—Mum doesn't approve." Finally, Ruksana stopped to take a breath, a sip of tea. As she did, her eyes moved back and forth between Mummy's face and mine before settling on me, finally. "Mum was right. Last time we saw each other, we were both kids, weren't we? She said we looked alike. But I didn't see it then. Now I do. I don't think anyone could doubt that we're related—aunt and niece."

I laughed now, not just to keep her company this time. "I don't think anyone would guess that. You're younger than me!"

"Only by a couple of years, yeah?"

I turned to look at my mother, to check if she was all right, without being too conspicuous about my concern. Her eyes were a little less pinched at the corners, her lips relaxed a bit as they opened delicately to take a sip of her tea.

Ruksana had turned to her, too. "You don't favor Aba at all, do you? You must look like your mum. You certainly are beautiful. And Aba was always talking about how beautiful your mother was."

Mummy nearly choked on the sip. "He—talked about my mother?"

"Oh, yeah. How could he not? He talked about *all* of you—he had to talk about your mum, too, didn't he?"

"How do you remember all of this? You must have been just a child when he died." I shrank a little at the accusatory note in my mother's voice.

But Ruksana, still cheerful, didn't seem to notice. "I was ten. And I remember everything I've told you about. But there's more to know, I'm sure, that you could hear if you talked to Tara and Adam. And my mother."

Mummy had nothing to say to this. We all sat around the table in silence, watching each other. I wondered what was going through Ruksana's head—whether this was all as lovely and nice for her as she was making it out to be. But there was nothing insincere about her that I could trace—and I was trying hard to look for some kind of inconsistency.

"Shabana?" Ruksana had my mother's full attention already, but she said Mummy's name in a tone so sweet and tentative that I felt my mother brace herself beside me for what would follow. "I know that my mother would love to meet you. It was—she's always regretted that you and Aba were—estranged. She's been so happy to be able to meet the rest of the family. Jamila, of course, we were in touch with even when Aba was alive. But Lubna, too, after he died. I know that you'll probably say no, but she would kill me if I didn't ask. Would you come with me? To my mother's house? To see her and talk? I was just a kid when Aba died, you're right—and I'm sure I only remember half of what *she* could tell you. About how much he missed you."

I remembered Belle then, the sincere warmth with which she had spoken to me, a sulky fourteen-year-old whose resentment, I realized suddenly, might have been more obvious than I'd imagined. And then it struck me—that Ruksana's warm effervescence may not have been as artless as it appeared to be, that no matter how much she may resemble her father, her nature came from her mother. She was charming and affectionate and had known just what to say to pique my mother's curiosity, to ease some of the anger she must have known her to be feeling.

After a long, thoughtful pause, Mummy shook her head and said, "No, Ruksana. Not yet. I'm—uh—glad that I've met you. But—I'm not ready for anything more. Next time."

Ruksana lit up at those last two words. "When will that be? Are you on your way to Pakistan?" I nodded for Mummy. "Then you'll be stopping here on your way back again?"

I waited for Mummy to answer, then rushed in to fill the gap of silence that lasted for just one second too long: "We'll be back in three weeks."

"Then, please, Shabana." Ruksana was pulling a little pad out of her purse. She scribbled a few numbers on it. "Take our numbers." She was pointing them out. "That's mine at college. That's Mum's. And that's Adam's. And, of course, Jamila has them all if you lose this. Please call us. We'll even get Tara to come over from Paris, if you could possibly give us some notice. Please think it over, Shabana. You won't regret it. I promise."

When we'd all finished our tea, after an awkward good-bye—even more awkward than the one from the day before, at Ahmed Chacha's, because there, at least, we had a script to follow, which provided a routine and rhythm that was familiar, if vacuous—we walked away from Ruksana. But not before she gave each of us a quick peck on the cheek and a tight hug. I felt myself stiffen slightly during the embrace, and forced myself to relax, an effort my mother did not even try to make.

We were on the bus, back on our way to the West End, when my mother asked, finally, "What is she like? Ruksana's mother? Is she very beautiful?"

I thought about her question as the bus lurched forward. We were upstairs now, out of sight of the passengers that got on and off at each stop. "Not beautiful, no. But attractive and very charming. A nice lady who you couldn't help but like. Like Ruksana."

"No. Ruksana is like my father." The last words sounded strange—the first time I'd ever heard her lay claim to the man she had hardly ever spoken of. "He was the most charming man you could imagine. Everyone loved him." Mummy was sitting by the window this time, and as she spoke, she turned her head to look out below at the shops that passed before our eyes, the tiny cars crowding the streets, hugging the left side of the street in a way that disoriented me so that I found myself leaning to the right.

"Will you call them on the way back?"

"No. I will not."

The only thing I could think of to say was what my aunt had said already. "He was human. He made a mistake."

"A mistake!"

"You never forgave him. Fine. But what about Ruksana? And Tara and Adam? What have *they* ever done? Why can't you accept them? Your sisters and your brother?"

"To accept them is to accept what he did. Some things are unforgivable, Saira—in my book and in God's. Remember that." Mummy had turned away from the window to look at me with eyes that were intense and alive with emotion. "Ameena is all right. She has such a good husband to take care of her. But you—you don't understand how worried I am for you, Saira. Promise me that you will keep an open mind. I will not rest until I know you are settled. With a good husband, like Shuja."

"Mummy. I don't want to get married."

"That's what everyone says. Before they meet the right man. You'll change your mind. You'll see."

I shrugged. "What if I don't?"

"You will."

"What if I want to do something else with my life?"

"What? What do you want to do?"

"I don't know yet. But—marriage isn't everything. Look at Big Nanima—"

"Big Nanima?! You think she wouldn't have traded everything for a husband and a family?"

"I don't think she would."

"Hmmph."

THE NEXT DAY, I snuck out early to meet up with Mohsin. Another pilgrimage to Speakers' Corner. I sat alone for a long time, the way I had wanted to five years ago. When Mohsin came, I stood up to give him a hug. His hair was short and neat, lacking any of the colors of the rainbow.

"You look different. All grown up. Good."

"You don't look so bad yourself." He pointed to the bench where I had been sitting, indicating that I should sit back down. "Don't be cross, Saira."

"Cross?"

"About what I'm going to tell you." He had a magazine in his hand.

"Are some of your pictures in there?"

"Yup. My pictures of Magda."

"That's wonderful, Mohsin!" He had been making a modest name for himself, getting published in fund-raising brochures mostly, for human rights organizations, hunger campaigns, and homeless shelters. "Why would I be mad?"

"Because I submitted the photographs with your piece."

"My piece? *Magda?*" I had written a few incoherent pages, pure speculation on the life and death of the old woman based on what I remembered of her, the photographs that Mohsin had taken, and all of the questions I had wished I had asked.

"I should have asked you, I know. But I loved it. And I met the publisher of this magazine and we got to talking. I told him about what you'd written, about the pictures I'd taken years ago. He published it."

"But—it wasn't—there was nothing in it. Just a bunch of what-ifs. And imaginary answers she might have given."

"They published it. With an introduction to explain that the pictures were of a real woman. Deceased."

It hit me then. "They published it?! In this?" I had already grabbed the magazine out of his hand, was rustling through it to find it—my name, under the title. Published! "I—I don't know what to say."

"You're not angry?"

"I—no! I'm thrilled."

He smiled. "I thought you might be." He stopped talking, giving me a chance to reread the story I'd written and sent him several months before. Then I bombarded him with questions. About the magazine, about him and what he'd been doing.

The last questions in my interrogation were about his family. "So you're really cut off? No contact. Except with Mehnaz, of course."

"Yeah. Mehnaz. I call my mum occasionally. Just to let her know I'm all right."

"But your dad—?"

"He said not to call him until I stopped being queer." I waited for him to laugh before I did.

"And—you're happy?"

"Never more. Work is great. But—I think it'll get even better in a couple of years. You still studying history?"

"Yes."

"Do you know what you want to be when you grow up yet?"

Bitterly, I said, "I know what I don't want to be."

"That's a start. You can't do your bachelor's in journalism at Berkeley, can you?"

"No. J-school is grad school only."

"Saira. I have an idea for you to think about. It came to me after you sent me that story. I'm a photographer—but not the artsy kind. I try to tell stories with my pictures. And—there are details behind those pictures that need to be told. I've worked with a few journalists already. And—I think you have what it takes to do the same. To write. Be a journalist. I thought, when you're done with school—that's in, what? Two, three years?"

"Yeah?"

"If you're interested, we could work together. Go out there and do it. Bear witness. I'll keep trying to make the contacts. And when you're done with your studies—you come join me."

"Oh, Mohsin! That—that would be fantastic!"

"I hoped you'd think so."

"I do! I do!"

"Your parents might not like it."

"No. They won't."

TWELVE

A FTER LONDON, EVERY moment with my parents on that
trip was hell. On the plane, on the way to Karachi, my mother bombarded me with tales of marital bliss and fulfillment as
part of a campaign which she rather pathetically imagined might
make me more receptive to the many mothers and sons I was
beginning to suspect she had lined up for us to meet. She alter-
nated these stories with expressions of hope and faith that I had
trouble digesting.

"In the end, Saira, it will not be about how you plan your life
or how I plan it. It is *kismat* that will determine the outcome. And
I tell you, believe me or not, I have a feeling that you are going
to meet your *kismat* very soon. Mother's intuition and faith tell
me this—because I have prayed so hard for you to meet the man
of your dreams, the man who will convince you that marriage is
what you want, I know we will find him very soon. Or he will find
us." We. Us.

The first thing I did when we arrived in Karachi was to visit

Big Nanima, who had moved into the flat she had kept for her retirement. She looked terribly old and frail, so much that I was afraid of hurting her as I held her to me, resisting the urge to squeeze her tightly, overcome, suddenly, by how much I had missed her. She asked about my studies, delving into the details of the curriculum of my classes like no one else had. She was disappointed by some of the things I had not read, recommending texts and literature I had never heard of, and delighted by others, writing down titles with which she was not familiar. She was retired from teaching at the college, but was still translating and adapting English literature for Pakistani television.

"Not that anyone watches our own Urdu dramas any longer. We have no culture of our own left—all everyone does is rent videos of Indian movies and American television shows. The young people here—I'm talking about the well-off children— are all hypnotized by what they think life is like everywhere else.

"No one is bothered by the fact that fewer and fewer of our children have food, shelter, education! I have spent my life in education—thinking that access to it would gradually broaden to include everyone. Hah! Instead, those with means only think about how to grab more for themselves and they do it without a second thought for all of the rest of our people—as if they are blind to their misery. We are not a country anymore—just a hellhole where tyranny and greed prevail. And all of those promises that have been broken—democracy, the constitution—how many times can such things be trampled in the mud before they become just forgotten words written on paper, which no one here even knows how to read, let alone implement? How much will our people suffer before they find something to fill the void of those promises? I don't know how it can ever be made right. Frankly, I'm too old and tired to even worry about it. Listen to me! Rambling on and on about things that don't concern you. Oh! It is so good to see you, *beti*! Tell me, how is Ameena? Is she happy?"

"Very. Shuja's a good guy. That's all that matters—in Mummy's view of the world."

Big Nanima tilted her head. "It is no small thing. To have a good husband."

I thought of what Mummy and Ameena had said about Big Nanima. "Would you—would you have given everything up—all of your accomplishments, your life—to have had a husband and a family?"

"Oh, my! What a big question you have begun with." Big Nanima was quiet for a moment, her hand on her cheek, giving my question serious thought. "I can't say there haven't been moments—long ago—when I wouldn't have done what you say. But—with the whole spectrum of my life behind me, I don't think I have any regrets."

I nodded happily.

Big Nanima moved her hand from her cheek to mine. "You liked my answer, eh?"

"Very much." I took hold of her hand for a long moment. And then remembered to say, "Mummy and Daddy said to give their *salaam*s. They'll be here in an hour, to pick me up, and they said they'll come in to visit then. But I couldn't wait that long."

"Bless you! I have been beside myself with excitement at the thought of seeing you—who knows when I'll see you next, whether I will ever see you again in this life? You see, don't you, how old I am getting? Too old! I should have been gone years ago. Every day I pray to God to take me soon, with my dignity still intact."

"Lubna Khala was complaining. That she wants you to move in with her and you keep refusing."

"Lubna is a dear, dear child. But as long as I have a choice, as long as I am able, I will cling to these walls. I am happy—she comes to visit every week and she sends the children to see me, too." She laughed. "I know they come because she tells them to. Even the new daughter-in-law. What do you think of your cousin's bride?"

"She's very pretty. And young." A year younger than me and married already.

"And completely cowered over by Lubna." Big Nanima shook her head as she laughed. "You would think, after what your *khala* went through with *her* mother-in-law, that she might have a more sympathetic hand over the poor girl. But none of us ever learn."

I agreed, having already noted how much Lubna Khala's household resembled the way things used to be when she was a younger woman, not yet the mistress of her own household—not while her mother-in-law lived and maintained control. Even Mummy had wondered over "why on Earth" her sister had chosen to get her son married and settled under her own roof.

"And—you're well, Big Nanima?"

"Oh yes. I am very well and very busy, *Mashallah*. Working on a new drama—an adaptation of *Wuthering Heights*. And I am in touch with many of my old students, too. Every week one of them stops by to see me. Some of them are doctors, lawyers, writers. Some of them visit when they come home from England or America, where they have settled, like your parents. It is wonderful to see them, even if it reminds me of how time has passed—to see those young girls all grown. Some of them are even grandmothers! Imagine!"

"Ameena sent this for you with her love." I handed her the box of handkerchiefs that Ameena had given me to pass on to our great-aunt.

"Oh, that naughty girl! Taking time to think of me! You tell her I love them. It's been too long since I have seen her—last when she and your mother came just before she was married. I want to see her before I die—tell her to forget about that old fan incident. That I love her as well as I love you." One of Big Nanima's wrinkled eyelids flashed shut in a slow but clear wink. "And what about you, Saira? You've told me about your studies. Do you know what you will do when you are finished?"

"I didn't. Until very recently. I want to write. To be a journalist."

"A journalist? Not fiction?"

I shook my head. "Maybe later. I want to show you something." I pulled out the copy of the magazine that Mohsin had given me, opened it, and handed it to her. Without saying anything, she read the story and studied the pictures with all the solemnity I had expected of her. When she was done, she looked at me for such a long moment and with such profound silence that I squirmed and said, apologetically, "It's really just a bunch of words to accompany the photographs that my cousin Mohsin took."

"Certainly—but the pictures themselves wouldn't have meant half as much without your words. I am very impressed, Saira. Your cousin Mohsin? Ahmed's son?"

I nodded.

"Ah. You are close?"

"Yes." Big Nanima's eyebrows lifted. "No, no, Big Nanima. Nothing like that. He—uh—he doesn't like girls."

"Yes. I'd heard."

I nodded toward the magazine she still held. "I haven't shown that to my parents."

"No? You think they won't approve?"

I shrugged.

"And are you happy with all of your mother's plans?"

"Her plans?"

"To find *you* a good husband."

"What did she do? Put out an ad in *Dawn*?"

"It's a big family, Saira. A huge network, which relays news from around the world, almost every continent. She's taken advantage of that network—to advertise your availability."

"So I've gathered. It's humiliating, Big Nanima."

"She wants you to be happy and well-settled."

"I want to be happy, too. But I can't do this."

"I thought as much." Big Nanima sighed and said, "Your mother is worried—you have so many choices, so many options. Those are choices she cannot relate to and it is always difficult to see those we love choose differently than we have chosen, to live differently and be different. Difficult from both sides. I suspect that your cousin Mohsin knows something of this—that you do as well, even if your mother doesn't realize this."

My eyes widened.

"I'm not asking for any confessions, Saira. But it is natural. You are a young woman from a different time and place. You have to decide what you want for your life. But don't be too quick to throw away all of the old to embrace the new. Make room for both, Saira. This old family network—it is with us when we are born, when we marry—as your mother is using it now—and when we die. It is not always a bad thing. Here people don't die alone in their apartments, unmissed and unnoticed for weeks, as I have heard happens in America. In our culture, you are defined by who you are to other people—someone's daughter, wife, mother, sister, aunt. I, who have *not* been all of those things, cling even more strongly to those I *have* had the fortune of being. With these bonds, there are expectations, yes. The price you pay. But there—where it seems people define themselves on their own terms, where there is no price to pay, no expectations that you are required to meet—there is also less chance of reward. Of being needed, wanted. Obligations. Duty. That is the price you pay. But you are paying for *something*. Something of value that it would be a shame to lose completely. I don't envy you, Saira. You have to decide exactly how many of these things you want to keep and bear the burden of. Don't alienate your mother. Your values might someday be closer to hers. All she wants is your happiness."

"Yeah. But she wants me to follow a script I can't follow, Big Nanima. You didn't follow that script."

"Not out of choice, Saira."

"But you've had a good life!"

"Never doubt it. But—what am I trying to say?" Big Nanima closed her eyes for a while. "I've had a good life. But the path I chose—whatever path anyone chooses—there will be times when life is not in our hands, Saira. At those times, we all need a—what did you call it? a script?—we all need a script to follow. If you have thrown the old script out completely, you will have to spend a lot of time writing a new script at that time—that would be a very difficult thing to do. Editing—that's something I can understand. But to reinvent the wheel? Why? What need is there of that? Marriage is only part of that script, Saira."

"Well, that's the only part I'm concerned with right now."

"Of course. But don't be too hasty about throwing the whole thing out, eh? Not without even knowing what the rest of it is about."

Big Nanima's words calmed me down enough so that I managed to muddle through all of the matchmaking efforts that Mummy subjected me to in the next few weeks. I watched them from afar, from a detached position in the room as part of the audience rather than a player in the performances that unfolded before me. So it was another Saira who talked to those mothers of eligible sons. Another Saira who sized up the guys themselves, most of them home for the summer from colleges they attended in Europe or America—*desi* versions of the college boys I knew and regarded less than highly. Two proposals came, carefully executed through respectable third parties. Two proposals from strangers whose faces I could not recall when their emissaries came to talk to my parents. I had to meet them before I said no—in my aunt's living room in a haze of awkward silence broken only by throat-clearing stammers from them and blank-faced stares from me. My mother railed against my indifference, but no stories of hers could change my mind.

In the last week of our stay in Karachi, Lubna Khala took us all out to lunch at Gymkhana, inviting Big Nanima, too. The lush, green grounds of the Gymkhana garden, where bow-tied bearers served the rich and privileged at tables set on the lawn, or in the open-walled pavilion that still housed heavy, dark, cane-backed chairs reminiscent of the days when this was a private club for the British, were a jarring contrast to the traffic and noise beyond the walls that contained them. Lubna Khala directed us to a square, clothed table near the steps of the pavilion. There were children there, shuttling back and forth between immaculately groomed, tastefully bejeweled mothers and shabbily dressed, gap-toothed *ayah*s that hovered at the perimeter and near the playground. The snippets of conversation that drifted from one end of the garden to the other were fascinating: talk of corruption and politics (apparently interchangeable terms), white money and black, export quotas, bridge, cricket, travel, and shopping hummed and hovered over us on our way to the table. Before we reached it, Mummy and Lubna Khala were stopped by an auntie they called Bunny, an old friend from Bombay, who greeted my mother with squeals and shrieks. My father was similarly waylaid by a childhood friend. Big Nanima and I seated ourselves and studied the menus that one of the waiters brought for us to peruse.

Having decided on our order—tomato soup, cheese toast, fish *pakora*s, chicken sandwiches, and tea—Big Nanima excused herself to use the washroom and I sat alone at the table to wait for everyone's return. I looked around to survey the familiar scene. Lubna Khala's treat at Gymkhana was something of a tradition on trips to Karachi. For her, it had always been a place to socialize away from home—a much-needed escape from her mother-in-law in years past. For us—Ameena and me—the large pool had been the attraction, a much-favored escape from the heat. As I'd gotten older, I had come to understand what it represented—an aristocratic refuge from the rabble, the status of membership there enhanced by the mystique of its past, when the only *desi*s allowed in were there to wait on tables and serve. There were other clubs like it in Karachi, some of higher status than others, but all of them with this foundation in common. They were the

residue of an empire that had not been replaced with much success, as Big Nanima regretfully lamented.

This is what I was thinking of when my eyes were drawn to
the center point in a group sitting and smoking inside the pavilion. There was a man there holding court, perched on the arm
of a chair, hands in motion, brow furrowed, issuing forth from a
face animated by a passion I was suddenly curious to find the reason for. He made his point and then fell silent, politely listening
to the response he had provoked. He shook his head and smiled,
turning his face to dismiss what his companion said. In the process, he caught me staring. His eyes held mine for too long a moment, forcing me to look away. Big Nanima returned. I stood to
help her be seated and chanced another look. He was on his way
over. Big Nanima saw the direction of my gaze and followed it.
The man waved and Big Nanima waved back, saying, while he
was en route, "Do you recognize him, Saira? He's Majid Khan. I
gave you his book to read last time you were here."

My interest, caught already, quickened. He was tall, with a
full, thick head of hair, lightly dusted at the temples with gray.
His smile was wide and brilliant, the creases at the corners of his
eyes evidence of heartfelt pleasure at the sight of my great-aunt.

"Adeeba Auntie! It's a pleasure to see you," said Majid
Khan—journalist, novelist, and winner of the Commonwealth
literature prize—taking Big Nanima's hand in order to bestow a
kiss upon it.

"Majid, my dear! How is your mother?"

"She's well."

He nodded at me politely as Big Nanima explained, "Majid's
mother was my student. One of my first. And best."

"And you, Auntie, according to my mother, are the reason

that I am a writer. It was her love of literature that gave rise to mine. You were the inspiration for her passion. My only misfortune was to have been born a boy, she says, making me ineligible to receive your teaching firsthand."

Big Nanima wagged her finger at him with a smile. "You are a writer! No doubt about it—twisting words to serve your purpose."

He grinned like a boy—an odd sight for a man whom I guessed to be not younger than forty.

"For how long are you here, *beta*?"

"A week only. I leave again on Monday, having learned—the hard way—that a long-term stay in Pakistan is not good for my health."

Big Nanima laughed appreciatively, a kind of laugh I had gotten used to, a head-shaking, joyless mirth that she issued forth when there was no alternative but to laugh. She turned to me to explain, "Last time Majid was here, he was stabbed. A direct result—we all know it is true—of his having done an exposé of the corruption of the Karachi police. They sent their *ghunda*s after him."

Majid Khan shrugged. "It's to be expected. Here—when you threaten someone's livelihood, they will make sure you know of their displeasure. And if there's one thing we excel at in Pakistan, it is the creation of *ghunda*s and terrorists."

"You will not come back to stay?"

"Not for the moment. The ground is unstable here—earthquakes, landslides, government coups—it all shifts beneath your feet too quickly for my taste."

"And where have you settled?"

"Settled? Nowhere, I'm afraid. I wander aimlessly, perpetually searching for a story to be told."

"Don't blame your restlessness on your profession, Majid," Big Nanima scolded. "A writer will always find a story—you need look no further than the tip of your nose and there will be something that needs to be said."

"Ah, yes—like the Austens and the Brontës, who made provincialism an art. But I insist on making the world my garden, Auntie, and that is a lot of ground to cover."

Majid Khan's eyes moved to embrace mine as Big Nanima said, "*Beta,* this is my sister's granddaughter, my great-niece, Saira Qader. She's visiting from America. And wants to be a writer. A journalist."

"A journalist? You'll have to leave America, won't you? There's not much left in the way of journalism there now, is there?"

I laughed.

Big Nanima said, "She's already been published. In a little magazine out of England."

"Have you?" His tone was a shade too polite to be categorized as bored.

"It was a very good piece." Big Nanima wouldn't let it go.

"If you say so, Auntie, then I have no doubt it was."

"I'm not sure Big Nanima's opinion qualifies as unbiased," I said, squirming a little at the thought of how many aunties must tell him daily about the talents of their writer nieces and nephews.

"Who published it?" Majid Khan asked me.

I told him the name of the magazine, wishing Big Nanima hadn't said anything.

One of Majid Khan's brows lifted. "But I know the editor of that sorry excuse for a magazine! A very good friend of mine. He insists on sending me a copy every month. What was your piece called?"

"'Magda.' It was a photographic piece. The writing was just a side thing."

"'Magda'?" He reached behind him to pull a chair up beside me and sat down. "I remember it. Very well, as it happens."

I felt myself flush—with pleasure, embarrassment, shock. "*You* read it?"

Big Nanima clapped. "You see, Saira? You want to be a writer—and you have been noticed by one the world has noticed."

"He didn't say he liked it, Big Nanima."

"Oh, but I did." Majid Khan managed to sound sincere.

Big Nanima clapped again.

Majid Khan was regarding me much as a scientist might regard a peculiar form of bacteria on a slide. "I'm not normally so impressed by young writers. Altogether too self-consciously clever, too pat, too neat. Creative nonfiction is particularly repulsive—blurring the line between fact and fiction in a world already unable to distinguish one from the other. Your piece, however—it was nothing but a list of questions and doubts. No attempt to provide any answers. A lament, really. You were painfully aware of your limitations—and played to them in a way that was rather interesting."

Big Nanima hooted with delight. "Ha! Forgive me, Majid, but I have known you too long to take you seriously on a soapbox. Don't be fooled by his stern manner, Saira. He has an image to maintain, after all. It was well disguised—the compliment he's offered you. But there, nonetheless."

Majid's nod was a concession to Big Nanima's crowing. "Keep

it up, Saira. Questions are all that matter. The answers don't belong to you. Too few journalists understand this in the rush to formulate a story."

He chatted with Big Nanima for a few more moments. Then— before Lubna Khala and my parents rejoined us—he left.

"That was—wow!" It was all I could say when he did. "I—I felt like a kindergartener holding up a crayon sketch of a house to Picasso."

"Nonsense! Picasso, indeed! You give *him* too much credit and yourself not enough."

THIRTEEN

❧

B EFORE I BEGIN," Majid Khan said, addressing an eager audience of Berkeley students during an extracurricular lecture that had been arranged to accommodate the undergraduates
among us, who did not have access to the man who was a guest
lecturer at the Graduate School of Journalism, "I have some questions for you. A journalist always begins with questions, no? And
because I believe there are some among you who aspire to be journalists," he paused to acknowledge the laughter and engagement
of those before him, "I hope and expect to be interrupted by *your*
questions as we move along. How many of you have heard of *Midnight's Children*?"

I looked around and saw that only a fraction of the audience
in the Dwinelle Hall auditorium raised their hands with mine.
"Okay. How many of you have heard of *The Satanic Verses*?"
More than half raised their hands. "And finally, how many have
heard of Salman Rushdie?" This time, every hand went up.

"That, my friends, is the difference between journalism and

fiction. Power. The power that transforms a relatively obscure—no matter how highly acclaimed—literary figure into worldwide headlines. The contents of Salman Rushdie's novels—his stories—will never, *never* have the impact that the story *about* Salman Rushdie had. There is a lot of posturing about this—about Rushdie's right to expression from one side, about the blasphemous nature of his work from another—but what he expressed was read neither by the vast majority of those who claimed his work to be insupportably offensive nor by those whom they, in turn, offended. *They*—those rioting hordes, those mullahs and fatwa-issuing ayatollahs—relied on the *news*. The same goes in the so-called Western world—so-called, because this kind of delineation, it seems to me, is a dangerous affectation that has nothing to do with the fact that we live in *one* world, all of us, with equal responsibility to care for it and equal opportunity to exploit and defile it. In the *so-called* Western world, few cared about Rushdie's novel per se. It was its effect that was the story, not its content. If that effect had not been reported on here, Salman Rushdie's book would have remained tucked away, however highly appreciated, in the literary niche where brilliant writing remains buried. Am I right? Can we agree on this? That there is more power in journalism than in fiction?" Majid Khan paused for a long moment.

My hand itched to be raised, my disbelieving eyes scanned the audience to find that no one else seemed to burn with the question that had formed in my mind. When I saw that I was alone, I raised my hand—slowly, tentatively. I had not come here expecting to expose myself to his scrutiny so soon.

"Ah—a question! Thank goodness—I was afraid that no one would challenge the premise I just constructed. Yes?"

"Umm—what you just said—isn't that only true in the short term? I mean—who remembers the news when they read a novel? The news at the time it was published? Does anyone know about the war that was taking place in the background of *Pride and Prejudice*? Even novels that seem to be grounded in the context of history can be read without much reference to the news of the day—like Tolstoy, for example. His stories stand alone—and most people who read them today have no idea what was going on in the newspapers at the time. Excepting what the authors chose to incorporate in the narrative of their characters."

"Ah, yes, the long view. You must be a history major."

I nodded as the audience laughed.

His attention was focused on me now, a specific face in a crowd. I saw his eyes narrow, his forehead crease. "I know you. 'Magda'? You wrote 'Magda'?"

I nodded again, resisting the urge to fan my face as the heat rose from chin to hairline.

"The long view," he said again, retracing his train of thought. "Who has time for that in journalism?" The audience laughed again, harder this time. "Your point is valid. But I won't back down from my premise. I began by asserting that the difference between journalism and fiction is power. It's true—what you said—that fiction lives a longer life. I will even argue that fiction is truer than journalism. But journalism is more powerful. And more dangerous. Because it is powerful, it is also attractive to power.

"Fiction is truer than journalism, you ask? But journalism is based on facts. Facts. What could be truer than facts? Well, facts are often disparate and contradictory. Their complexity eludes our understanding. How to assimilate them—these unruly, misshapen entities? Journalists are reporters. Reporters are supposed to report. The temptation to do more than report is irresistible, however—all for a good cause, of course. To clarify, explain, contextualize—to help people understand what we ourselves do not. So, journalists are in the habit of putting facts together so that they make sense, fitting them into the frame of a story. To construct something out of chaos. But when you build a story, you choose which blocks to use, which not to use. You decide how they are to be arranged, what shape they will take. Journalists become architects. And who can say what an architect is? A glorified engineer? An artist? A little of both? An artist?—you ask in surprise and disgust. But an artist must create. A journalist merely reports, you insist. I disagree. Journalists also create. Journalists—those among them who become architects—are the designers of buildings and neighborhoods, which their audience will inhabit and occupy. Mainstream media is like this—actively involved in the design of endless tracts of cookie-cutter homes, two-car garages, white-picket fences, and well-tended lawns surrounded by pretty bouquets of carefully arranged flower beds. There is no room for weeds there—contradictions and complexities that threaten the order of the pattern. But weeds grow anyway, and journalists in America, with very few and brave exceptions, work hard to avoid them and ignore them—at best. At worst, they help to point them out as ugly, unwanted growths worthy only of being destroyed. That is what journalism is today. Know this. Be under no illusions.

"The problem is that weeds have names, too. Any botanist will tell you what they are. There are facts to be learned about them—statistics, processes of survival, which are quite remarkable in their own right.

"What kind of building will you design? What will the neighborhood which you construct look like? Which facts will you use? And which will you ignore? If a fact falls in the forest, and no one hears it, will it make a sound? Oh, yes. Because there is *always* someone else in the forest. Those facts that we dismiss because they do not fit into the pattern of the stories we write, they cannot be eliminated, no matter how hard we try, no matter how much we may love the neighborhoods, the houses, the buildings we have constructed. The other facts—those blocks which have been discarded—are still there, bricks in the hands of other people in the forest, who do see them and hear them, whose lives they inform. Take care. Those bricks can become weapons.

"I am a journalist. Fully aware of my own limitations, aware that I will never be able to overcome them. I am as susceptible as anyone else to the business of construction. I am a product of my own specific culture, and in that culture I find justification for my point of view, already formed. Many of you may know what *shaheed* means. In the lexicon of most people—Muslims and non-Muslims alike—a *shaheed* is a martyr. Someone who dies for a cause—the cause of Islam. There it is—a word, ready to be used and which is used by those desperate enough, or crazy enough, or depraved enough, depending on your point of view, to need such a word. But the root word of *shaheed* is 'witness.' That is also the root meaning of the Greek word *martyr*. That is the kind of journalism I aspire to practice. Merely to bear witness. Not to make sense, not even to understand. Because when I try to do those things, I become an architect, the constructor of meaning and truth, a storyteller. When the need to ascribe meaning becomes overwhelming, I write a novel. That is the only time I allow myself to be concerned with telling a story. A work of fiction—the only context in which I am interested in the Truth. Capital T.

"In journalism, truth is too easily rendered irrelevant, subject to the design and construction of facts. In fiction, *facts* are irrelevant, subject to the storyteller's quest for truth. Truth is dangerous. The novel is the most subversive expression of truth there is. Because the greatest truths can be hidden in the fiction of a novel.

"In Shia Islam, there is a principle of self-preservation, called *taqiyya*. When the truth becomes hazardous to your health, you can lie. Go undercover. That is what fiction is—truth obscured, less susceptible to manipulation because it is hidden. My friend Salman is a brilliant writer. Hide-and-seek, he's not so good at. Because he chooses to hide his explosive truths in very dangerous places—too close to open flames where they ignite and divert attention from the message of his stories."

Again, the audience laughed. He was a good speaker, but I'd heard that already from friends in the journalism department who were taking his class. I paid close attention to the whole of his speech. But I ventured no more questions through it or after, when others raised their hands. I knew—because he had recognized me—that I would have the opportunity to ask more in a less public forum. When the lecture was done, I lingered in my seat. I didn't have to wait long. He approached as soon as the little crowd that had gathered around him—about the same size as the one I had first seen him in—dispersed.

"Adeeba Auntie's niece?" His hand was extended.

I took his and spared him the effort that the furrow of his brow indicated. "Saira Qader."

"Saira. Yes. Have you been writing?"

I hesitated, then said, "Um. Not really."

He nodded knowingly. "Nothing you want to share yet." He paused. "You didn't enroll in any of my classes."

"I couldn't. I'm an undergraduate. A senior."

"Ah." Our eyes were locked together, had been since he'd approached. "You didn't ask any questions—after that first one. I didn't scare you off?"

"No. I figured I'd ask more later."

One eyebrow lifted, a little too self-consciously, I thought, giving the appearance of cultivated surprise. "Coffee?"

I picked up my bag and led the way. We went to Au Coquelet, my favorite café in Berkeley because it was open late, had a restaurant in the back, and was the only one I knew of with a liquor license. It was also farther away from campus, making the journey there, on foot, a long one.

Majid Khan kept up a slow and steady conversation the whole way to the café, mostly downhill, along curving pathways that led through some of the prettiest parts of campus. I nodded and listened—less rapt than I had been at Dwinelle Hall. I worried about stupid things, I remember, like what to call this man. He was old enough, technically, to be my father—though he was younger than mine. (I knew this because I had looked it up.) Old enough to call uncle. But the title didn't fit—he was too youthful, and that was not how I saw him. He was a visiting lecturer at the School of Journalism, so I couldn't call him "professor," and, as far as I knew, he didn't have a PhD, so "doctor" was out.

We passed Krishna Copy Center on the way to the café, down University, past Shattuck, along with Viceroy Indian Restaurant, Long Life Veggie Chinese, Papa's Persian Cuisine, and McDonald's. At Au Coquelet, I hesitated before ordering, wanting desperately to know what he would order first. I turned backward and made a great show of looking at the fruit tarts, waving him forward when the server asked, for the second time, if we were ready. He laughed and ordered a carafe of red wine—the laughter fading quickly when the woman behind the counter asked to see my ID. I handed it over proudly, having passed that milestone and put away my fake one months earlier.

Majid Khan. I was sharing a carafe of wine with Majid Khan. He wanted, he said, to know all about me. He recalled, again, my story—even remembering the photographs that had accompanied it, asking who the photographer was. I told him about Mohsin, about his plans and mine. He was an excellent journalist, ferreting out information I didn't realize I possessed.

At the dinner hour, we were still there, at Au Coquelet. We ate something—pasta—and drank some more wine, achieving a steady and decorous level of intoxication that left our speech free of slur and our gait free of sway. As the evening progressed, we spoke less and less. His eyelids became heavy, closing like a hood over his eyes so that his thoughts were difficult to read—making me feel breathless and exhilarated at the same time. Silence reigned, now, but we remained where we were. Suddenly, it was closing time—1:30 AM—and we were forced to leave, forced to resume some semblance of conversation, though I don't remember what it was about. We headed uphill to the North Side—where I shared a house with close friends whose affection had survived the close quarters of dorm life in our first two years at Cal, and where he was renting an apartment for the duration of the semester he was spending at North Gate Hall.

My house came first. We stood outside in silence, having lapsed back out of the pretense of forced conversation. Then I said, "You asked about my writing."

By the light of the streetlamp, I saw him nod.

"I—I have some things—rough drafts, really. That I'd like you to read. If you would."

"Of course!"

"Will you come in?" I had turned already to unlock the door and ushered him inside. He waited in the living room while I went upstairs to find my stories.

He was on the couch when I returned, his long legs sprawled out in front of him. He held his hand out and I handed him a folder, which he opened.

"'Ballroom Dancing.' 'The English Teacher.'" He was reading the titles out loud. The third one made him pause. He looked at me as he said, "'Bearing Witness'?"

"What you talked about this evening. Funny coincidence, huh?"

"Coincidence? Happenstance? At my age—people become superstitious. They no longer believe in coincidence. They begin to believe in fate. In *kismat*." His eyes were running down the pages of my writing as he spoke, absentmindedly, making me feel naked and vulnerable in a way that I knew all writers would recognize.

I laughed nervously. "Do you? Believe in fate?"

"Absolutely not." He was replacing the papers in the folder. "My choices—good and bad ones—are my responsibility." He held up the folder. "Are they fiction?"

"No. Creative nonfiction, I guess. They—they're about people in my family. My two grandfathers. And my great-aunt—Adeeba Anwar."

He stood up suddenly, slapping the folder of stories shut, making his way to the door. We said good-bye there. And that was it. Except that it wasn't.

I knew already. I knew it was more than that—had designed it to be so by giving him the stories, which would be the excuse, if I needed one, to stay in touch.

I didn't need the excuse. We met again two days later—by chance—at Three C's Café. I was there first, with two of my roommates—a *desi*, Smita, American-born like me, and Lamiya, who was half-Arab and half-Iowan. He entered alone and took a seat without seeing me. Smita gave me a pointed look, the same kind we always gave to alert each other to the presence of another *desi*—a warning, I suppose, to not speak in the broken Hindi-Urdu that we occasionally used as code and that we would have to translate later for Lamiya's sake.

Under her breath, Smita said, "Gorgeous. Think he's a grad student?"

The restaurant was tiny and I was afraid he'd hear me, so I didn't explain—suddenly self-conscious because I hadn't told them about him already. That was when Majid Khan saw me. I felt his gaze catch, from the hyperconscious periphery of my vision. He rose and came to stand beside us.

"Saira."

I nodded, still not knowing what to call him. I introduced my friends to him and told them, "This is Majid Khan. He's lecturing at the J-School."

"Wow! Oh! Majid Khan!" That was Smita.

Lamiya, who was majoring in engineering, had no idea who he was.

After an awkward moment, I asked him to join us and was surprised when he did. I don't remember what they talked about, only that the conversation flowed between Majid Khan, Smita, and Lamiya, through the arrival and consumption of our blintzes and crêpes, and despite the conspicuous silence that I maintained and that Smita and Lamiya would tease me about, mercilessly, later. Smita stood first, showing us her watch by way of explanation. Lamiya joined her, on her way to the library, where I had planned to be with her, studying for midterms. But I stayed where I was. So did Majid Khan. I didn't watch them as they left. Neither did he.

"I read your stories."

I braced myself.

"You are a leech, Miss Saira. You have stolen the stories of your family and made them yours." He watched my face to gauge my response, but bracing myself had worked. I could feel the blankness of my own expression, consciously maintained as my mind struggled to understand what Majid Khan was saying. "That is what a writer does. You have listened, observed, researched, and reported. But you have also stepped out of line—an inevitable temptation, I suppose. One of the dangers of creative nonfiction. You are too presumptuous, putting words in the mouths and feelings in the hearts of people that you have no way of knowing are accurate. Yet, you have done it in a way that seems to honor them, with such sympathy that I can almost forgive your literary hubris."

I released the breath I had been holding and smiled. "Almost?"

"Go ahead—smile, laugh, you cheeky girl. From now on, you do all the talking. I refuse to give you any stories of *my* life to steal and make your own."

"But what's wrong with that? Putting yourself in the place of the people you're writing about, so you can write from their perspective?"

"What's wrong with it? Where will it end? You can't *feel* your way through facts. If you do, every last pretense at objectivity is gone. You made your grandfather a hero—"

"Not a hero—just human."

"—what if you were writing about a murderer? Or a terrorist? Would you put yourself in their place, too?"

I thought about it. "Yes."

"Would you, by God?"

"Yes. I would. Everyone has a story."

"That's true—and that would be absolutely fine in a novel. But in journalism, you have to maintain your distance. You can't bear witness if your eyes are full of tears. You'll be blind—blinded by emotions."

"But—as long as I'm crying for *everyone*—the innocent victims as well as the bloodthirsty terrorists—what's wrong with that?"

"You'll be accused of bias. By everyone."

"So—you think a journalist has to stand back and take the humanity out of every story so that no one will accuse them of bias? Nobody does that. Everybody chooses sides."

"Bad journalists do. Good journalists stand back. They tell facts—all the facts, please, regardless of who you're offending. If you're feeling your way through—you're lost. You don't know what objectivity is."

"There's no such thing."

"Of course there isn't. Not pure objectivity. But that is the goal—"

"What's the point of having a goal that's unattainable?"

"Miss Saira!" Majid Khan banged his hand on the table.

I banged mine so that it landed right next to his. "Mr. Majid!"

"Mr. Majid?" He fell silent. "Is that what you've decided to call me?"

"You started it."

"I did. To maintain my distance."

"Is that necessary?"

He laughed. "Don't you think it is?"

"No. I don't." Our eyes were locked in some kind of struggle.

"I remember that look. A shameless teenager stared at me in just that way once. In Karachi. At Gymkhana." He laughed at whatever he saw in my face.

It was my turn to laugh. "I'm not a teenager. Not anymore."

"Saira, this is ridiculous. You're half my age. Go home and be a good, respectable girl. Instead of hanging out with rogues like me."

"I don't want to be good. Or respectable."

"Then find someone your own age."

"I don't want to."

"Saira, this will never work out."

"I know that. I don't expect anything to come of it." I moved my hand an inch to the left, so that it was touching his. "The here and now will do."

FOURTEEN

M Y BRIEF AFFAIR with Majid Khan, the defining relationship of my college years, did not remain the secret I had
planned it to be. And with discovery came consequences. Painful
consequences from which I had to escape.

Exile. I found haven in the unlikeliest of contexts—in the aftermath of forgotten wars, in the midst of ongoing conflicts, in
the miseries of forsaken peoples. After I graduated from college,
Mohsin and I traveled the world, bearing witness, with his camera
and my words, to the callousness of humanity's indifference.

But exile, even when it is self-imposed, is by definition tem-
poral. When Ameena summoned me home, I did not hesitate to
comply.

Daddy opened the door when I knocked, letting out a yelp of
surprise so subdued that I knew the urgency of Ameena's call had
been sincere. Any awkwardness I may have felt at arriving, un-
heralded, after five years of absence, was dispelled by the sight of
him—a gray and grim shadow of what I remembered him to be.

I asked him for all the bleak details, and knew the whole truth when he was done. Mummy was dying.

I made my way to my parents' room. There she was, a small, shriveled shell of life. I stood and stared for only a second before her eyes opened to see me.

Her hand came out from under the covers, reaching out as she said, "Saira. You're home. My little girl is home." She started to sit up, I was at her side, fluffing up pillows and smoothing blankets around her, with one hand only, the other firmly in her grip. She moved over and patted the space at her side. I climbed into bed with her and rested my head on her shoulder as she stroked my hair and wiped my forehead clean. "I have worried so much about you, Saira. The places you've been! The risks you've taken! My fearless little girl. That is what you have always been, Saira—fearless, fearless, heedless of danger."

I was crying so hard that her words seemed to come from a great distance. I knew what I owed her—an explanation, excuses, contrition—all that I had not offered before.

"Mummy, I—I'm sorry—I—"

"Shhh. Shhh, Saira. No tears. What is done, is done. You are here with me now—thank God—and that is all that matters."

"You're not angry, Mummy? About why I went away? That I stayed away so long?"

"Of course not, Saira. I knew why you went. I understood. You kept in touch. Those letters you sent were from so far away. They made me realize and learn what I should have learned long ago. About anger and forgiveness."

"I wasn't angry with you—I told you—"

"I know. I was speaking of myself, Saira. The anger I felt at my father. Who was human, I know. I learned that from you, from your stories, which opened my eyes. See? Here they are." She pointed to a copy of my first book at her bedside. "The one you wrote about him—you made me see. How I wasted the last years of his life. But I acted on what I learned. I wrote and told you what I did."

I nodded, my hand on her wet cheek.

"Let me show you"—she was reaching for the drawer at her bedside—"see these?" Pulling out photographs and letters. "They're pictures of my sisters and their families—Tara and Ruksana. And of Adam." She had separated one photograph from the rest. "This is Ruksana's son. Kasim. Born last month. I didn't have time to write to you about him. She named him after our father. You see? I am in touch with them all, Saira. Even Belle. There is no room—no time—in this short life, to stay angry and hold grudges."

I knew about it all—about the trip she had taken to London two years before, about the visit Ruksana, Tara, and Adam had made to Los Angeles in return. But I made her tell me again, the new ending to an old story.

"You see, Saira? I've been busy in your absence."

"How is Ameena?"

"She is well—she and Sakina and Shuja. They left only an hour before you came. You know that they live here now? Only two miles away? They moved soon after—but you know this already."

We fell silent.

Resting her head back against the pillows, closing her eyes to block the pain and weariness of her illness, Mummy said, "I have read everything you've written. Such beautiful, horrible stories. From Rwanda to Chechnya. From Mozambique to Afghanistan.

I want to hear it all in your voice, now. Instead of reading it from a distance."

On these words, Mummy's eyes closed again. I kissed her forehead before standing up. "I'll tell you everything, Mummy. Later. You should rest, now."

She squeezed my hand for a second, then let go. "Yes. For a little while. I'll rest. And then, you'll tell me all of your stories."

Before I left the room, Mummy spoke again. "Saira?"

"Yes, Mummy?"

"The reason you went away—? Will you be able to—"

"I'm fine, Mummy. I'll be fine." I shut the door gently, hoping I was right.

Another reunion awaited me in the kitchen. Ameena was there, and whatever I had anticipated feeling at the sight of her flew from my mind, so changed did I find her—not her features, though, which were remarkably the same.

"A *hijab*?" I was stunned to see her in a scarf, every hair tucked out of view. "You wear *hijab*?"

She nodded as she embraced me, but I had to step back to take in how she looked. What she saw in my face made her laugh nervously. "You don't approve."

The fact that she wasn't asking made me realize how transparent my feelings were. I reined in my expression and said, "It's not my place to approve."

She didn't answer, and the subject was added to a list of others, begun long ago, which we never talked about.

"Daddy called you? I thought I wouldn't see you until tomorrow."

"I had to come right away. I didn't want to disturb you while you were with Mummy. It must have shocked you to see her."

I nodded and bit my lip. "Thank you for calling me, Ameena."

"I knew you'd come."

"Of course."

"Saira—when you went away—"

I cut Ameena off, sensing that she was going to venture into the vicinity of that forbidden list. "It's so good to see you, Ameena. When will I see Shuja? And Sakina?"

"Tomorrow. But—are you—?"

"I can't wait! How old is she now?"

Ameena was silent for a long moment. And then took my cue, however reluctantly. "She's five. In kindergarten."

"And Shuja? He's happy in L.A.?"

"Yes."

"Tell me all about them." My voice was bright and cheerful, incongruously so, given the scene I had just been a part of and the fact that I had been away so long.

THE NEXT MORNING, I woke up, keeping my eyes shut, to the feel of her breath on my face. Little, shallow breaths. Very slowly, I opened my eyes to the sight of a small face, inches from mine, peering at me with wide, curious eyes of its own.

Beyond my room, I heard Ameena calling, giving a name to my intruder, "Sakina! Sakina, where are you?"

Footsteps sounded in the hallway. The door opened. "There you are, Sakina! What are you doing?" My sister's whisper was loud and raspy. "I told you not to disturb—you see, you've woken her up!" Ameena was in the room in an instant, her hold on Sakina's hand tight and firm, tugging her away from me in a motion that was protective. "I'm sorry, Saira. Go back to sleep."

Sakina was looking over her shoulder as her mother tugged her out of the room, eyes twinkling and lips twitching with a mischievous humor that left me breathless.

A short while later, I came into the kitchen, in desperate need of coffee in a house where only tea was available. Shuja was there.

He embraced me, saying, gently, "It's good to have you home."

"It's good to be home. Why aren't you at work?"

"The same reason Sakina was able to wake you up this morning. It's Saturday."

I was going through the kitchen cupboards in a vain search for instant coffee. Out of the corner of my eye, I saw a little forehead peek out from behind the dining-room doorway. Eyes, on me, followed.

Unaided by the needed boost of caffeine, I had to manufacture the heartiness in my cheerful greeting, "Well, hello there!"

I heard a giggle as the forehead and eyes were retracted. A moment later, a conversation began, two sides of it conducted by the same voice. "Is she really your aunt?—Yes, her name is Sairakhala.—And you've never met her before?—No, never.—Why not?—Because she lives all over the world.—Do you like her?—Of course I like her. I love her. She's my Sairakhala.—Then why don't you talk to her?—Because I'm shy.—But she doesn't know that. She'll think you're rude.—No she won't. She knows. She's Sairakhala.—Do you think she's gotten you a present?—Of course! She's my Sairakhala."

Shuja's eyes met mine, his lips twitching, the rest of his face contorted into a bizarre blend of emotion and query that I could not answer.

I opened my mouth to reassure the voices that their expectation was not in vain. Ignoring Shuja, I said, to myself, "Who is that little girl who keeps popping in and out of sight?—Don't you know? That's Sakina!—Oh! Sakina! Well, why doesn't she just come and introduce herself?—I don't know. Maybe she's shy.—But if she stays far away, how will you give her the presents you have for her?—I don't know. I guess I will just have to wait for her to want to be friends.—But how long will you have to wait?—I don't know. Not long, I hope."

A hand gripped the frame of the door, closely followed by feet, legs, and the rest of my alarm clock. The quest for coffee forgotten, I squatted down to Sakina's eye level and regarded her as soberly, as curiously, as she had regarded me earlier. We stared at each other for some long, torturous moments. Finally, a giggle burst through the solemnity of her assumed expression and my eyes were relieved from the torment of remaining open and neutral in response to hers, which were intense and inquisitive. I looked up to gauge Shuja's reaction to my ice-breaking techniques. He was smiling and nodding.

I crooked a finger to invite Sakina to follow me back to my room. There, she watched me rummage around in my bag, looking for the dolls I had brought for her, from all over Asia and Africa and parts of Europe. She took them wordlessly, running her fingers over their dresses to explore their textures. A movement in the doorway caught my attention. I looked up and smiled when I saw Ameena.

She smiled back at me with moist eyes and said to Sakina, "Have you thanked Saira Khala?"

Sakina came close to me, put a thin arm around my neck, and whispered, in my ear, "Thank you, Sairakhala."

"You're welcome, Sakina."

"Come, Sakina, Nanima is asking for you. You can show her your new dolls."

After a while, Ameena and my father helped Mummy into the living room, Shuja bringing up the rear, carrying the IV stand within range. I watched them arrange her on the couch and surveyed the evidence of my mother's weakness, Sakina's restless feet carrying her in and out of the room in a patter of steps and a chatter of song that played on in the background. We all sat together until Mummy fell asleep. Then Ameena and her family left, promising to return later in the afternoon. I must have fallen asleep soon after.

When my eyes opened, Mummy was still asleep and Daddy was still in his armchair, his face veiled from my mother's potential sight behind a newspaper—but not from mine. From my angle in the room, I saw his face clearly, saw his hand reaching up, from time to time, to wipe his eyes. I had never before seen my father cry. Every once in a while, he would lift his eyes from the newsprint he was pretending to read, and gaze at my mother, unable to stem the flow of tears that he was trying so hard to hide.

My instinct, learned from him, was to flee the room. Daddy had always melted away into the background, remote and absent through all the controversies and trauma of the past. It occurred to me suddenly that my father's relationship to me and Ameena could only be traced through Mummy. He had opened the door to welcome me to my mother's deathbed, without one reference to my having been away for so long. All of our lives, it had been her job to interact and intercede, his only to pay the bills and provide. When she was gone—where would that leave us? Where would it leave him?

I fought against instinct and approached him, putting my

hand on his arm. He didn't look at me, his eyes still on the paper that rustled a bit in his hands. After a few seconds, he let half fall into his lap as he loosened his grip and moved one hand to rest on mine. A squeeze, a sniff. That was all.

"DADDY KNOWS?"

"Of course he knows."

I took a moment to absorb what Mummy told me. I was lying next to her on her bed about a week after I had returned from exile. Such a long time passed in silence that I was surprised to turn and see her still awake, her eyes on my face.

I said one of the things that had been on my mind since I came home, "It's strange to see Ameena in *hijab*."

"Hmmm," Mummy said, her lips pursed in the way they so frequently had because of something I said or did.

"You don't like it?"

"I don't agree with it. The idea that a woman has to cover her hair. Modesty, yes. But not *hijab*. There was no such thing when I was growing up. Some women wore their *dupatta*s on their head when they went out—conservative women. From conservative, old-fashioned families. I don't understand what this new fashion is about. It's like a uniform. A declaration of one's piety."

I laughed. "Like a bumper sticker."

"That is what I told her."

"And?"

"She said it was something she had to do. She has become very religious. Since you went away. She feels guilty, I think."

I sat up in bed. This had not occurred to me. "She has no reason to."

"Doesn't she? Whatever you say, you are not at peace. Anyone can see that, Saira. You avoid her."

"No I don't. I don't."

"Yes. You look through her. You don't see her. And the whole thing is festering."

"It's—been hard. Coming home. That's all. I knew it would be."

"That's why you kept away for so long." Mummy's hand was on my forehead. Smoothing, caressing.

"You remember when you used to write on my forehead?"

Mummy nodded.

"What was it you used to write?"

"An *ayat* from the Quran. *Ayatul Kursi*. A prayer for protection. Ameena does the same thing for Sakina."

"Does she?" I could feel Mummy's fingers begin to trace the script, right to left. "I'm glad."

THAT HAD BEEN one of Mummy's good days.

There were bad ones, too. Days when her pain was so bad that nothing seemed to help. On those days, I did as she requested—what she had asked me to do on the afternoon of my return. I told her stories—stories of what I'd seen and written about over the course of my exile. War, hunger, poverty, death, destruction. Mummy hung on every word, meditating on the suffering of others in a vain attempt to distract herself from her own. Hours would pass before she could finally manage to close her eyes and sleep.

One day, as the tension on her forehead eased and I saw that finally she would be able to rest, Mummy's eyes turned to Ameena sitting in the chair by the window, and she asked, "Where's Sakina?"

"She's at home."

"You've been here all day, Ameena. Go home. Take care of Sakina. Don't neglect her because of me. Saira is here to take care of me."

"She's all right. Shuja is with her."

Mummy smiled. She closed her eyes and said, "Shuja. He dotes on that child. I think he loves her even more than he loves you, Ameena. And that hardly seems possible." I tried not to see the wringing of my sister's hands.

We waited, Ameena and I, for a few minutes before quietly leaving the room, leaving Sakina's old baby monitor on so we could hear if Mummy called out. Ameena followed me into the kitchen and watched me put the water on for the tea that I had resigned myself to drinking. The silence was dangerously awkward, carefully cultivated by me and reluctantly respected by Ameena.

With relief, I saw her reach for her bag and scarf. Watched her put it on, tucking her hair under it carefully. She was getting ready to go home. Back to her life.

I took a deep breath and said what I had been planning to say: "You have nothing to feel guilty about, Ameena. That's why you wear *hijab,* isn't it? Why you've become so religious?"

Ameena smiled gently and said, "You've been talking to Mummy."

"She's wrong?"

Ameena cocked her head to one side. "Maybe not."

"Please don't feel guilty, Ameena. It's such a useless emotion."

"How could I not? I drove you away from us."

"You didn't do that."

"Yes I did, Saira. If I—"

"There's no if, Ameena. Only what was. What is. You have nothing to feel guilty about."

Ameena took a step closer to me. She put her hand on my arm. "What I feel guilty about is that I have no regrets. I'm not sorry, Saira. If it all happened again, I would do the same thing." She put her face in her hands. "What kind of sister am I—that I would do it again? Put you through it all over again? Even though I know you regret it."

"No. I have no regrets."

I met her eyes, saw the struggle in them, the doubt, the fear.

The last took me by surprise. "You're not—afraid of me, Ameena?"

The quick intake of breath was my answer.

I shook my head, put my mug down, and took her shoulders to give her a shake. "You have no reason to be afraid. I promise. I have no regrets."

Out came the breath and the tension in her shoulders eased as she nodded, wiping at the corners of her eyes.

I put my hand on Ameena's cheek, tucked a lock of stray hair back under her scarf. Without thinking, I asked, "Will Sakina have to wear one of these when she gets older?"

Ameena took a step backward and paused for long enough to make me realize what I had done.

"I'm sorry, Ameena. It's none of my business. How you choose to raise your daughter."

"Whether Sakina chooses to cover or not will be up to her."

I held my hand up. "I'm sorry. It's none of my business." I

picked up Ameena's car keys from the hook where they hung in our mother's kitchen. "Here. Mummy's right. Go home. Be with Sakina. Give my love to Shuja."

"Saira—"

"I'm sorry, Ameena. It was a difficult day. With Mummy. And, I suppose, it's only going to get worse."

Ameena opened her mouth again, saw the look in my eye, and then reached forward to give my arm a rub. "Get some sleep."

"I will."

FIFTEEN

SOME LONG MONTHS after my return home, months when Mummy struggled without complaint through the last race between morphine and pain that is the final stage of cancer, she died.

In the first days and weeks after, every morning was the same. I woke to the sound of my father's sobs, loud and inconsolable. Barely breathing, I waited for the storm to pass, postponing movement and motion until after it subsided, trying to avoid violation of the carefully constructed privacy of his grief. An hour later, at breakfast, there was never any sign of it on his face or in his demeanor. He resumed the façade of his life the very day after the funeral—going to work and coming home, watching television, and reading the paper. Our interaction fell under this category, limited to formal greetings and good-nights, no references to my mother or the grief that we should have been able to share. The only contradiction to his outward composure was the fear I saw in his eyes whenever I talked of leaving. Then, the assumed calm of his routine would give way to an anxiety he tried to hide. And

I knew—instinctively, not from anything he said—that my departure was something he dreaded.

More than a month had passed when Mohsin called to ask when I was going to rejoin him—rubbing salt in the wound of my awkward captivity with news of an exciting story he thought we should tackle.

I was working on my laptop, at the dining table, when Daddy came home. He looked for me when he did, calling my name the moment he walked in the door.

"I'm here, Daddy! In the dining room."

He came and stood in the doorway, which opened from the kitchen. "Oh. Are you working?"

I shrugged. "Sort of."

He entered the room and sat down at the table across from me. "Writing?"

"Not really. Sketching out some questions to ask for something Mohsin's working on. He wants me to join him soon."

"You're not leaving already?" There was that note again, of panic, which he couldn't quite seem to contain.

"Not yet. But I'll have to. Eventually."

Looking out the window, he said, as if in reference to the weather, "I—I can't bear the thought, Saira. Of being alone."

I came around the table and took a seat beside him. "You won't be. Ameena's here. So close. And I promise I'll come and visit. Not like before."

He was shaking his head. "That's not the same. I've never lived alone. I don't know how to do it." He was tracing the grains of wood on the table where we sat. "I don't know how he did it. My father. I've been thinking of him a lot lately. He had no one at the end."

"He had his work."

Daddy shook his head. "I have work. That's all I have. It's not enough. It couldn't have been enough for him." My father's eyes met mine. "I promised him I'd go back. You know that. You wrote about it in your story—'Bearing Witness.' But I didn't keep my promise. He died alone." The breath Daddy exhaled was ragged.

"But *you're* not alone, Daddy. You have me and Ameena. Sakina and Shuja."

"I have been a cold and distant father."

"No!"

"Don't deny it. It's true. I know it. Your mother—she always complained. That I wasn't involved enough. And now—you and Ameena will go on as before. I will see her often, with her family. You, less often, when you visit me now and then. But you are both as distant from me as I was from him. I feel bad, now. About coming to America. Staying here, when I said I would go back. But it was easier to stay. I didn't think about him and what he might have needed."

"Daddy—"

He held up his hand to stop me from speaking. "It's all right. I'm not complaining. I know you have to go." He stood and shuffled out of the room.

I followed him into the living room and surprised myself with my next words—an idea I had toyed with and discarded as unfeasible. "Daddy—why don't you come with me?"

"What? Where?"

"To India. We'll meet up with Mohsin. Then, we're going to Pakistan." I didn't tell him about Afghanistan after that.

He raised his eyebrows. "Go with you? To India?" He frowned down at the remote control in his hand. And then put it aside, very deliberately, without flicking on the television as he had planned to do. He turned his face up to look at me as he said, sounding surprised himself, "Yes. I think—I'd like that."

WE WENT TO India first, to Bombay—which is what Daddy and Mummy had continued to call the city of Mumbai, even after its name was officially changed—where Mohsin was waiting. At first, Daddy was our guide, showing us the house where he was raised, the schools he and Mohsin's father attended. Later, he tagged along with us as we worked, interviewing patients and doctors at women's clinics all over the city for a story on selective female abortions.

At one of these clinics, Mohsin and I introduced him to Dr. Asma Mohammed.

"It's an honor to meet you, Dr. Qader. At long last."

My father looked from Dr. Mohammed's face to mine, not understanding.

I let her explain: "I met your daughter—and your nephew—three years back. They found me here, in this clinic which your father founded."

"My father?"

"He was our neighbor."

Daddy frowned.

"In the flat that he lived in at the end. I was just starting college when he shifted to our building. He was a great man. A mentor to me. The reason I became a doctor. He spoke of you often."

"Did he?"

"Indeed." She waited for some response from my father. When none came, she said, "Would you like a tour?"

My father nodded. And we followed. I watched him assess the facility, taking stock, perhaps, of what his professional life might have been like if he had fulfilled his father's wishes. He paid close attention to Dr. Mohammed, asking questions about the kinds of services offered at the women's clinic.

At dinner that night, in the restaurant of our hotel, he was unusually quiet. Daddy didn't come out with us the next day, claiming to be tired. When Mohsin and I trudged back to the hotel in the evening, Daddy was excited. He'd taken a cab back to the clinic, had spent the day there with Dr. Mohammed—Asma, he called her.

"She's incredible—that woman. She told me how you two helped her create their fund-raising brochure. It's beautiful—the pictures, the personal stories. Tell me—what do you know of her? Is she married? Does she have children?"

Mohsin's eyes met and held mine for a moment, their widened state conveying a curiosity that I caught and registered before answering my father. "She's a widow. Her husband died years ago. No kids as far as I know."

My father spent the next few days at the clinic with Dr. Asma Mohammed.

One morning, after watching my father burn his tongue in his hurry to finish his tea and dash off to the clinic, I turned to Mohsin and said, "Do you think—?" Mohsin was familiar enough with my inquiring mind to know where I had stopped myself from going. He answered me with a shrug, and I felt my own shoulders lift in answer to his.

———

WE WENT TO Karachi—where I had been several times since the husband-hunt Mummy had dragged me on when I was still in college. Karachi, my cousins always tried to convince me, had changed. All the way from the airport to Lubna Khala's house, they would point out the proof of progress: McDonald's, Pizza Hut, KFC, Dunkin' Donuts, shopping malls, boutiques, bridges, and flyovers. To my eyes, they were hollow symbols set up within the familiar and still shocking sight of open garbage pits and dirty rag-clothed and limb-severed beggars—bitter signs of stagnation and despair that my cousins, and everyone else, seemed not even to notice.

Big Nanima was what kept me coming back, the reason I had not avoided my aunts and cousins in Pakistan, like I had my family in America. She was eighty years old. Since she had broken her hip a year before, she was living with Lubna Khala, having sold her own flat and relinquished the independence she had fought to keep for so long. She used a cane to walk, now, and shuffled forward into the foyer of Lubna Khala's house to greet us when we arrived.

She reached up to put her hand on my father's shoulder. "*Beta*—we have not been the same since we heard. It is a cruel thing, to have to live long enough to see my children die before my eyes. Shabana was my sister's daughter, but she was my child, too, and I remember her and miss her with every breath that I take. But this is a temporary world. *Inna lilaahi wa inna ilaihi raji-oon.*" (From God we come and to God we return.) "Shabana was very fortunate. To die surrounded by those she loved and in the lifetime of her husband. She died a bride and not a widow." Then Big Nanima turned to me. "Saira. *Beti*. You are not alone. You don't have your mother, but you have your mother's family to love you and care for you. Always." She hugged me to her, put her paper-thin cheek against mine, and wiped the tears I had not noticed trailing down my face.

Mohsin was already in Peshawar, making arrangements for our next story. I had only a few days in Karachi, days I spent with Big Nanima, leaving my father to spend his time with my other relatives—Lubna Khala's family, Mummy's cousins and his own—to talk of the old days in Bombay.

Big Nanima never spoke of the old days, because she was still too vibrantly involved in the world around her. "The best thing about reading your stories, Saira, is that it makes me feel that at least we are not alone—there are places in the world more miserable, even, than here. What this country has come to! That an old lady is not allowed to take a walk on the street of the house she lives in."

"Not allowed?"

"Not allowed! Lubna says it is not safe. Ha! Safe! In my own neighborhood, I took a walk on the streets every day for all of the years that I lived there. But now, here in this walled and gated fool's paradise, I am confined—a prisoner. The only place I am allowed to go for a walk is to another walled garden, getting in the car to be chauffeur-driven from one fortress to another. Everyone is afraid—the kidnapping and the carjackings. It gets better and then worse again. We have a few months, a year even, of relative calm—when only a few cars are hijacked, when no one *we* know is kidnapped, when the only people being butchered are strangers whose names we don't recognize when we read them in the newspapers.

"And then—all it takes is a spark—and the whole thing lights up again, exploding and exposing what has been there all the time, simmering just under the surface. This is no way to live. Children don't play outside anymore. They are shuttled back and forth from schools and homes and clubs, all guarded by armed men in uniforms. In my neighborhood—before—*all* the children played on the streets. Together. The children who lived in walled houses, in flats, the children of servants. Now, there are some children who have never felt the air outside! Even that is filtered by those obnoxious air-conditioners that drown out the sounds of the street. All anyone can talk of is how to get out. Laborers line up for visas to the Gulf. The rich all have green cards ready, or are applying for immigrant status in Canada. Everyone lives with one foot on the ground, gathering up their money and profits with one hand, and packing it all into a suitcase with the other, the other foot set on the steps to an airplane out of here. How will anything change?"

Every day, she muttered the same complaints as we walked around the Gymkhana garden, which, like the garbage pits and the children who lived among them, seemed to stay the same, year after year. After a few rounds, we would sit down for some tea or cold drinks.

On one of those days, when she and I had sat down and ordered tea, I told her about Asma Mohammed.

"You think he will marry her," Big Nanima said.

"I don't know."

"Would that bother you?"

"I don't know. It shouldn't. Should it?"

She didn't answer me for a moment, stirred her tea vigorously before raising the cup to her lips a little unsteadily. "No. It should not. But it would be understandable if it did."

"Hmm."

"What about you, Saira? Are you going to be a gypsy for all of your life? Forgive me, but I have a right to ask. Your mother is dead. Your *khala*s are worried."

"I know." They had tried to set me up with an eligible bachelor within hours of my arrival.

"You were hurt? By a man?"

I laughed. "No. That's not it, Big Nanima."

"Then? Your work—it *is* important, Saira. But you shouldn't let it consume you."

"You called me a gypsy. That's what I am. I don't have time to commit myself to anyone."

"And that is not something you will regret? Later?"

Her question was in the wrong tense. The answer I repressed was a bittersweet mixture of regret and remorse already realized, processed and assimilated into who I was. Later was not something I worried much about. I shrugged—a defiant gesture of ambivalence that was forced and familiar.

"How is Ameena?"

"She's fine. She's in *hijab*."

"Is she? Hmm." Big Nanima shook her head. "It's become quite a trend, hasn't it? An international revival, the reclamation of what *my* generation cheerfully cast off. How strange it is—to live long enough to see the wheel go 'round again. She must be busy, eh? Taking care of her little one? She must be four years old?"

"She just turned six."

"Six already? She's started school."

I nodded.

"What is her name?"

"Sakina."

"I wish you had a picture of her to show me. You must tell Ameena to send me one, eh?" We were interrupted by an old student of Big Nanima's. I watched them speak for a moment and then excused myself to use the restroom. When I came back, the student was gone, but Big Nanima was still not alone. I paused, coming down the pavilion steps onto the lawn, when I recognized the man seated next to her. Majid Khan. He stood when he saw me and remained standing until I sat down.

Of course, I had seen him a few times over the past years, the first of which had been mildly awkward—he had been a perfect gentleman, gallant and flirtatious. Less so the second time, taking his cue from my own unaffected manner. Our paths were bound to cross again and again. We were in the same profession, after all. Though our angles were different. Even when we covered the same region or conflict, it was rare that we met.

"Saira. It is so good to see you." The changes in him were subtle. There was a little more gray and some of the old, fine lines had deepened alongside new ones that had appeared around his eyes. He was as lean and tall as ever. I saw that he was doing a similar inventory of my face, and turned to look at Big Nanima, who was looking back and forth between us both.

"Adeeba Auntie told me about your mother. I am so sorry, Saira, for your loss."

"Thank you."

"How have you been? Last time I saw you—where was it? Kosovo?"

I nodded.

"Do you remember, Auntie, that it was you who first introduced us, right here in this very place? Back when Saira was still a child—a novice! Now, when we meet, we meet as equals."

"Hardly." I glanced at Big Nanima again and, seeing her eyes on me, I realized that I had been searching Majid's face a little too carefully, looking for something I had not bothered to look for the last time we'd met. "What have you been up to?"

"You think I would tell you? The competition?"

I laughed. "I'm small potatoes. I always will be. You follow the big shots around. My angle is the little people."

"It's only a matter of time—you'll be called to account, too. That's what success does, Saira. It gives you access."

"I don't want access. Not to the game players. I want to report from the pawn's point of view."

"Hmm. In any case—I'm not doing any reporting right now. I'm working on a novel."

"Are you?"

"Yes. No one seems to be interested in what I have to say as a journalist. You know what I mean."

"I know exactly what you mean."

"Lately, when I try to write a news story, all I can come up with are dire warnings and perilous prophecies."

"What kind of warnings?" Big Nanima had decided to stop watching us and join the conversation.

Majid shook his head. "It's all nonsense, I'm sure, Auntie." Then, he turned to me again and said, still to Big Nanima, "This is the one who needs to be warned. Can't you stop her from exercising her suicidal tendencies, Auntie? Chechnya, Rwanda—have you never met a massacre you didn't like, Saira?"

"Her work needs to be done!" Big Nanima, who had often expressed the same doubt and worry as Majid, rode in strong for my defense.

"Yes. Have you seen her book, Auntie?" Big Nanima nodded. "*Collateral Victims*. I bought a copy. Full-price."

I flushed. "So you're the one. Not my book, anyway. Mohsin's book. It was a pictorial essay."

"With your commentary."

"The words were superfluous. The pictures spoke for themselves."

"But you told their stories. You made them come alive. All those grieving women—widows and mothers—and children, orphaned and mutilated. How do you sleep at night?"

"It was wonderful writing." This, warmly, from Big Nanima.

"No doubt about it. You haven't done anything personal? Since your first collection of stories?"

"No. Haven't had the time."

"And what are you up to now, Saira?"

"We're heading for Afghanistan."

"Again? I can't quite picture you in a burka."

"The funnier sight is always Mohsin with a beard."

"I was there a short while ago. Afghanistan. Interviewing Mad Mullah Omar about the destruction of the Buddhas at Bamiyan." Majid paused. "Be careful, will you?"

Big Nanima cleared her throat, rather loudly, and said, "More warnings? You've teased us enough, young man. Whetted our appetites with talk of peril and danger. I insist on hearing these prophecies of yours."

Majid leaned forward, bracing his weight on his elbows. "I suppose I have nothing clear to say—that's why I hesitate. The facts are all out there. But there's a story in progress. A climax is coming." He leaned back and waved a hand to encompass our location. "This place—look how peaceful it is. How pleasant. Pockets of space like this one dot the landscape. But what is really going on here? Another general is in power in Pakistan. And the whole Muslim world is a pot on a stove, roiling and boiling, about to overflow."

"So? What's new?" Big Nanima's eyes were narrowed. Her question wasn't a challenge, merely a question.

"I'm uneasy. That's all. When I am writing a novel, I like to know what the end of my story will be before I begin. That's not always possible. Even in fiction. In real life, it's bloody impossible. I know this. I have always been comfortable with uncertainty. But now—there is something different. Too much power on one side. Too much anger on another. Power, by its very nature, is blind to the destruction it causes. And anger is too easily exploited and transformed into hatred—a process that has begun and which we see the results of on one side of the world already. You see? I have nothing concrete to offer you, Auntie. Conjecture, speculation. Nothing of note. Still, I find myself holding my breath—"

It took me a moment to realize that I, too, was holding my breath. I exhaled and laughed. "What kind of a novel are you working on? Suspense?"

He laughed with me, and Big Nanima smiled, too. "A love story, actually."

"A love story?" Now I was laughing even harder.

"Yes! A classic, historical love story. Set in Mughal India."

Even Big Nanima was laughing now, shaking her head in disbelief.

"*Et tu*, Auntie?" Majid's attention was called by a man waving at another table. "Saira. Adeeba Auntie. It has—as always—been a pleasure." He stood and kissed both Big Nanima's hand and mine and left.

I stared after him with a smile still on my lips. A smile abruptly ended when Big Nanima asked, "You and Majid Khan? When did that happen?"

"I don't know what you mean."

"You silly girl. I can see it. Was it very long ago?"

"Very long ago. Ancient history."

When we got back to my aunt's house, Daddy wanted to speak to me. He followed me into the guest room I occupied.

"Saira, I have something I want to tell you. Something awkward, I'm afraid."

I braced myself—then said, "Asma Mohammed?"

"You—how did you know?"

"A good guess. Have you declared your intentions to her?"

"Yes. By e-mail. Just today. She's accepted my proposal. I'm going back to Bombay. Tonight."

"Tonight?"

Daddy nodded.

"She won't want to move to the U.S."

"No. I will stay in India with her. We'll visit Los Angeles regularly, of course."

"Of course. Daddy?"

He had an unseemly kind of glow on his face. "Yes?"

"You don't think it's too soon?"

"To come back? To keep my promise to my father? Not too soon at all."

"I mean, too soon after Mummy."

He winced briefly. Then shook his head. "No. I don't think

so. The reason I came with you—I had a crazy idea already in my head. To come back and pick up where I had left off. To do something for someone else. And—"

"You found Asma."

"Yes. She's a doctor. She's already doing what I want to do. She has no one. I have no one."

"It's meant to be." I wasn't sure if I was being sarcastic.

Daddy wasn't either. "You—you're upset?"

I sighed. "No. Are you going to call Ameena?"

"Hmm? Yes." Daddy frowned. "No. You do it. Call her. Would you?"

"You're afraid of Ameena?"

"Well, this is an awkward conversation to have. Once is enough, I think."

I frowned. "They should be back from Florida?"

"Yes. Sakina's school will have started."

"I'm leaving, too. The day after tomorrow. Won't you call her? Tell her yourself?"

Daddy shook his head.

I sighed again. "I'll send her an e-mail."

SIXTEEN

~ᘓᘔ~

Daddy's departure from Karachi was so sudden that I was left alone to deal with the leave-taking, gift-bearing relatives that paraded in and out of my aunt's house the next day, as they usually did whenever I left Karachi. This time, they were hungry for information. Word of my father's engagement had circulated and the fishing lines were cast so boldly that I lost no time in sending off an e-mail about Daddy and Asma to Ameena, before she could get the news from the likes of some Razia Nani–type relative who might call to commiserate, congratulate, or both.

At some point in the early evening, I wandered into Big Nanima's room, finding her holding court with the next generation—Lubna Khala's grandchildren and their cousins. She had them rolling on the floor with poop-and-fart stories, the kind she had entertained me with before I graduated to literature and political science. When she had reached "the end," she shooed the children out of the room and patted a space on the bed next to her. She put her arm around me, pulling me close, pressed her cheek against mine.

"Don't feel bad about your father, Saira. He is not being disloyal to your mother. And neither are you if you accept his new wife."

"I know that. In my head, I know that."

"But not so much in your heart?" Big Nanima sighed. "Where our parents are concerned, we are always children. Like your mother was about *her* father. It took her more time than it will take for you to accept your father's happiness. Because his will come at no cost to anyone else. That is the best kind of happiness. The kind few are privileged to have." She took my chin in her hand and opened her mouth to say something. Before she could, she cocked her head to one side, listening to the sound of voices coming from the hall outside. "Go, Saira. Your Lubna Khala is calling. More guests have arrived."

I sighed.

"I know it is difficult, but they mean no harm, Saira. Go. Grit your teeth and say good-bye."

The house was packed at the six o'clock evening hour. The lounge was filled to capacity, the TV blaring at the request of the older, hearing-impaired CNN-junkie uncles present, and I was grateful for the excuse of the volume, which made conversation downright impossible, preparing myself mentally for the risks and dangers that my journey with Mohsin would entail.

Suddenly, the rhythmically calm assertions of the British-accented CNN International newsreaders were interrupted by a note of panic and disbelief. All eyes in the room were glued to the television screen, on the image of a skyscraper in flames. A few moments later, we saw an airplane, the second one, flying into the twin of the first building. The gasps and shouts were loud enough to draw Big Nanima out of her room. Her eyes singled me out in the crowd, making me realize the pose I had assumed, my hand clenching and unclenching, clutching at my abdomen in a universally feminine gesture that I had witnessed and written about many, too many times—this is what women all over the world do when confronted with danger. Mothers, clutching at their wombs, where life is conceived and nurtured, a primordial plea for protection offered whenever life is threatened and attacked.

Big Nanima knew this. She had read everything I had ever written. Her eyes on my abdomen made me still my hand.

She came closer. "Saira? What has happened?"

Mute, I pointed to the image of horror and destruction taking place on the other side of the world. It was September 11, 2001.

SEVENTEEN

❦

DESPERATELY, I TRIED, in those first few hours after the planes hit the Twin Towers, to call Ameena, to make sure she was safe. She and Shuja and Sakina. I knew they had to be back in California after a vacation spent on the East Coast. But I would not rest until I was sure.

"They were—were they going to stop in New York on their way home from Florida? I think they were. Oh, God, I can't remember!" The room was still full of people, but I was speaking to myself, my eyes fixed on the television. Big Nanima was there, watching me pace the length of Lubna Khala's lounge with phone in hand.

"Relax, Saira. They must be home. Far away from all of that." She waved her hand in the direction of the horror on television. "You said yourself that Sakina's school would have started already."

"I know, I know. But I just have to be sure. And—who knows? Who knows what will happen next?" The sky was falling. In New York, in Washington, in Pennsylvania.

The rest of the night and the morning that followed, I spent in front of the television, like all the millions of Americans at home and those around the world who did the same. In terror, in grief, I pressed my knuckles into my mouth and, through the aid of the footage that rolled around the clock, tried to put myself there, at Ground Zero, in body and in spirit to feel, in solidarity, the panic of those last moments of the thousands, the frantic worry of those left behind to search, to pick up pieces, to grieve. All against the backdrop of a completely foreign digestion of the same events among people who were not American, who could not really understand the pain of what it was to be an American on that day and on the days that followed it.

Reaction in Lubna Khala's lounge varied widely as crowds of people seemed to continue to wade in and out of the flickering light of the television screen. It was what people did in Pakistan—in good times, in bad times, and as a part of everyday existence—they gathered to eat together and argue, to live out their lives in the public forum that an extended family provides. The phone rang off the hook as friends and relatives, far more desperately close to Manhattan than me, despite the thousands of miles of ocean and land in between, sought and relayed news back and forth from sons, daughters, brothers, and sisters who worked in the city that was the center of the world.

And then there were the armchair analysts, people like my second cousin's husband, who said smugly, when the first few hours of muted shock had faded, "Well, then. Now America will know what it feels like. What it feels like to face death and destruction, the kind they deal out every day and everywhere else, the bloody imperialists! Now they will know what it feels like to suffer."

Or my aunt's husband, who clicked his tongue, shook his head, and mourned, "Such shame! The shame that these so-called Muslims have brought upon us!"

One of his sons, my first cousin, asked, "What are you going to do now, Saira? You can't go to Afghanistan. They'll be dropping bombs there. Masses of them. And you can't go home, either. You know what they did to the Japanese during World War II, don't you, Saira? You watch and wait to see how they treat you now."

"And what about the rest of us, eh? You think we won't all be painted with the same brush? Wait and see how they punish us, see how they will bomb Muslims everywhere. Bomb us into oblivion," his father added.

Lubna Khala objected, "Surely not. You heard President Bush. He has said it already. He knows. Islam is peace. Islam is not what these madmen have done. He knows that." But she didn't sound convinced.

Finally, almost twenty-four hours later, I made contact.

"Ameena? Thank God! I've been trying to reach you for hours! You're okay?"

Ameena's voice was small and stretched thin. "Yes. But, Saira, we were just there! In New York. I can't believe it. I can't believe what's happened! It's unspeakable."

"Sakina's all right?"

"She's fine. She's in school. I kept her home yesterday. I don't know why. I—I didn't want her to be away from me."

"So—you're all all right?"

"Yes, Saira. We're fine."

"Did you get my e-mail? About Daddy?"

"I did. He's in India?"

"Yes." The phone crackled for a few long moments while I tried to think up something else to say.

"And you? You're off again with Mohsin? To Afghanistan?"

"That's the plan. I—I was supposed to go yesterday. But—I couldn't leave without hearing from you. I have to rebook a flight to Peshawar. We go on across the border next week."

"Is that a good idea, Saira? To go there now?"

"I—it's what I do, Ameena."

"Yes. Well, be careful."

"I will."

"And keep in touch. Please, Saira. Mummy's gone. I—I worry about you. Let me know that you're safe."

"I will. Give my love to Shuja. And Sakina."

The phone crackled again, then beeped, signaling the end of time for the call I had booked, before going dead.

When I had put the phone down carefully on its cradle, Big Nanima shuffled into the room and put her hand on my arm. "You've spoken to Ameena? They're all right?"

I nodded.

"Now you can rest. You haven't slept, Saira."

Two days later, I was still in Karachi, unable to take the steps necessary to get on with the business of my life—telling stories that no one wanted to hear.

Mohsin called several times, urging me to hurry. I said something to him that I had not realized I was feeling. "I—what if you do this story without me, Mohsin?"

"What do you mean?"

"I was thinking about going home."

"What are you talking about? You know there'll be a war here. In Afghanistan. It's just a matter of time. What's happened over there—no one's story is going to be forgotten there, Saira. You know that. It's what will happen here that has to be covered. You've delayed long enough. Waiting to get word from Ameena."

"You're right." I closed my eyes, wondering at where this doubt was coming from. "Of course you're right."

Still, I hesitated. There was backlash in America. Snippets of tragedy totally overshadowed by the mass calamity still unfolding. Big Nanima showed me the article in *Dawn* on the day before I had finally determined to leave Karachi to join Mohsin. A Sikh man had been murdered. Mosques had been graffitied and firebombed. There were little attacks all over the country, swallowed up into the back pages of history.

"Saira," Big Nanima said, "you must call Ameena. You must tell her to take off her *hijab*."

My eyes widened at the implication of her suggestion. "I—I didn't even think of it. You're right. I'll call her in the morning. Before I leave. But I don't think she'll listen."

"Of course she will. There's no point in taking risks. The world is full of crazy people. She has a daughter to think of."

I nodded.

"Come. Let's go to Gymkhana. I haven't gone for a walk for days and if I don't use these old legs, they will stop serving me at all."

Gymkhana. That was where we were when the call came from California. Lubna Khala called the club. She had us tracked down and brought home.

Shuja had called, Lubna Khala told Big Nanima and me. To say that Ameena had been shot.

EIGHTEEN

I DON'T KNOW WHAT kind of string-pulling my uncle had to engage in to get me on a flight home within hours of Shuja's phone call—bribery and name-dropping had something to do with it, I'm sure. The airport terminal in Karachi was pandemonium—crowded with rich and angry young men and women eager to get back to the United States for the start of their Ivy League semesters, frustrated by the backlog and delay that three days of grounded U.S.-bound flights had caused. Classes would begin without them.

Before I left, I called Daddy in Bombay, though he was unable to respond to anything I told him, a string of words that meant nothing, because neither he nor I had witnessed the truth of them the way we—the whole world—had witnessed the truth of towers burning and crashing, of mothers and fathers and sons and daughters eviscerated by a hatred that had massive implications. What Shuja had called to tell me was about hatred on a smaller scale—hatred that only a few would mourn, hatred that only Sakina had witnessed.

No, we could not yet absorb this truth. There were only words and phrases that reverberated in my mind for the duration of my journey—backlash, hate crime, gunshot, surgery, coma, a prognosis that was not good, and Sakina. Sakina was there. Seated and belted into the car when Ameena went round the back to load groceries into the trunk and was accosted by a man spewing epithets—raghead! towelhead!—raging on about revenge. A random spree—the man had been out hunting, shooting people at gas stations and mini markets. A Hindu. A Sikh. At least with Ameena, his aim had been a little less misdirected. The others had survived.

And Ameena will too, I told myself, over and over again, in the charged atmosphere of my journey through three airports and thousands of miles around the Earth. Over the sound of the cargo doors slamming shut underneath us, the rattling wheels of beverage carts rolling down the aisle, the crackle and pop of the pilot's announcements, the whispered exchanges among the passengers. Over the smell of the canned, recirculated air of the cabin, the aroma of the mini meals served to those of us in economy, and the scent of too much eau de cologne that some passengers availed themselves of in the lavatories. Over the feel of rough, fire-retardant seat upholstery, static-sticky blankets, paper-covered pillows, and the cold, metal touch of the button that reclined the seat. These sensual details might otherwise have been tinged with the awareness of what it must have been like for the passengers of those other doomed flights, if my own focus was not wholly consumed by thoughts—some random and some very painfully specific—of my sister.

I thought of my last conversation with her—on the phone, three days earlier. Of the call I had planned to make at Big Nanima's suggestion. And I remembered the last time I had seen Ameena—the awkwardness of that parting. The relief of it. The guilt. Mine and hers. And the cause of both, standing, oblivious, at her side.

When I landed, I took a cab straight to the hospital. I found Shuja sitting alone in a waiting room. He didn't stand when he saw me and said nothing when I took the seat next to him, waiting—hoping—for him to tell me what I had tried to convince myself. That Ameena was all right. That she and Sakina were both all right.

After a stretch of silence that I was too afraid to violate, Shuja spoke, in a tone that I both recognized and denied—a tone that sounded the same in all the languages I had heard it in before. One that signaled shock. Trauma. Pain and loss yet unassimilated.

"No one saw anything. Sakina was there. But she didn't see it happen. She heard a man's voice. And a gunshot. By the time she got out of the car, he was gone—thank God! Ameena was on the ground. Bleeding out. She was covered in blood. So was Sakina."

I couldn't bear it any longer—that my next words had to be questions. "Shuja? She'll be all right? Tell me, Shuja. Please. She's okay?"

He looked at me then. Really looked at me for the first time since I'd arrived. "No. She's gone, Saira. Ameena's gone."

NINETEEN

A MEENA WAS DEAD. I had not reached her in time. Hours later, after Shuja and I collected Sakina from his aunt's house—Nilofer Auntie's home, where Sakina had stayed since the shooting, where Shuja had stayed years before, during those months of courting Ameena—we let ourselves into my parents' house, the three of us, because Shuja could not yet face going home.

I was scooping tea leaves into the kettle when he entered the kitchen. "She's asleep?"

Shuja nodded. "I put her down in Ameena's old room." He sat down at the kitchen table and put his head in his hands. "I should have told her. I should have told Ameena to take off her *hijab*." His voice was flat and distant.

I shook my head. "You can't blame yourself," I heard myself say. "I—Big Nanima told me to tell her the same thing. But—it was too late—" My voice trailed off at the sight of Shuja's face caving inward. I put my arm around him and squeezed his shoulders.

After a while, he pulled away and began to speak again: "I didn't like the idea at first. When she began wearing *hijab*. All I thought of was what people must be thinking of me. That I was some kind of chauvinistic, Muslim oppressor. It took me a while to admit that to myself. But—after Sakina—she wanted to be the best person she could be. To deserve the gift that we had been given. I knew how she felt. I was the same way. I started working out and eating right. I read everything I could on parenting. We both did. We felt—both of us—that we had to earn the right to be parents. Does that make sense?" He didn't wait for an answer. "She was always so good. After Sakina, she became even better. A better wife. A better human being. A better Muslim. When I realized—what my own objections were—that people would think less of *me*—I laughed at myself. She had the right to decide. What she would wear. But I should have said something—after what happened. Done something. To protect her. It's my fault that she's dead."

"No, Shuja. It's not your fault."

"I've lost her, Saira. I've lost Ameena. And with her, I've lost everything."

That was when I should have said something, anything, to reassure him. That all was not lost. That he had Sakina. But I didn't. Because I couldn't. Ameena was gone—leaving behind no script for me to follow.

When I looked up, Shuja's eyes were on me, but I looked away, unnerved by my own silence.

He stood up. "I should go."

"You won't stay here?"

"No. I—I have to go home."

"Sakina?"

His eyes were on me again, asking a question I couldn't answer. After a barely perceptible pause, he said, "Let her sleep. It's better for her to be here."

AHMED CHACHA, GRAVE-FACED and smirkless, standing in for my father, who wrestled with a grief that rendered him incapable of travel, was the first among a steady trickle of relatives who came. They staggered their visits in well-coordinated shifts—those who could, the British nationals among them, who needed no visas. He stayed for a week, just long enough for Ameena's body to be released and buried. Ameena's body. The subject of a murder investigation that had yielded no arrests.

Ahmed Chacha left and Zehra arrived as Shuja went back to work and Sakina resumed school. Then, Mehnaz was dispatched. After the uncle and the cousins, it was the aunties' turn. First, Ruksana came with her baby, Kasim—an auntie by definition only, representing the branch of Mummy's family that had only recently been reconciled. When Ruksana left, more than a month after Ameena's death, Jamila Khala and Nasreen Chachi came together—the last scheduled visitors. They cooked and cleaned, preparing two weeks' worth of food, which they packed and labeled and stored in Mummy's freezer in a spectacular grand finale of support.

Shuja came every night, establishing the routine that we would cling to when all had gone. On the aunties' last day in Los Angeles, they gathered—Jamila Khala, Nasreen Chachi, and Shuja's aunt, Nilofer Auntie—conferencing together in hushed tones that were silenced whenever I entered the room. When Shuja came that night, they cornered him while I made tea in the kitchen.

Carrying the tray in from the dining room, I stopped when I saw them and stood immobile and unnoticed. They were all on the sofa—Shuja, his face in his hands, Nilofer Auntie on one side of him, her hand on his shoulder, Jamila Khala on the other, a hand on his knee, Nasreen Chachi perched on the arm of the sofa next to her—all of them with their backs to me.

Jamila Khala said, "*Beta*. I know that your grief is still fresh. We are leaving tomorrow. Otherwise, we would have waited to tell you what we have to say. But we must tell you this—even if you are not ready—for Sakina's sake. She needs a mother. You must marry again. It's what Ameena would have wanted." One of them handed Shuja a tissue from the box on the table in front of them.

Shuja said nothing, his shoulders shaking.

From behind, I saw Jamila Khala's eyes turn to Nilofer Auntie. A visual nudge made Nilofer Auntie clear her throat and say, "Jamila is right, Shuja. You know that. Better than anyone else. You lost your parents when you were so young. You know what it is to grow up without a mother."

It was Nasreen Chachi's turn. "We tell you what Ameena's mother would have told you if she were still alive. *Beta*, Saira is here. She is not married. It is the best solution. Who else can love Sakina as much as her mother did? Who else but Saira? My husband—Ahmed Chacha—he lost his mother, too. When he was only a baby. You know about this?"

Shuja shook his head, blowing his nose into the tissue.

"His mother died when he was only six months old. And then his father married his wife's sister. Ahmed's *khala*. He never knew his own mother. But he never felt her loss, either. Because my mother-in-law—Nadeem's mother—raised him as her own. He was her sister's son. As Sakina is the child of Saira's sister."

Shuja raised his head and stared straight in front of him. His back was to me, so I couldn't see his expression.

The tray was getting heavy. And the tea cold. I came fully into the room, set the tray down on the table with only a slight rattle of china, my face heated from the feel of my aunts' probing eyes, actively gauging what I might have heard.

"I'm really tired. I'm going to bed." I didn't look at Shuja. "Good night."

He stood up, too. "I should get going. I have work in the morning. Nasreen Chachi. Jamila Khala. Thank you so much for everything—for being here when Sakina and Saira and I needed you most."

TWENTY

I AM BACK IN bed, having tried and failed to get back to sleep. I have survived the night, the memories of what has led me to now. But the past is catching up with the present, both of them only partially deposed. There are left-out details to reckon with yet—facts in the forest that I have chosen not to hear.

I look at the clock. Four minutes have passed since the last time I did. In two minutes, the alarm will ring its unnecessary call to wake. Before it does, Ameena's daughter emerges from her room, which is opposite mine. I hear her pause wordlessly in the hallway, on her way to the bathroom next door. I sit up in bed to let Sakina know I am awake, willing her to enter, hoping desperately that she will not. I feel the shrug of her shoulders, hear her move on.

I pull myself up and replace my pajamas with sweats before following her and beginning my morning monologue of false cheer. Every morning, it's like this. Like I'm on a job interview, unsure of what to say—trying to be what I think she needs with no idea of what that is.

I help her pick out her clothes before going into the kitchen. There is breakfast to prepare, a lunchbox to pack. She comes in fully dressed and takes a seat at the table. She sits in silence, shoveling oatmeal into her mouth while I cradle my mug of coffee and talk, talk, talk. I feel guilty for talking. I know she would prefer I didn't. I smile at her. She doesn't smile back. I shudder, just a little, at the burden of her reticence. We are strangers, forced together. Circumstance is the culprit in her case. Duty and obligation in mine.

It's time for the bus. I carry on my chatter all the way to the stop. The bus comes. She boards. I wave her good-bye. Wordlessly, she waves back.

I let myself back into my parents' house and pause in the foyer, listening to the silence. My feet remember that there is a morning ritual, lately established, yet to be performed. They take the necessary steps out of the room, down the hallway, and into the living room to a console table overflowing with vivid Kodak moments. My eyes brush over the pictures of my childhood and Ameena's. There are some of Sakina, which my eyes overlook, a trick I have mastered through years of practice, stopping, instead, to focus on the large frame in the center. Here is the Ameena of my dream—draped in a brilliant red chiffon fabric embroidered with gold thread that matches the jewelry that drips from her ears, neck, wrists, fingers. Her hair is swept up and away from her face, accentuating high, heavily rouged cheekbones, which would be garish if they were not matched by an equally heavy application of makeup on the rest of her face. Bridal makeup. *Desi* bridal makeup, which is a category all of its own.

Her expression is obediently forlorn, belying the sparkle of happiness that shines out of her eyes. "Don't smile or laugh, Ameena, on your wedding day. It would be immodest. A bride must appear to be shy. Even sad. To be leaving your father's home is not something to celebrate" had been Mummy's words to Ameena on the morning of her wedding. Strange, old ideas relevant to a strange, old world. Beside her, Shuja, the groom, is under no such constraint. His dazzling display of teeth is unseemly in light of Ameena's feigned distress.

The phone rings. I answer and am unsurprised by Shuja's greeting, his concerned interrogation on how Sakina's night had passed, how her day began.

"Did she finish her breakfast?"

"Yes. The whole bowl of oatmeal."

"She got on the bus all right?"

"Yes." I have nothing more to say and he has nothing more to ask. He will be with us in the evening, like every evening, soon enough to ensure Sakina's health and welfare firsthand.

"Don't forget the parent-teacher conference. Today. At four o'clock."

I slap my head and walk to the kitchen, where Shuja has kept Ameena's calendar. I find it there, the appointment we marked together. "You'll be there?"

"Of course. Mrs. Walker said she'd watch Sakina, so make sure you get her there in time to make it to school. Please."

"I will."

"I'll meet you at school at four."

The connection is severed.

I gather up Sakina's breakfast bowl and stack it in the dishwasher. As I refill my mug with coffee, the phone rings again. I reach for it eagerly.

I pick up and hear Lubna Khala's voice from Karachi. "*Beti*, how are you and Sakina?"

"We're fine. How is Big Nanima?"

I hear the crackle of long-distance as Lubna Khala hesitates before saying, "She's—she is worse, Saira. Confined to bed. She has not woken up for days. The doctor says she is not suffering. That it's only a matter of time."

I close my eyes and rejoice—this death will be gentle, cradled by sleep. Not torturous or violent, like the others I am still grieving.

"Is Daddy still in India?"

"Yes. He called today and asked me to call you. He wanted me to tell you, Saira—he and Asma were married this morning. In Bombay."

"But—I thought—after what's happened—I've been waiting for him. To come home."

"I know, *beti*. He says he cannot come. Not now."

"Not now? Then when?"

"He will come. Next year, perhaps. In the meantime—if there's anything you need—he said to tell you—that you must let him know. Money. Anything. He will not sell the house. Not yet. It is yours to live in as long as you like."

I say nothing. What can I say? Lubna Khala fills in my silence with words of consolation. "You have to understand, Saira. He—he has suffered a lot. His mind was made up already, Saira, you knew that."

"Yes. I knew."

"Your mother—she would have understood, Saira. She would have given him her blessing."

Mummy. "She's been dead less than a year." I say the words and cannot believe them myself.

"*Beti*—what can I say?" The impotence of Lubna Khala's sympathy is one I can relate to—how to console the daughter of a dead sister? But her task is less complicated than mine.

TWENTY-ONE

❧

I SPEND THE NEXT few hours in a frenzy of housekeeping. Two loads of laundry, folded and put away. Bathrooms scoured, tables dusted, carpets sucked clean of dust and debris. The kitchen swept, mopped, and wiped down, made ready for the groceries I go out to purchase. Then, I shower. And dress with more care than I have in weeks. I strap on my watch and see that there is still too much time to spare, evidence of the manic pace that I have kept in vain to drown out the calls of the past, to shrug off the burden of choices I have made, which must be reckoned with in the present.

I cannot sit and wait for the bus to return Sakina home. I get in the car and drive around until it is time to go to the school, which was mine and Ameena's. I park and wait for the bell to ring. When it does, I stand near the bus so that I can catch Sakina before she boards. A playground supervisor is there to move things along. Sakina appears and puts her hand in the one I have offered her.

The playground lady smiles and nods. "Mommy here to pick you up today, Sakina?"

The connection of our hands is severed. Did I pull away? Did she?

In the car, I tell Sakina, "Mrs. Walker will take care of you for a little while this afternoon. I—your dad and I—have an appointment with your teacher. For a conference."

She says nothing. I glance at the clock on the face of the car stereo and see that there is time for a detour. "How was your day?"

Sakina nods, too wearily for a child her age.

"You wanna go for ice cream?"

She nods again, with such an effort that I know she agrees only to humor me.

I watch her lick listlessly at her cone and throw my own cup of ice cream away only half-eaten. It is the only thing I have had to eat all day, I suddenly realize. But the realization is unaccompanied by any form of hunger that I can recognize. I drop her off at Mrs. Walker's house and head back to school.

Shuja's car is not in the lot. I make my way to Sakina's classroom and wait on the bench outside the door. At four o'clock, Mrs. Myers opens the door and lets out the three-thirty parents. They look relieved, as if Mrs. Myers has assured them of something they themselves had doubted—that their child was all right and not in any danger of flunking first grade. I stand and greet Sakina's teacher.

"Hello, Mrs. Myers. I am Saira Qader. We met about a month ago."

Mrs. Myers nods. "Sakina's aunt. Won't you come in?"

"Uh. Shuja—Sakina's dad—is supposed to meet me here." I stand awkwardly, looking out across the playground at the parking lot in the hopes that I will see Shuja there, hurriedly striding toward us so that I won't have to begin this discussion with Sakina's teacher by myself.

"Why don't we wait for him inside?"

It would seem strange to refuse, though the urge to do so is overwhelming. I follow Mrs. Myers into the classroom and take the seat she indicates, folding myself awkwardly into the chair designed to accommodate the small body of a six-year-old.

"How are you all holding up?"

My eyes meet her sympathetic ones and a door in my throat seems to slam shut. I nod, the way that Sakina nods, wordlessly. Now, I understand. Sakina doesn't say anything to me because she doesn't know what to say. Mrs. Myers moves her hand to cover mine and I resist the urge to flinch. The sympathy of a stranger. Again, I can relate to how Sakina must feel with me when I occasionally try to touch her—a hand on her head, a pat on the back—through the chatter I subject her to.

I hear the door open behind me and the relief that shoots through me is powerfully palpable. Shuja is here to lead us through this. He sits down and Mrs. Myers pulls out a file, shares samples of Sakina's work, and guides us through the carefully constructed language of the report card, which she hands to Shuja. I understand the three-thirty parents' expressions of re-lief—Mrs. Myers thinks that Sakina is motivated and intelligent, a high achiever who takes pride in her work.

She asks if we have any questions. Shuja asks a few—the kind a parent should ask. How can we help her? Is there anything she needs to work on?

And then he asks what other parents don't need to ask. "Is she—does she seem to be coping with—with her mother's—with what happened?"

Mrs. Myers takes a deep breath. I realize that I am not the only one who has been dreading this conference. "I—well—you've told me already that Sakina is seeing a counselor. I wanted to share something with you. Something that you might want her counselor to see." From the file, Mrs. Myers pulls out a booklet, construction paper–covered newsprint that has been stapled together. "This is Sakina's daily journal. The students write and draw about their day. What we've done, how they're feeling, what they like and don't like. And why. They've learned to use the word 'because' in order to make their sentences more complex." Mrs. Myers is flipping through the pages, going backward, as she speaks. "As you can see, Sakina writes very well. With a lot of detail and attention to spelling and grammar and punctuation. Above grade level, really. She proofreads and checks her own work and reads everything she writes back to me."

Both Shuja and I can see already what Mrs. Myers would like us to see. In every entry, Sakina has written what is expected of her. *Today we had music. Today is Monday. I like to read. I like stories. I like school because I like to learn. I am happy because we have PE today. I am happy because it is Friday. I am very happy because today is pizza day. I like pizza a lot because it is yummy. I am happy because I love my dad. I am happy because I love my mom. I like my doll.*

In every entry, Sakina has drawn a picture. The same one every day. A picture of a woman lying on the ground. She is wearing a scarf on her head—a *hijab*—and there is a splash of red color on her chest. A little girl stands beside her. There is a gun in the picture, floating over them both. Off to one side, there is a man standing alone. On the other side, there is a woman. Shuja? Me?

I close my eyes. Here it is. What I look for on her face in the middle of the night. But the schedule of Sakina's subconscious is out of sync with mine. The images that haunt me by night stalk Sakina by day.

Mrs. Myers is still speaking. "What she writes about and what she draws about—they're completely unrelated. When I have asked her to describe what she has drawn, she'll only read and reread what she has written. I haven't pushed her. She was there, I believe? When it happened?"

Shuja looks at me helplessly. I nod.

"She's still staying with you?" Mrs. Myers is asking me.

I nod again.

"Will she be going home again soon?" It is Shuja's turn to be questioned.

He doesn't answer.

I open my mouth. I want to explain. But to explain something, you have to understand it yourself.

More sympathy wells up in Mrs. Myers's eyes. "This is—I know this is difficult. But I just thought you should know."

I have to say something—to know something. "She—she doesn't talk about it. With me. Hardly talks at all. About anything. Does she—does she talk here? At school? With you? With her friends? Not about this." My finger taps the open page on the table. "About anything? Other things?"

Mrs. Myers's hand is on mine again. She is nodding. "She's fine. In every other way. She participates in class. Laughs and plays at recess. Other than these pictures, you'd never know what she's been through."

That hurts. I remember the way she lit up at the sight of Mrs. Walker when I dropped her off. How she chatters on and on with

Shuja when he comes in the evening. Her reticence is personal. It's not that Sakina has withdrawn from the world. It's only me she won't respond to. I find myself taking quick, shallow breaths and feel light-headed. Shuja sees and pushes my head down between my legs. "You're okay, Saira. Take deep breaths." His voice is clipped, businesslike. He asks Sakina's teacher, "Do you have a brown paper bag?" Mrs. Myers goes to the supply cabinet and gets him one. Shuja opens the bag, squeezes the top portion of it into a neck, and gives it to me, saying, imperiously, "Breathe in and out of the bag. It'll help."

TWENTY-TWO

❧

OUR CONFERENCE TIME is over and we are seen to the door. The four-thirty parents are waiting outside.

"Are you all right?" Shuja's hands are in his pockets, his eyes narrowly focused on me.

I nod.

"You want to get coffee?"

"Yes!" I hear the eagerness in my own voice. Anything to avoid going back to Mrs. Walker's. Back to Sakina.

"Let's go in my car."

"No. I'm okay. I'll follow in mine." It isn't mine really. It's Mummy's car. A Honda Accord. I like driving it. More than Daddy's. I like to put my hands on the wheel she used to steer herself with. That is what I think of when I drive.

I pull into a space one removed from where Shuja has already parked. He waits for me to get out of the car and we walk together into the coffee shop halfway between his house and my parents'.

We sit down and order coffee. His is black. Mine is milky and sweet from the raw sugar packets I have opened and dumped into it.

I stir mine vigorously and say, "Shuja," an opening for a conversation neither one of us wants to have.

Shuja's jaw tightens slightly before he says, "Have you heard from your dad?"

So he has entertained the same idea that I have. That Daddy will arrive and solve this ridiculous, unspeakable impasse. King Solomon–style, I suppose.

I shake my head. "No. But Lubna Khala called."

I see him brace himself—the absurd auntie solution to every problem, which has already been offered, has made him wary, too. "What did she say?"

"Daddy and Asma are married."

Shuja frowns. "Lubna Khala told you?"

I nod.

"I'm sorry, Saira. Your dad should have called you himself."

"Yes. He should have."

"You knew he was going to marry her. He told you."

"Yes. I knew. But—I—I wasn't surprised. Shocked. But not surprised. If that makes sense?"

Shuja nods because he is supposed to. But it doesn't. Make sense. Of course it doesn't. Nothing does.

"Saira." It's his turn to pretend to move.

My turn to resist. I cling to the subject at hand in order to do us both the favor of avoiding the lump under the rug. "I'm the one. I know I've told you this already. I'm the one who introduced them. Asma and Daddy."

"You told me."

"I—I wasn't upset about it. Not when he told me he was going to marry her. That he was going to stay in India."

"But you're upset about it now."

"Lubna Khala said that Mummy would have given her blessing."

Shuja takes a sip of his coffee. He sets the cup down on the saucer. And rests his chin on one hand. Every move is deliberate and thoughtful. As if he were running through a patient's symptoms in order to be able to make a diagnosis. "I think she's right."

"What did Ameena say? When she got my e-mail?"

"She was surprised. Uncomfortable. Relieved, for his sake."

"Did she tell Sakina?"

Shuja frowned. "No. I don't think she did."

"Will you tell her? Tonight?"

"Saira. You should tell her. He's your father."

"Shuja. I can't talk to her. She won't let me in."

He stares at me for a long moment and I see the conflict in his face—the inverted, mirror image of what I feel.

Reluctantly, he asks, "Do you *want* her to let you in, Saira? Maybe she's waiting for you to let her in first."

I don't have any reply to give him. And the silence descends upon us again.

Shuja closes his eyes. He opens them. What I see in them makes me want to shrink away.

Too politely, he says, "Is there anything you'd like me to pick up for dinner?"

"No. Thank you. I'll cook up something."

"Thank you, Saira. For everything. For taking care of Sakina."

"You don't have to thank me for that, Shuja. For anything."

"Saira—"

"Shuja—"

We have begun at the same time. Both of us wait, deferring to the other. And realize, at the same time, that neither one of us really wants to say anything. Too much hangs in the balance.

Shuja stands up, tosses some bills on the table, and walks out of the restaurant without a backward glance.

I try to rein in the pace of my breathing. Panic hovers at the edge of my consciousness as I realize how close to the edge Shuja is, too. It occurs to me, suddenly, that he and Daddy were equals for a while. Both of them widowers. Daddy's bereavement had been a needy one. And Shuja's—his suffering is twofold. I don't know how to help—I know, in fact, that I am part of the problem.

A little while later, I am in the kitchen with Sakina. She is at the table, working on her homework while I stand at the stove, stirring what I hope will be a palatably healthy meal. I have told Sakina about the conference with her teacher. I set the rice to simmer and have a seat at the table to look over her work. She packs up her pencil and eraser, her crayons and glue.

"Sakina, I have something I want to tell you."

She lifts her face and her eyes meet mine so directly that I have to resist the urge to look away. "You know that Nana's in India? Well, he's going to be there for a while. He—he's gotten married, Sakina."

Sakina's nose wrinkles. She looks down at her papers. Begins to shuffle them together, to put them carefully into her folder, and I am afraid that this news, too, will be greeted with silence.

Her eyes are still cast downward and I barely hear the words she utters, "But. Nana is already married. To Nanima."

"Yes. But—Nanima's not here anymore. And he's very lonely. So—he found a very nice lady. And asked her to marry him. They'll visit us soon. Maybe early next year."

"So?—he's not married to Nanima anymore?"

"He—he is. But she's not here. With us."

She looks up and I see it all. Clear and undisguised. The hurt. The bewilderment. I realize what I have done, the worry I have caused her. The parallel I myself drew—at the café—has not escaped Sakina's thoughts.

"Will Daddy find a new wife, too?"

TWENTY-THREE

SHUJA PUTS SAKINA to bed as I hover in the doorway of Amee-na's room. This is a nightly ritual. When he is done, we make our way to the family room. I sit on the couch and Shuja sits in one of the recliners. He clicks on the television and we drown ourselves in what passes for war coverage. Pundits and experts from around the world are called upon to offer their august opinions. A familiar face flashes on the screen, offering somber admonition to deaf ears.

"It's him, isn't it, Saira? He's the one." Shuja nods toward Majid Khan's talking head.

I close my eyes. This is the first question. There will be others, I know, that I will not know how to answer. I only know how to ask them, to turn the answers into stories that bring alive the gory, inconvenient details that others would rather forget. This story is one I left behind. That is how Ameena and I agreed it would be. But she is dead—leaving me stuck in the aftermath of what she convinced me to do. In any case, what I remember is not a story—

merely a series of snips and snatches, disparate memories that I have severed from significance, like the sound bytes that comprise the news playing on in front of me.

Majid Khan. I remember saying good-bye at an airport. The semester was over and so was the affair. He took me in his arms and gave me a final kiss. I turned from the departure gate and saw Ameena standing there. I was caught.

I was home for Christmas and violently ill. Stomach flu, I told Mummy, even though I had begun to suspect. Then, back in Berkeley for my final semester, Ameena showed up for the lecture I ran away from before. She took one look at my green face and headed out the door, returning shortly with a bag from the drugstore, forcing me to confront what I already knew. When the blue line appeared, I was strangely calm. I knew what I would do. An appointment at Planned Parenthood was all it would take and I had no qualms about it.

Ameena was quiet. I didn't know what she was thinking—whether she would tell Mummy my secret. She was quiet. And thoughtful. And had secrets of her own. Four inseminations. Five attempts at IVF. As she told me all of this, the look in her eye was not hard to understand—something I had to look away from because I knew what it meant. This time, I had something that she wanted.

I made the appointment. But Ameena came again. What she asked was not something I thought I could do. But she begged and pleaded, her beautiful face enhanced by the trail of her tears. How could I deny her? What difference would it make to me? I canceled my appointment. By the end of that semester, I resorted to wearing baggy clothes that would not serve their purpose for much longer. Hiding the shape of what was taking form inside of me—the shape of what I thought would make no difference. I felt her move. And I realized, too late, what it was I had committed myself to.

Mummy knew. She broke the angry, months-long silence to tell me—arriving at the hospital as my labor intensified. *Do you know what you are doing, Saira? Do you understand what you are giving up?* She held my hand, going back on her word to never forgive. Writing the words of the prayer on my forehead—praying for a safe delivery.

When I was done—when Sakina was born—she held her grandchild and brought her close to me. *Look at her, Saira. Hold her. You can change your mind. Ameena does not realize what she has asked you to do.*

I shook my head. *No. I can't hold her. I can't take her in my arms. If I do, I'll never let go. She's Ameena's child. Not mine.*

When I open my eyes, the news coverage has shifted to scenes of destruction from a hurricane that has hit Cuba.

Shuja is speaking, and it is no effort to divert myself from my memories in order to listen to his.

"I was absolutely against it. That day—when Ameena came home and told me what she wanted to do. Which was ironic. Because I'm the one who had suggested adoption in the first place."

I am listening. But I cannot respond.

It doesn't matter. He is ready to talk and what I feel or think seems to be of little importance. "After our third try at IVF, I told her. It was futile to try anymore. But she was adamant. Every time, she believed it would happen. I went along. I gave her the shots. I watched her go through the torture. Of hoping and believing. I had given up myself. Medicine had failed. There was no explanation. No reason the specialists could ever give us for why we couldn't conceive. Unexplained infertility. What a ridiculous diagnosis. I am a doctor. I can understand cancer and disease. They have a cause. There's a pattern to them that you can understand at least, even if there's no cure. But our medical verdict was so absurd. Unexplained infertility. That was what kept Ameena's faith alive. If science had no answer, then the answer had to be found somewhere else. In the realm of miracles and faith. But after that fifth time, even Ameena had a hard time understanding. Until then, she didn't want to adopt. She—she wanted us to have a child of our own. But a few months had gone by since that last failed try. And she had stopped talking about trying again. Then—she came home that day utterly convinced. That this was the answer to her prayers. I tried to talk her out of it. I told her we should adopt, yes, but not this child. Not yours. But she wouldn't listen. So—I agreed. Thinking that you never would." Shuja stops talking and waits.

What can I say? "I'd already made the appointment. To have an abortion. When she asked—begged—I hated her. For putting me in that position. No matter what I said—it would always be there, between us. If I had said no—the question would have lingered over us forever. It seemed—it seemed so little. I had something I didn't want. To destroy it, knowing how much she wanted it—it seemed so churlish. So wasteful. In the end, I couldn't say no. I tried to. But I couldn't."

"She never told me. About him. Only that she'd seen you with him. At the airport. That he was a *desi* man. Does he know?"

I shake my head. "No! No. He doesn't."

"Don't you think he has a right to know?"

"No. I—as far as I'm concerned—it never happened. I got pregnant. I would have had an abortion."

"But you didn't. You had her, Saira. You had Sakina. You carried her inside of you. And gave birth to her."

I close my eyes again briefly. Then, I open them and say, with more hostility than I intend, "It's a bit late, isn't it? To be worrying about him now?"

He has no answer to that. Of course he doesn't. The answer is the whole point—the whole crux of the story. Now. Who could have ever conceived of now? It occurs to me to ask, "So—if Ameena didn't tell you, how did you know it was him?"

Shuja shrugs. "I guessed. I—I don't know how. You mentioned him once or twice. That he was at Berkeley. After Sakina was born, Ameena bought all of his books. She read them. And kept them on the shelf. I pulled one of them out one day. When Sakina began to grow. There was a picture of him inside the jacket of the book. I saw the resemblance."

The resemblance. Yes. I had noticed it, too. That day at Gymkhana. In passing only. A detail that registered. But that was before now. Now.

Finally, Shuja breaks the stalemate. "What are you going to do, Saira?"

I look at him. His eyes are bright with the tears he won't shed. His hair—is it grayer? And those lines on his face, the grooves around his mouth—the result of the ready smile and easy laughter that I had seen as smug and mocking when we first met—are they fading? Yes. At least when compared to the creases on his forehead, the result of the fear I hear in his voice—the same fear Ameena had felt, the kind that had hovered over us since the day her daughter was born. He won't put words to that fear—to do so would be to assert a claim he is afraid I will challenge. But he wants to know what I am going to do. *You*, he said. Not *we*.

"I don't know, Shuja. Tell me. Tell me what I should do."

He shakes his head. "I can't tell you. I don't know either."

I cannot stand it. I am desperate to see him smile again and laugh. "There's always that other option. The one the aunties proposed."

But he doesn't laugh. Or even smile. He nods his head. And says, "Yes," as if in answer to a question I haven't asked.

TWENTY-FOUR

❧

S HUJA IS LONG gone—leaving me to wrestle with a bad joke that fell flat. I prowl around the house, in a vain attempt to avoid the vision of death that descends upon me nightly. Vain, because the phone rings. It is Lubna Khala. Big Nanima is dead. I lie down on my bed and let the tears flow.

A little while passes and I am there again—at Gymkhana. *The ghosts dance, the glasses clink, and the walls shrink. Big Nanima is there, issuing her warning. So are Nanima, Belle, and Dada. A gunshot sounds. Ameena falls. There is Sakina, beside me, her arms outstretched. And the gun? Where is the gun? There it is—hovering over us, in no one's hands tonight.*

I wake up, again, from my nightmare. Bathed in sweat. Breathing hard. Resigned to the sleepless routine that will follow. I close my eyes and long, once more, for the touch of my mother's hand on my forehead.

I get out of bed and begin to make the quiet, nightly journey to the room across the hall, but am suddenly diverted by my longing. In Mummy's room, in the drawer of her dresser where she kept her prayer rug, I find a copy of the Quran. I look up the verse—*Ayatul Kursi*—and find the words. *Bismillah ir Rahman ir Raheem.* "In the Name of God, Most Merciful, Most Compassionate," I read, in English and in Arabic. *He knows what lies before them, and what is after them, and they comprehend not anything of His knowledge save such as He wills.* I trace the words with my finger, over and over again, and realize what I did not before. That not all questions can be answered. That some truths are beyond the capacity of our minds to understand.

Then, my feet resume their original purpose. I approach the bed where Ameena's daughter is asleep and stare down at her for a moment. Quietly, I sit down on the bed, remembering when she was born—this child, conceived in Ameena's imagination, whose life I would have ended before it even began. But these are secrets—details—I can now never disclose. Because they will be forever wrapped in the tragedy of Ameena's death. Sakina has lost her mother. That is the end of the story she will know—a story that leaves no place for me as her mother, because to claim that place would be to kill her mother all over again.

But there is another way, one there is plenty of time to contemplate and that has no bearing on the assertion I have yet been unable to make. I remember something else—*the greatest truths can be hidden in fiction.* That is what Majid Khan had said before she was conceived.

Sakina stirs in her sleep. "Mommy?"

I force myself not to recoil. I see the glint of the whites of her eyes and know that she is awake. "No. It's Saira Khala. I'm sorry."

Her hand reaches up. She touches my cheek.

"You're crying."

"Am I?" I lie down next to her.

"You can't sleep?"

"No."

"Did you have a bad dream?"

"Yes, Sakina."

She is quiet for so long that I think she has gone back to sleep. But she hasn't.

"I have bad dreams sometimes."

"You do? What do you dream about?"

I feel her shoulders shrug next to mine. "I don't know."

"You know that you can come to me? If you ever wake up in the night?"

"I can?"

"Of course."

She is quiet again, but now I know that she is not asleep.

"I miss Mommy."

"I miss her too, Sakina. Very, very much."

"Did your dream make you afraid?"

"Yes."

"Mommy used to write on my forehead. When I was afraid." Her hand reaches up and her fingers trace a random pattern on my forehead. "But I don't know what she used to write. Do you?"

I recite the words for her. *Allahu la ilaha ill huwa, Al-Haiyul-Qaiyum . . .*

"Do you know what the words mean?"

I hesitate. "I think they mean that there are many things that we can't understand. The past. The bad things that have happened. Like what happened to Mommy. And we become afraid. Of what might happen in the future. It's okay to be afraid. But we have to keep hoping and believing."

"We do?"

"We do. That's what Mommy would have wanted us to do. To keep hoping. And trying our best to be good and do good. Even when we're afraid."

Sakina moves a little closer to me. And I can resist no longer. I take her in my arms. I hold her close. Whatever it takes, I will never let go.

ACKNOWLEDGMENTS

Many debts were incurred along the journey that led here. First, to all of the teachers who taught me to read and write, to think and to feel—foremost among them, Dr. Nahid Angha and Dr. Ali Kianfar, whose teachings of the heart continue to enrich my life.

With gratitude, I wish to acknowledge all of the support and input offered by friends and family along the way: from Anabel, Sudha, Zafar and Preeti, Roya and Khaled, Nuzha, Michelle, Shaila and Vishal, Patty and her mother, Marianne and John, Hina, Simi, Pam De Ferrari, Valerie, the teachers and students of Olive Elementary, Raissa, Mariyah Khala, Mumtaz Auntie, Papa, Fazila, Batool, Farah, and Hani. Thanks also to JoAnn and her friends at the Santa Rosa Symphony League for their patronage of art in all its forms; to BJ Robbins, my agent, whose early and abiding confidence kept me at it long after I alone would have given up; to Laurie Chittenden, whose keen insight and bright enthusiasm made editing painless; and to Juliette Shapland, Brenda Segel, Lisa Gallagher, Will Hinton, and the team at William Morrow for the ride of my life; to Daddy, who believed enough to refuse to read a word until he could buy a copy of his own. (Hope you paid full cover price!)

And finally, I am grateful to those who walked along on every step of the journey, who I am blessed enough to be able to take for granted—to Mimi and Mummy, for inspiration and for reading and listening to every word in every draft; to Khalil, whose birth was the excuse I needed to begin writing again; and to Ali, for all of the above, for earning the right to say I told you so like no one else, and for far more than I can ever express.